Advanced Praise for

LIGHTNINGSTRUCK

Full of mystery, tension, and the very real and often turbulent history of rural South Carolina, *Lightningstruck* is an engrossing and enchanting story.

—Tim O'Brien, National Book Award Winner
and author of *The Things They Carried*

It's rare these days to find a good poet who can also write fine fiction. It turns out Ashley Mace Havird is one of these. I read *Lightningstruck* with great pleasure, and felt entirely in the spell of her prose. I won't soon forget Etta McDaniel and her journey.

—Richard Bausch, author of
The Stories of Richard Bausch and editor
of *The Norton Anthology of Short Fiction*

What a rich witness of a culture and a world.

—Stanley Plumly, author of
Orphan Hours and *Posthumous Keats*

MERCER UNIVERSITY PRESS

Endowed by

TOM WATSON BROWN
and
THE WATSON-BROWN FOUNDATION, INC.

Lightningstruck

To Madeline —

A fellow traveler in the art!

Ashley Mace Havird

ASHLEY MACE HAVIRD

Belhaven

Sept. 27, 2016

MERCER UNIVERSITY PRESS | *Macon, Georgia*

2016

MUP/ P540

Books published by Mercer University Press are printed on acid-free paper
that meets the requirements of the American National Standard for
Information Sciences—Permanence of Paper for Printed Library Materials.

ISBN 978-0-88146-596-9
Cataloging-in-Publication Data is available from the Library of Congress

Winner of the 2015 Ferrol Sams Award for Fiction

For David

and

In memory of Phil Mace and Mattie Bostick

CONTENTS

I crossed the evening barnlot, opened
The sagging gate, and was prepared
To go into the world of action and liability.
I had long lived in the world of action and liability.
But now I passed the gate into a world

Sweeter than hope in that confirmation of late light.

Robert Penn Warren, *Brother to Dragons*

LIGHTNINGSTRUCK

PART ONE

1: Lightning

May 22, 1964

Even before my horse got struck by lightning—a crazy thing all by itself—the world had gone stark raving mad. I saw it on TV: the President's funeral after he was shot and killed by an unshaven man who was himself gunned down on live TV; colored marchers fire-hosed and beaten by white policemen; churches with children inside bombed and reduced to char and rubble by the Klan. Crazy. I saw it at home: my own world changing—thanks mostly to the gift of a horse that was anything but the horse of my dreams—pushing me off-balance the way bullies did my little brother on the school playground.

Technically the horse wasn't even mine anymore. There had been an accident back in March—a terrible one—and my father had talked one of the tenant farmers into taking him off our hands.

That tenant, Jesse, lived alone at the opposite end of the field that stretched behind our house. He already had a pen right next to his shack; the old horse wouldn't be any trouble. But Troy, true to habit, refused to stay where he was supposed to. Right away he started wandering back to his old home, the barn that used to house mules in the pasture beside my grandfather's house. There Troy, now that he was cast out, seemed to have decided he belonged after all. Nobody could figure out how the horse, who surely couldn't jump a fence, kept escaping from Jesse's pen.

But that day in late May when the thunderstorm hit, he *was* in the pen, standing still as a statue, according to Jesse, with sheets of rain slamming against him.

It was after school on Friday, and I was curled on my bed absorbed as usual in *Ancient Wonders of the World*. When boots stomped on the porch, and then the doorbell rang, and a fist knocked, I figured it was one of the Scurlock boys, drunk already (the weekend had begun) and primed with some made-up story about needing money. I looked through my window. Not a Scurlock but Jesse.

Cleo, who got to the door before I did, now hurried off for towels. Jesse looked like he'd just come out of the creek. "Your papa home?" He was breathing hard, as though he'd run all the way here. "The old horse. He's down, lightning-struck." Jesse's shirt stuck to his big heaving chest and to his heavily muscled arms. Drops fell from his tight silver-and-black curls and off the end of his nose.

Cleo spread bath towels on the tiles of the entryway and put another around Jesse's shoulders. She patted his face and neck as if he were a baby and couldn't do it for himself. "Drowned rat," Cleo mumbled. "You going to catch pneumonia."

Cleo had worked for our family since I was born and used to fuss over me the way she was doing with Jesse. But not anymore.

Papa, just then home from work, came towards us through the den. Besides farming with my grandfather, Mr. Mac, he had a town job lending money to other farmers.

"That old horse down, Mr. Frank." Jesse was still trying to catch his breath. "Crack of lightning shook the house, made the ground jump up. I look out and there I see Troy knocked over on his back. He ain't moved."

"Is he dead?" I asked. "Really dead?"

"Got to be. Or near about."

A half-hour later Dr. Fowler, the veterinarian who looked after the cows and whatever dogs and cats took up with us, came splashing up in his white-roofed brown Impala beneath the pecan trees that lined the driveway. While Papa and I waited to crowd in beside him, he lifted a case rattling with glass vials off the front seat and slid it onto the back seat beside Jesse. "Don't let this fall off, you hear?"

I had never seen an animal who'd been struck by lightning, only trees stripped naked and bleached, like skeletons scratching at the sky. Would Troy be a skeleton? Who wouldn't be curious? But more than anything I wanted to see for myself that Troy was finally dead and gone, out of my life as though he'd never come in the first place, bringing with him one catastrophe after another.

Dr. Fowler's car smelled like dogs and hospital disinfectant and the rotten-fruity red medicine I had to take for a week along with Will to keep me from getting the pinworms he'd picked up from no telling where. As we hit the ruts and bumps of the dirt road that skirted the field, the glass bottles clinked. I turned to look back. Jesse was gripping the case with both hands.

Once we veered off onto the track that cut through the field towards Jesse's house, the tires spun. We were going to get stuck. I'd bet anything. Just as well, then, that Will was missing the excitement. My brother hated getting stuck. Right now he was probably on his way back with our mother from seeing the doctor in town. Yet another ear infection. Dr. Fowler gunned the motor.

Jesse's yard was a muddy mess. We had to wade clear around to the other side of his house, the side near the trees, to reach the pen. Jesse carried the case, and Dr. Fowler, in green coveralls, had his leather bag. The rain was still falling steadily. No one had thought to bring an umbrella.

The odors hit me so hard I could almost taste them. Before I even saw Troy, I smelled the rotten egg of burnt hair, the charcoal of scorched meat, the odd new-penny smell of what must have been electricity from the lightning. I pushed my forearm against my nose and tried to keep the rain from running into my mouth, bringing with it the thick smell. I struggled not to gag. The men coughed and cleared their throats. Jesse held a handkerchief to his face.

Lying there on his side, legs stuck out stiff and straight, Troy looked dead. Surely he was dead. Lightning had seared him in a bizarre pattern. Like a swollen meandering river, the raw red-black wound ran along his exposed side and down both legs. Around his belly and over onto his back, the flesh and rust-colored hair looked singed as though from a shotgun's scatter. The horse wasn't moving. His eyes were open, but he didn't seem to see anything.

Dr. Fowler pulled a stethoscope from his bag. He crouched for several minutes, then shook his head. He started to get up but stopped mid-stand. He cocked his head as though he heard something in the pattering rain. Again he crouched. He lifted Troy's front leg away from his body and asked Jesse to hold it up. In a manner that called to my mind Cleo's palms kneading biscuit dough, Dr. Fowler pressed his hands just beneath the shoulder joint. Then, lacing his fingers together to make a fist, he hit Troy's upper chest hard—one, two, three, four times. He forced the lids up from both eyes and shined his little flashlight into them. He listened again with his stethoscope. He cocked his head. Again he hit Troy's chest. One, two, three, four. Again he listened.

He stood and wiped his face. He looked first at my father and then at me. He was short for a man and I was tall for my age; we were almost eye level. "Son of a gun's alive. In shock, but alive."

The vet gave Troy a shot with a needle so long it made my knees wobble. He wiped his hands down the front of his coveralls. "He's blind, probably deaf. He may recover, partly. No way to know for sure."

Troy's legs twitched. The twitches turned into kicks, and after a few tries he worked himself to his feet. He huffed and tried to shake his muddy mane, but something was wrong. His head hung crooked to the left, as though drawn by a magnet to the wound, and swayed from side to side. He stumbled, tried again to shake himself. But his body wouldn't cooperate.

"I've seen this only once before, an animal surviving a lightning strike, and that was a 3,000-pound bull. Troy got lucky. Lightning came up from the ground. Went in here." The vet pointed to Troy's left foreleg. "Went out here." He gestured to the rear leg.

"What's wrong with his head?" I asked from behind my arm.

"It's spastic, Etta, because of the blindness; there may be some paralysis. As I say, it might wear off. But old Troy'll never be the same."

I thought this over. Perhaps that was a good thing. Troy couldn't possibly be any more disagreeable than he had been.

Dr. Fowler shook his head and grinned, showing his white teeth, unstained by cigarettes. He and my friend Margot's mother were the only grownups I knew who didn't smoke. "Troy must have twenty years or more on him—and lived through this. That's something."

The rain had slowed into a fine mist. Dr. Fowler reached into his case—Jesse was still carrying it—and handed a jar of big orange pills to my father.

Papa had been off to the side, talking quietly to Jesse. The two men—without so much as a word to me—had reached an understanding.

They walked Dr. Fowler back to his car. He scribbled something in a little notebook, tore out the page, and handed it to Papa—not Jesse. The men rocked the Impala out of the mud, which had splattered all the way to the car's white roof, and Dr.

Fowler drove away. Jesse tied a rope around Troy's neck and handed the end to my father, who handed it to me.

Papa and I led Troy along the farm road towards the pasture beside Mr. Mac's house. Every few minutes we had to stop and wait for the horse to untangle himself. Troy kept stumbling, one leg crossing in front of the other. He couldn't straighten his neck, even with the rope around it, but kept it lowered and curved to the left.

The mist turned back into rain, a slow and steady drizzle.

"If he survives—and you know he might not—nobody's going to ride this horse again. Not even Will," Papa said. We were sloshing through puddles in the muddy road. "But if Dr. Fowler's right, and he lives, he's your responsibility, Etta. You were the one who asked for him."

I bit my tongue. I never asked for *this* horse, I wanted to say.

I had had a fit for a horse. I had nagged my parents for months. Then, on my eleventh birthday back in August, I got my wish. His name was Jim Dandy. To make him mine, I changed the name to Troy. In *Ancient Wonders of the World*, there was a picture of a wooden horse on wheels, the Trojan horse, outside the walls of Troy. New name or not, the old horse would not be mine. He defied me at every turn. Long before the accident in March that wasn't my fault, though I blamed it as much on Cleo as on Troy, I had wanted nothing so much as to be rid of him. Now it seemed I was stuck with him after all—Troy was mine, but not as I, or anyone else, would ever want a horse to be.

"Be careful what you wish for," Cleo liked to say. She had sayings for everything.

My shoes squished. I could hardly watch my step and lead Troy at the same time. My feet seemed to find the deepest puddles. Drenched, with my clothes glued to my skin, my last-year's overalls halfway up my calves, I felt ridiculous.

I glanced over at Papa, who was scowling and swinging his arms, the way he did when some worry latched on inside his head. His springy, copper-colored hair had come alive in the rain. His ears stuck out. I patted my own hair, as if to smooth it down—it had gone to frizz like my father's, had pulled loose from my braids to fall into my eyes. At least I didn't have his ears like Will did. At least my face wasn't covered with freckles—only my nose.

Sometimes I leaned over my bedroom dresser and touched my nose to the mirror. I stared at my eyes, willing them to turn blue like my mother's. Around the pupil was a thin gold band that never got wider but bled into a dull brownish green. Hazel, Mama called it, which was not even a real color. I did have her high cheekbones, though. They'd been passed down from my mother's father whose ancestors included a Cherokee Indian princess, or so the legend went. There was nothing more to the story—my mother claimed to have no other details—but cheekbones with even a skeletal legend were better than nothing.

Papa shook his head, and droplets flew. He slapped at his sopping shirtsleeves. "Your horse is just about the last straw. First he kicks little Trudy—could have killed her—now this. I might as well tell you, Etta. I have my eyes open for a job in a city. Columbia, maybe Charlotte, maybe even Atlanta. Will needs specialists who aren't a hundred miles away."

"Good," I said. "I like cities, and I hardly ever get to go."

It was true. Even though painful surgeries were what took Will to Columbia, I envied my brother those trips. Last year, when he was there for an operation, he'd found in a downtown department store the book that introduced me to archaeology. Despite its having come from Will, *Ancient Wonders of the World* became my favorite book ever. I pictured Columbia as a place of wonder, where you could find treasure as easily as turning the pages of an illustrated book. So, yes, moving there would be good.

Yet no sooner had I said it than I had second thoughts. For what that book showed, as well as riches, were empty stretches of land—deserts, plains—not a lot different from the fields that stretched for acres behind our house, and buried below which there were *wonders.* Not just anyone could find buried treasure. But I was going to be an archaeologist, and before long I'd have all summer to become one. We couldn't be moving soon!

And there was Mr. Mac to think about. And Cleo. Suddenly it hurt to draw a breath. I wouldn't miss Cleo, I told myself—Cleo who claimed that Will and I were her "children." Before the accident that wasn't my fault, the one with Trudy, I would have felt that leaving Cleo was like leaving a mother. Why, she might as well have been my mother, since my own had pretty much given all of her attention to Will since he was born. But now I didn't care. Cleo had failed me, betrayed me even. Her constant presence was a burden.

It was different with Mr. Mac. I had always been his "hard rock"—still was, though I was having trouble coming to terms with the new interest he was taking in Will. Recently Will had begun to show a talent for baseball. He was playing Little League, and our grandfather never missed a game and afterward never missed a chance to brag on Will. Sometimes, when he bragged on Will to me, it seemed he was implying that I was in some way deficient, that he was challenging me to measure up to Will, much as Cleo was forever praising Will's "sweet temper'ment" while criticizing my "bad" one. Mr. Mac's interest in Will as a boy threw me off balance—not as Cleo's betrayal had done, but at least a little. Still, it wasn't as if he were paying me less attention than before, not exactly, and I relished my weekends with him out on the farm, reveled in the chores we did together—especially when Will was sick or at ball practice and it was just the two of us.

All the same, if we did move, at least I'd be done with this chore of a stinking horse.

"I'm ready to move," I said, but not so loudly as before. "Good and ready."

Troy went right into the mule barn and stood there, bobbing and swaying his crooked head. From across the fence, my grandfather's screened door whacked shut. The wooden gate creaked open. Mr. Mac joined us and folded his arms over his belly, which had grown so plump lately that it hid his belt buckle. The rain didn't seem to faze him. "That was some kind of branding iron marked the old fellow," Mr. Mac said, chewing on his unlit cigar. He smiled, but the corners of his mouth turned down as they always did. He lifted his hat and resettled it upon his nearly bald head. "Horse going to have his way. Nothing we can do about it."

Cleo wasn't so philosophical. Especially when Troy went on living. "I gots to look at old Lightningstruck every morning on my way here cross the pasture. And every morning I gets the same evil eye. Dead and brought back to the living. Ain't natural. He been down to visit the Devil and come back up, so now he got one eye cocked down to the Satan world and one eye looking up at this one. Ain't natural. He's a hant-horse, that's what."

Troy was blind, I tried to tell her. He wasn't seeing anything. But Cleo refused to be corrected. And finally one afternoon, when I went to give Troy an orange pill stuck in an apple, I found, much as I hated to admit it, that Cleo was right; the old horse could see. What was more, though I couldn't have put it into words then, it occurred to me that somehow the stark raving madness of the world, which had seemed for almost a year now to keep me off-balance, lived in this gruesome horse, whose one good eye, so Cleo said, was evil. Yes, Cleo was right; the old horse wasn't blind. Nodding like a drunkard, Troy rolled his good eye until it settled on me and focused, locked me in his vision and kept me there.

2: Third Eye

I hadn't left my room. It was late morning in the middle of summer, and I was hungry—really hungry. I sat in short pajama bottoms on my bed, the fan directed straight at me, its hot breeze riffling the pages of *Ancient Wonders of the World*. Sweat slicked my bare chest. What had happened yesterday? And *how*? Out in the tobacco field, with Will and Troy, what happened was a puzzle, and the way I had acted was more puzzling than anything.

Will was no doubt in Columbia by now; he'd left with our parents at dawn for the second of the two-part operation on his harelip and cleft palate. And I was stuck with Cleo, who was vacuuming the den, from the sound of it…and humming. Behind my closed door, here I was practically melting, practically starving, but clearly Cleo couldn't spare a thought for me.

I made myself focus on my book. I'd read it so often I could imagine myself now as each archaeologist in turn: sometimes Arthur Evans, who excavated the Palace of Knossos on Crete, home of King Minos and the Minotaur; sometimes Howard Carter, who discovered the Egyptian tomb of King Tut; but most times Heinrich Schliemann, who found the lost cities of Troy. Schliemann all but stepped from the page and fit himself into my skin.

It was a miracle—a pure miracle—the way he'd discovered beneath a landscape as dull and dry as any field on our farm the nine buried cities of Troy. Wiping the stinging sweat from my eyes, I scrutinized for the twentieth time the photographs of King Priam's Treasure—silver goblets and vases, gold cups and diadems, copper axes and daggers. I stared at the picture of Schliemann's stiff-looking wife draped in the jewelry that had belonged to Helen of Troy. How could she keep such a serious expression? I would have been grinning like a fool. I studied pictures of the site. Nothing dramatic, no fancy ruins: just scrub wood and weeds. I pictured the fields and swampland behind my own house.

I raised my right hand, as people did when swearing to tell the truth on the *Perry Mason* TV show. I, Etta McDaniel, would make a real find—just as Schliemann had. And this would restore the balance of my world, which really meant putting me back in its center.

For it seemed everything was going wrong. And all because of the old horse, Troy. But what to make of him after yesterday, when he appeared so far from his pasture like the hant-horse Cleo insisted he was? Was he trying to communicate something to me at last? Maybe—just maybe—I had gotten through to him.

Holding on to that half-hope, I dressed in a hurry. Without a word to Cleo, I left the house, slamming the front door behind me.

Troy stood right outside the barn, scolding me with his good eye for being late. He turned and hobbled inside. I scooped feed into his bucket and, when he lowered his head to eat, reached out to touch the dusty forelock between his ragged-looking ears. He backed away, shaking his head and stomping at the ground.

"What's it going to take for you to be on my side? I'm sorry, okay? I'm *sorry* I wanted you dead for keeps."

At first, back in May, what had lured me to him after he survived the lightning strike—apart from my having to give him medicine—was morbid curiosity. The charred, salmon-edged wound oozed for days. I would feed him dutifully, then study with sick fascination the flies wading in the wide, slimy river gouged into his side, branching like veins of lightning from shoulder to hip and down his legs.

A notion had come to me in those early weeks after Troy's injury. Dr. Fowler had never seen a horse survive that sort of strike—it was "something"—and what was more, if Cleo was right and the horse had come back from the dead, then Troy was *something*. He was special indeed. A journey like that could have given him powers. Troy would never be the horse I'd dreamed of. But if I could nurse him back to health, he might decide to be my horse after all. He might let me harness his powers, whatever they were. Then, he'd be *more* than the horse of my dreams, whatever that might prove to be.

I'd begun working with him in earnest. In hopes of straightening his gait, I would stand just inside the fence and hold out a carrot. He'd move grudgingly, crookedly, towards me from the barn, one leg crossing in front of the other. "That's it…that's it! You're doing good," I lied.

"You're not a devil-horse, are you?" He was probably deaf, but I gave him the benefit of the doubt and talked sweetly. "You want to be a good horse, don't you? You're *my* horse. Not Will's."

For some reason, before the lightning had put an end to it, Troy had tolerated Will on his back, even as he tried to buck me off. Will bragged about this and wouldn't let me forget—even though, when it came to horseback-riding, Will could take it or leave it. His interests were narrow: ball-playing and fishing and gluing together little cars and airplanes.

I had tried to restore Troy's vision by waggling a peppermint in front of his left eye. That iris stayed lodged in the back corner, as though permanently staring at something behind him, but somehow the right one, bulging and crazed-looking, could see exactly what was going on. The old horse would snap his head around and snatch the candy with his whiskery muzzle. If I edged too close to the wound, Troy, despite the bribes, bared his ugly, brown square teeth.

Troy had made no progress, none that I could tell. He limped and stumbled when he walked; he leaned hard when he stood. His head fell at an angle; his left eye refused to heal. The gash along his side was still raw and even bloody-looking in places where Troy, rubbing against the walls of the mule barn, had scraped off lingering scabs. Somehow instead of shrinking, it seemed to be spreading. And his temperament was as rotten as it had always been.

Until yesterday there had been no sign of change. And now, standing with him in the barn, I wondered if I'd imagined what I'd seen. Troy appeared to be just as crippled as ever.

"I really mean it. I'm sorry. Cleo thinks you're a devil-horse, but I don't. Not now, anyway. I'm stuck here with her, you know, while everybody's at the hospital with Will. And she's got no use for me. Everything is mixed up."

All the while I talked, the old horse ate his feed, leaning to one side, his crooked head rocking the bucket. Sunlight spinning with dust motes streamed in through the spaces between the wide boards, hit the spider webs that hung between the rungs of the ladder to the hayloft, and illuminated the farm tools propped in one corner. It shone onto the wound that stretched across Troy's side. His reddish hair was matted around it. Flies danced.

"You're not just any horse," I began. "A horse that comes back from the dead knows things, sees things." It occurred to me how Troy could direct his powers. "If you can see how to get out of the pasture, I'll bet you can see what's hidden underground. Secret things. Treasure."

❧

Get out of the pasture was what Troy had done. The day before, when Will and I were racing each other in the tobacco field near Boggy Swamp, the old horse, lame though he was, had simply appeared, like some sort of supernatural being, and laid on me his eye that was not evil but something *more*.

It was late in the afternoon. We'd been with Mr. Mac, checking the tobacco barns where leaves, in 150-degree heat, were curing. It was Will's idea to cool off in the irrigation showering the field beside us. Even this late in the growing season, Mr. Mac was irrigating because of the drought. It hadn't rained—rained hard—since May, the very day in fact when lightning struck the old horse. Aluminum pipes stuck up just higher than the tobacco, and water spewed out in circles from sprinklers at the top that knocked around one way, then back the other. A network of connecting pipes ran along the ground between the rows. If I stood on tiptoes, I could just see beyond the field the roof of a long-abandoned tenant shack, Aunt Charlotte's house.

"Go on." Our grandfather nodded. "Just keep in the furrows and out the tobacco." Mr. Mac walked across the dirt road and headed for the barn on the opposite side.

"Let's have a race!" Will grinned. Playing Little League, he'd surprised everyone not only by hitting balls but also by stealing bases almost every game. For a little kid, Will was fast.

I didn't feel like racing, especially in a field made muddy from irrigation. "Chicken," Will said. Kicking off my shoes, which suddenly today were too tight, I agreed to run as far as the end of the irrigation line. I'd win, as always—of course I would.

I caught my breath. What *was* that? Far off, where the tobacco met the banks of the ditch that marked the Aunt Charlotte field, a movement, a rusty blur. Troy? Impossible. He could barely walk. The best he could manage was pathetic, a crooked hobble.

I turned to get Will's attention, but he was touching his toes, stretching. Some good that would do—I was two years older than he was. I looked back; the figure was gone.

Barbed wire enclosed the pasture. And nowadays the gate stayed locked. What could it have been that looked like Troy?

Will and I positioned ourselves in the furrow left wide for the tractor and tobacco drag. I wiped the stray hair out of my eyes. It never stayed put in my braids the way it was supposed to.

"On your mark, get set, go!" I yelled before Will could beat me to it.

My first steps sank inches into the mud. For a second I was back in the muck of Jesse's pen, trudging towards the horse I had hoped was dead. Here in the field, the harder I tried to run, the deeper I sank. Worse, I kept tripping on the hems of my brand new overalls. Why hadn't I worn shorts? In no time Will, in short pants and weighing almost nothing, sprinted past me. He threw his shoulders forward. His knobby knees pumped up and down.

Still, I knew I'd win. One of his bare feet would step on glass or a wasp.

"Slow poke! Look who's a slow poke!" Will hollered back at me.

Soaking wet, my overalls dragged so heavily it felt like hands were reaching out of the ground and pulling them down—pulling me. I stumbled, nearly fell.

"I win!" Will yelled.

I was having a growing spurt that was mostly in my legs, so my mother had bought my overalls too long on purpose. This defeat—the first race I'd ever lost to Will—was her fault. But it felt more like Troy's. I could feel on my cheekbone the pressure of Troy's eye, like a bruise coming.

"I *let* you win. Because you have to get operated on. Now look here, we're going to race back to the barn." I rolled up my pants legs as far as they could go.

"This time I'm going to say 'on your mark,'" Will said.

I held on to my pants, which kept them from rolling down but slowed me even more. As before, every footfall sank deeper and deeper. Every passing shower of the irrigation system seemed to cripple me further. Something—a splat of mud or a gnat—got into my left eye. But I could see with my right eye Will crashing against the side of the barn, raising his arms, and jumping around like he was Jim Thorpe—All-American.

"You cheated!" I fought to catch my breath. "You started before you said 'go.'"

"You're just mad because I beat you. Twice."

I felt for my pocketknife, a hand-me-down from Mr. Mac—too dull even to whittle with. I pictured myself waving it at Will, then jerked my hand away, balled my fist. I'd lost. And lost more, it seemed to me even then, than just a couple of races.

"Cheater," I said.

"Jealous."

Across the road, our grandfather was talking to Lamar Scurlock. A sharecropper, he drove a turquoise truck with a white hood and doors. He was leaning against a turquoise fender. Mr. Mac depended on Mr. Scurlock, but his three grown sons were sorry workers who were always getting in trouble with the law. Mr. Mac continued to talk, his back to Will and me. He hadn't seen me lose—at least there was that.

I scooped up a handful of mud. Will's clothes clung to his skinny body. Beneath his wiry curls, his ears stuck out just like Papa's did.

In the heat and pitch dark of the last barn we'd checked with Mr. Mac, Will had shined his flashlight under his chin, and in the yellow light, for just a second, his face became a mask, one of Schliemann's beaten gold death masks in *Ancient Wonders of the World*. His ears popped out like cup handles. The scar through his upper lip gave him half of an engraved mustache. "What's my name? What's my name? Rumpelstiltskin is my name!" he had squawked, stomping around in a circle.

"Agamemnon," I'd said under my breath.

But out here in the field, he was just a goblin—an ugly, cheating little goblin. I wanted to yell it. It was all I could do to keep from yelling it, the way kids at school might have done. But no matter how mad I got with my brother, I never called him names that brought attention to his face. That would have been more than mean; that would have been evil.

Even so, I packed the mud like a snowball. Then I packed some more. When I threw it, the bits of brick and gravel would hurt and hurt bad.

"You do—you throw that—and I'll tell." He was panting.

Will's breathing worried our mother; sometimes I saw her listening outside Will's bedroom door at night. But his breathing problems hadn't slowed him down one bit. They didn't slow him down in Little League when he was stealing bases or running to catch a pop fly. Just an act—that's what they were.

I drew back my arm and narrowed my eyes at Will. Behind him, far off in the green edge of the woods, a flash. An eye? I couldn't shake the feeling that I was being watched. But no, it was like the reflection of sun on metal. Something stirred—a deer, most likely—at the edge of the woods that bordered Boggy Swamp. But what about a deer could give off a flash of light? Legend had it that Francis Marion, a hero of the Revolution, the Swamp Fox, had—with his band of guerilla fighters—launched from these very swamps his surprise attacks on the redcoats. Why had that leapt into my mind right now?

A figure emerged. An animal, twisted and hulking. No doubt about it: Troy.

"Don't—you—dare," Will said between breaths, his skinny chest heaving. He still stood beside the barn, an easy target.

My hand—as if it did so on its own—mashed the mud, mashed it hard, against my face. Brick fragments scratched my cheek. Grit got into my mouth. I spat and pulled clots of dirt from my hair. I wiped my hands down my chest.

My cheek stung. How had this happened? I scanned the woods bordering the swamp. Nothing but trees. Troy—he'd put a spell on me, then vanished. What else but a spell could have grabbed my mud-filled hand and slapped it against my own cheek?

Will's eyes widened. His face turned so red all his freckles ran together. I knew that look—he was on the verge of tears.

Now in the barn with Troy, my stomach growling—it must be nearly noon—I watched the old horse finish eating from his pail. Again I reached for his forelock. I lowered my voice, picturing an illustration from my book of Greek myths. "Zeus, the god of the sky, has a third eye. Right in the middle of his forehead. Lightning comes out of it." Maybe, I thought, your blind eye and good one together make up a third. I tried to look at Troy's two eyes at once, the seeing one whose deep brown iris swam jerkily on its yellowish globe, and the blind bloodshot one whose squashed iris seemed to be inching backwards into his head—the effort made me feel queasy, even unsteady.

"I was going to be nice to Will," I claimed, as much to myself as to Troy. "He always comes back from his operations swollen and sore. He can't eat anything but applesauce, and he can't leave the house. But if he's fixed this time, once and for all, it'll be worth it."

During the school year, the other children never got tired of poking fun at him. A harelip and cleft palate. Hardly as serious as water on the brain—Darlene Love's baby brother was born with that condition. Then there was poor Tammy Truluck, the teenaged mongoloid daughter of our church choir director. And Mr. Grimsley at the appliance store with his withered arm. For some reason, maybe because they saw him every day, the children at school were driven to torment Will. And as his older sister, I had to come to his defense. I had no choice but to make enemies of people I'd rather be friends with—in fact, desperately wanted to be friends with—the popular girls with their smart mouths, their cruel and clever insults. In truth, Will's disfigured face embarrassed me. At the same time, I felt his defect was partly my own. These confused feelings, they complicated my life; they made me angry.

"Why did you jinx me? You found a way to come back from the dead. To come back to me." This time my fingers touched the coarse hair that fell between the old horse's eyes. "Here's what I think. I think the way you followed and jinxed me is a test. You want to know if I'm ready, if I'm worthy of knowing what you know. I didn't mean to be so ugly to Will."

Troy turned his head just enough to stare at me with his good eye. "I can see straight through you," he seemed to say. He shook his forelock from my fingers.

"I lost my temper when Will won those races."

Troy kicked at the loose hay on the floor of the barn. He snorted, then whinnied. He took a step forward and nudged at my shorts with his nose. One thing he knew was that I still had raisins in my pocket. I held out several on my palm.

"I never could get rid of you—you weren't going to let me." For a second I pictured myself as Zeus—well, not as Zeus exactly but as a goddess, a woman in a sheet-like dress and shiny bracelets and bolts of lightning in each hand. It was as if I had so wanted to be rid of Troy that I had hurled the lightning and Troy had defiantly refused to go, to die.

"OK, then—be my horse." I felt more than ever bound and determined. "I'm going to make you mine," I said.

I lifted my hand towards his blind eye. Troy knocked my wrist hard with his nose; he gobbled up the spilt raisins from the ground.

He'd hit the bone; pain shot to my elbow. "You think you can push me around and call the shots? You think you can scare me and I'll back off?" Tears rose in my eyes. "What do I have to do to make you mine? Do I have to show you I'm not scared—is that it?"

I reached out again to touch his forelock, and this time I grabbed it. He jerked his head away, leaving me with a sweaty hand smeared with grime. "You will help me. I'll show you I'm…I'm worthy. And you will help me find what's *under*."

Troy huffed and limped out of the barn. Then he lurched around and looked back, his crooked head bobbing. He seemed to know and hold it against me that I'd wished him dead. I was ignorant and foolish, he seemed to be saying. I couldn't make him do one thing he didn't want to do.

3: Wandering Spirit

July 8, 1964

"It's fixing to rain, and I got lines out full of clothes." It was late afternoon when Cleo barged into my bedroom. After my visit with Troy, I'd grabbed a half-empty box of Frosted Flakes and parked myself on the floor, leaning against my bed. "Come on. We got to walk over to the house and pull them in. You can make yourself helpful."

Beneath her white headscarf, which hid every strand of her hair, perspiration beaded on her round, dark brown face. She ran her hand over her forehead, then wiped the skirt of her apron. Cleo had always been plump, but recently it seemed to me she'd shrunk. Maybe it was because I had shot up so fast. The two of us were almost the same height.

"How you breathe in this shut-up room? It's het up like a tobacco barn."

Far-off thunder rattled in the sky. Wishing I'd eaten the leftovers Cleo had put out—even if it had meant sitting with her in the kitchen—I laid down my book. I would learn their secrets, the archaeologists'. I would. At least if it rained, I'd have a better chance of finding Indian relics in one of the several nearby fields that still held them and sometimes gave them up. Mr. Mac had promised to take me to look.

Mr. Mac, who almost always ate his midday meal at our house, must have gotten his "dinner" at Walter's Store today instead. I hadn't been able to keep from blurting out that I'd seen Troy in the field, so he and Jesse were taking the entire day to walk the pasture line and repair the fence. No telling when he'd be free to take me relic-hunting.

"It's not going to rain, Cleo." I pointed to the cloudless sky through my window. "Look." The last thing I wanted was to be alone with Cleo. There was a pressure that weighed on the two of us when we were together. It was like the weather—a distant storm that threatened to come but never did.

"I'm not willing to take that chance. Get your shoes on."

"I can go barefoot."

"You want your feets full of stickers, step barefoot in Troy mess, you go right ahead."

I thrust my toes into my Keds. "They don't fit anymore."

Cleo kneeled down and pushed my heels into my shoes. "They'll do. Now come on." Breathing heavily, as if something hurt, Cleo took a long time standing back up.

"What you do to your face, Etta? Look like a cat got you."

I nodded.

A year ago, I would have run ahead of Cleo, skipping sometimes, across the pecan orchard and all the way through the pasture. But now I dragged behind her, kicking up dirt—you never knew what might turn up—until we passed Mr. Mac's house and reached the gate. Carefully Cleo unlocked and then relocked it behind us. Before the incident with Trudy, there had been just a latch, but now there was a padlock that only Mr. Mac, my father, and Cleo had the key to. If Will and I were by ourselves, we were forced to climb the slatted wooden gate.

Troy stood beside the barn and stared cockeyed at Cleo and me. The hairless pink edges of his purplish wound wore the sheen of a scar and caught the western sun. Cleo whispered something under her breath and shook her head. She looked back at me. "You stay close till we get past Mister Lightning-struck. If he's getting himself out this pasture now, no telling what he'll do."

"His name is Troy."

"You ought to keep clear of him, else you be lightning-struck, too."

I can take care of myself, I said silently. And it's a good thing I can when one minute you take care of me like you always did, and the next—for no reason—you don't.

Troy twisted his head, rolling his right, faultfinding eye at me. My toe caught on a clump of weeds; I stumbled, caught myself. I stared back at the old horse. "Trying to jinx me again? Not after yesterday."

I hurried to catch up to Cleo. Past the barn, the two of us waded through tall yellow wildflowers, smaller blue strawflowers, and purple passionflowers attached to vines. A gnarly sweet gum marked the passageway through a wall of trees to Cleo's house.

It was all but invisible, the narrow opening that led through the tangle of scrub trees and bottlebrush grass to a deep and weedy ditch. Cleo and I had to take turns crossing over on the slab of a board that made a footbridge. On the other side, surrounded by vines covered with fat blackberries, was a pitcher pump with red paint flaking off. Just beyond that was the house.

I had been here before, sometimes with Cleo, cutting through the pasture, sometimes with Mama or Papa the long way around on the rutted drive from the highway, through pines and scrub wood. Like the other tenant houses, Cleo's was made of unpainted wood, sagging and small. But on both sides of the cinderblock steps that rose to her front porch grew bushes filled with tiny white blossoms that smelled like lemon and roses mixed together. Noisy bees hovered. Nestled as it was in a small clearing in the pine woods, Cleo's house seemed like a place in another country, or a cottage in a fairy tale.

Cleo walked to the far side of her yard where her clothes were hung from lines tied to pine trees. "Almost dry but not quite," she said. "Two hours if it don't rain."

"Two hours!"

"If it don't rain."

"But it'll be dark then, or almost. And Mr. Mac said he'd take me to look for arrowheads."

"He knows where to find you if you ain't to home. He and Jesse going to be at that fence line till the sun down anyhow."

I stabbed the toe of my shoe into the ground. My own fault for blabbing about seeing Troy out loose.

"But if it rains," I persisted, "afterwards, I mean, he'll want right then to take me. Right after a rain's the best time. Buried things come to the surface."

Cleo said nothing. She didn't understand, or else she didn't care about the urgency I felt. Archaeology—the word itself seemed magical, and I had taken to pronouncing it slowly to my-self, each of its five syllables distinctly, over and over until it be-came a song that could almost work like a spell and draw treasure from its hiding place. I had no words to convey this urgency to Cleo, and even if I tried to, wouldn't Cleo come back at me with some saying about the treasure you find—how it might not be the one you seek? Well, whatever I found, I knew it would be special, mine alone to find, and it would prove that I was special. Like Schliemann, I'd unearth something like Troy—the ancient city of Troy—from the boring-looking fields and scrubby woods around my house.

Cleo had left newly canned tomatoes and blackberries out in her kitchen. She needed to check on the seals, then do some washing up. She hauled a bucket from under her porch and pumped it full of water.

My own house, built right after I was born, was brick and modern and smelled like nothing. But Cleo's house was filled with the smell of a fire's having smoldered for years, mingled with the spiced peach smells of cooking. I breathed in deeply—I couldn't resist—taking in the comforting mixture that sometimes clung faintly to Cleo's clothes. The room we'd entered from the porch held almost everything a house needed—a fireplace, a bed, two tables, two chairs, and a huge wardrobe with leafy designs carved on the doors. Cleo cranked up her old-timey record player and went into the kitchen, the one other room. "I'm climbing up—on the rough side—of the mountain. I'm looking for—my starry crown," a choir scratched out. Cleo knew all the words and sang along in a low voice while she clanged pots and pans. She was heating water on the stove.

My stomach growled. Was I ever going to get anything besides stale cereal to eat today? It seemed babyish to ask.

One by one, I chewed sandy raisins pried from the bottom of my pocket and flipped through Cleo's records. They all felt heavier and thicker than the albums at my house. Bessie Griffin, Sister Ernestine B. Washington, the Original Blind Boys of Alabama. Only colored church music.

A grouping of cloudy photographs in plain black frames sat atop the table near a window. They were all black and white: grown couples I didn't recognize, a youngish man in a suit, a semicircle of women and girls dressed up for church. Evelyn, Cleo's niece, stood in a group of other young women all wearing white dresses; it looked like a sort of ceremony. And there was a sleeping baby holding a flower. Why sleeping? I wondered. Who was she—or he? And where was a picture of *me*?

There was only one picture of Cleo, and it was strange. She didn't look like herself at all. She stood posed in front of a painted screen—a fake house with columns across the front. She wore a dress made of dotted swiss, a sheer, dainty fabric I knew from a Sunday dress of my mother's. Four necklaces were strung around her neck. But strangest of all was the thing on her head. It was white and fell to her shoulders like a tea towel. From beneath it, onto her forehead, crept little corkscrew curls. I wasn't sure I'd ever seen Cleo without her regular headscarf, which she wound like a turban. The picture reminded me of the portrait of

Schliemann's wife decked out in jewels from Priam's Treasure, the fancy headband and necklaces that didn't fit her dark clothes and solemn expression.

I had the photographs of Cleo and the sleeping baby in my hand. I was on my way to the kitchen for an explanation, but the walls stopped me: faded comics from the newspaper and advertisement pages out of magazines.

The horn of a cartoon tin soldier tooted, "Spray FLIT! Rid Your House of Roaches Bedbugs Ants."

Two fat ladies dressed up in old-fashioned suits declared, "OUTWIT the scales that say you're STOUT—Lane Bryant Style Book FREE."

"*Amelia's Favorite Dish is my Fried Chicken with Biscuits*" proclaimed "the mother of Amelia Earhart, World's Most Famous Woman Flier." The gray-haired woman looked both sweet and slightly scary in her red-flowered apron. She was nearly eclipsed by an enormous platter of chicken and Royal Biscuits and peas and carrots. Even that fake-looking food made my mouth water.

All of these pages pasted onto the walls, pictures that I had ignored in the past—they were like the illustrations in *Ancient Wonders of the World* of the walls of Egyptian tombs, the profusion there of hieroglyphs and paintings. Amelia Earhart's mother—why, she could be one of the ancient mourners bearing grains or fruit for some dead queen or pharaoh's afterlife.

"Cleo!" I hollered, "I've been meaning to ask you, how come you got all these funny papers on your walls? And magazine ads? My book…"

"They keeps out the drafts," she called back. "And they cheerful."

Not if they remind a person of a tomb, I thought. "You need some new magazines, Cleo. These are old as the hills."

"Look on the wall next to the warderobe. That's this year's.…I'm gone walk that milky white way—oh Lord, some mm-mm-hm. I'm gone walk that milky white way mm-mm-hm days," Cleo sang from the kitchen. For the first time in months, her singing and humming weren't setting my teeth on edge.

The newer wall-coverings were mostly Sears Catalog pages. But among them was a black-and-white picture of a colored man staring through the bars of a jail. A preacher! The caption underneath called him Reverend.

I had never heard of a preacher in jail. I called out to Cleo and told her so.

Cleo stood in the doorway, wiping her hands on her apron. "Dr. King just doing what he's called to do. Trying to help the colored folks take one step up the Jacob Ladder. Some of the white folks don't like it, so they throwed him in jail.

"He's out now, though. Like the 'postle Paul—traveling everyplace, spreading the truth. You mind Reverend Hughes. He gave these pictures out to everybody in the congregation."

How could I forget that Sunday last summer at Cleo's church? There was talk of the colored preacher who was leading his people to the Promised Land. "Moses," I said. "Not Paul."

"Mmm…" Cleo nodded.

I remembered now having seen Dr. Martin Luther King on TV; I'd heard my parents and other grownups mention him, too. Margot's parents called him dangerous. I pictured the fear that showed on colored people's faces on TV and in magazines, the anger on white faces.

What did Cleo mean when she spoke of Jacob's Ladder? What truth was Dr. King spreading?

Even as I was on the verge of asking, I pressed my free hand against one of the dark, heavily scrolled doors of Cleo's wardrobe, and my thoughts left the Reverend Dr. King. It had always been there, this massive wooden piece of furniture. I had never given it a second thought. But now I imagined treasure: the necklaces Cleo wore in the picture, earrings and bracelets made from shells or rare stones, a long-forgotten box of coins.

"Cleo," I began, "do you think…inside here…?" I rubbed the wood, my fingers spread.

At a knock on her screened door, Cleo smiled, showing her dimples. It was Jesse, come to pump some water.

"We just back on the west side of the Aunt Charlotte field," he said. "Found some bobwire needs patching. Must be where that Troy be getting through." He leaned around Cleo and nodded hello to me.

Cleo got two mason jars from her kitchen, stepped out onto the porch, and gave them to Jesse. She put her hand on his shoulder. "Why don't I fix you all some sandwiches. You got to be hungry."

"I 'preciate that, but we been at the store. No time to waste if we going to finish this evening."

My heart sank. Almost certainly there would be no Indian field with Mr. Mac—not today, anyway.

"Well, you needs a hat," Cleo said. "Get sunstroke out there without a hat."

She hurried back in and pulled a key from her apron pocket to unlock one door to the wardrobe. Standing on tiptoe, she reached onto the top shelf and came back out with a man's straw hat. Not a farm hat, but a dress hat. It looked ridiculous on Jesse, far too small. Besides, this late in the afternoon, there was no need for a hat at all. Cleo laughed and took it off. "Enough of this foolishness. Go pump your water."

"Why do you have a man's hat?" I asked. All I'd been able to see inside the wardrobe were shelves of clothing.

"Curious, why you want to know every blessed thing?"

The pictures of Cleo and the baby were still in my hand. I slapped them facedown on the table and went outside, letting the screened door slam behind me. I sat on the porch steps. For those few minutes before Jesse showed up, Cleo had seemed like her old self, talking to me about Dr. King in her open, teacherly way. I was even feeling my old goose-bumpy pleasure in hearing Cleo sing. Then Jesse came and ruined it. And reminded me how hungry I was.

I didn't care, I told myself. I didn't care who were in those pictures or where the silly hat came from or what else was inside the wardrobe or anything Cleo had to say to me. So what if Jesse was Cleo's boyfriend? Still, when Cleo had put her hand on Jesse's shoulder, I felt it like a jab in my stomach.

"You going to chew that finger right off?"

I jerked my hand away from my mouth. I hadn't realized that I was biting my nails. I was trying to quit.

"Here." Cleo handed down to me two other mason jars. "I'll go in and find us something to eat."

I sighed as though pumping well water were a chore. In fact, I loved the pebbly feel of the metal handle that curved like a swan's neck. The water came up cold from the belly of the earth and tasted slightly of the good silver my mother used at Thanksgiving and Christmas—the heavy silver that had belonged to Mama's mother, Henrietta. I'd never known either of my grandmothers, though I was stuck with that one's name.

Cleo returned with plates of sweet cucumber pickles, sliced tomatoes, and biscuits stuffed with hard salty ham. She sat beside me on the porch and stretched her legs out over the steps. I used to try to make out numbers or letters on the coin that was threaded by a wire around Cleo's right ankle. Which was heads? Which was tails? No way to tell. The dull metal was as smooth as glass.

Any number of times, I had asked her about that penny around her ankle. But Cleo claimed she'd had it so long she thought she'd been born with it. "Maybe my mama," she guessed. "Maybe Aunt Charlotte."

I was eating too fast to talk, even if I'd wanted to. My mouth full of biscuit and sweet pickle, I looked past the flowering bushes with their butterflies and bees, to the sheets and aprons and one yellow dress moving in the slight breeze. The threat of rain, if there ever was one, had passed. With my mind's eye, I watched a magic breath from the pines turn the yellow dress into a golden horse, the horse Troy was supposed to have been.

When I was younger, even a year ago, I might have shared this little bit of daydream with Cleo. Cleo would nod and add to my story. Then I would add to Cleo's part. On and on we would go, spinning a tale.

But now I was too old to waste my time making up fairy tales. Only real-life stories mattered now, stories about archaeologists and their excavations of mythical sites. It would be a long time before I saw how my appetite for fairy tales had made me hungry for myths and the stories of the archaeologists who unearthed the world of those myths—a long time before I understood the short distance from magical golden horse to mythical winged horse, the immortal Pegasus.

Cleo stood and stretched, putting her hands on her lower back. "Aunt Charlotte wants a visit."

"Aunt Charlotte's dead. You mean Jesse, don't you?"

The sun had gone low. I didn't know what time it was, but crickets and tree frogs were singing all around us. Too late, I thought with bitterness, too late to hunt for relics.

Cleo gave me a hard look. "Aunt Charlotte died on this very day twenty years ago. She wants a visit. You don't want to go, Etta, you can sit right here."

This new Cleo didn't care one bit whether I was disappointed or not. She didn't even care whether I walked with her to Aunt Charlotte's house.

Sulking, I followed her past the garden and the outhouse, into the woods where a path began. It was deep with pine straw, but not quite deep enough to keep out the weeds and briers. Bright green cords laced with yellow teeth rose from the ground and fell from the branches above them. We crouched to pass under a pine that had fallen across the path into the fork of another tree. A second pine had fallen along the path as well, revealing a root bed swarming with ants.

Cleo was beating an arc in front of us with a long stick. She warned me, as she often did, of snakes: the coachwhip snake that would wrap itself around a tree and whip you with its long tail, the hoop snake that bit its tail and rolled like a wheel right over you.

A whippoorwill called.

"Whip poor Will," I mimicked.

"Watch your mouth," Cleo snapped.

I had no idea when we might come out, the trees were so dense. But suddenly we were emerging into the pinkish light of sunset. To the left of the opening rose a tall stand of bamboo, and to the right sat the tumbledown shack that had been a fixture in the distance all my life. I had never seen it up close. Around it were clumps of weeds and parched-looking wildflowers, scattered jars and shards of blue glass. Next to the porch, almost beneath it, lay a bucket, its bottom rusted through.

The barbed wire, which Mr. Mac and Jesse had gone to mend, separated the Aunt Charlotte field, a hayfield where the grass was now knee-high, from a strip of woods, beyond which lay the pasture. The men were nowhere in sight. The break must have been where the fence divided the pasture from the west end of the tobacco field; if so, I couldn't see them for the woods. But

I could see, beyond the drainage ditch, where Will and I had raced the day before and Troy had jinxed me. My dark mood blackened.

Cleo warned me to watch my step. "This been standing since slavery days."

The porch was half-gone. Inside, some of the floorboards had rotted so that in places I could see the ground. Patches of violet sky showed through the holes in the roof. But the shack itself was oddly clean and free of debris. It was as though someone swept it.

Suddenly I felt better. No telling what I might find when I came back to excavate, which I was immediately determined to do.

Cleo reached into the rolled sleeve of her dress for her packet of tobacco, then down to her stocking for the paper. With her usual precision, she tapped tobacco the length of the paper, rolled, and licked it from end to end.

"Aunt Charlotte had a healing hand. Your grandmammy would have died right off without my aunty and her potions and her praying."

I had to think a minute. Grandmammy? Cleo was referring to Miss Lila, my father's mother.

Cleo stood, quietly smoking. "Feel it?" she asked.

"Feel what?" But suddenly I did feel a light breeze that made me shiver, though here it was July.

"Shush," Cleo whispered.

It was the breeze, rattling the bamboo—or was it a bird, fluttering somewhere against the roof? Just where the sound was coming from I couldn't tell. Again I shivered. Without thinking, I grabbed Cleo's hand.

"Aunty, we here to pay you a visit. This here's Etta, Miss Lila's own little granddaughter. Isn't she a pretty thing? Smart, too. Maybe one day she'll have a sweet temper'ment. Her little brother having an operation. Little Will have a right sweet temper'ment…"

Eyes were staring at me. The broken-out windows, the holes in the roof were eyes; the doorway was an eye. Cleo didn't say another word; she just stood there smoking.

I tugged my hand free and went back outside. Breathing deeply, I looked all around. Where was Troy? It had been his eye on me. My feet felt glued to the ground next to the porch. I listened hard. The rotting floorboards creaked—Cleo was taking her time. Finally she appeared and eased herself off the porch.

"Why'd you have to go and tell Aunt Charlotte…about my temperament?"

"Baby, you got a stubborn streak. One day gone trip you up. Blessed are the meek—remember that. They shall inherit the earth."

"You don't understand anything about me," I said.

I stared hard at the stand of bamboo. It wasn't raining, but the sound of rain was coming from inside it.

"Troy—I knew it! He's in there spying on me."

"He'll be full of ticks if he is," Cleo said matter-of-factly, as if she were talking merely about a real horse and not a haunted one, a "hant-horse." She has other ghosts on her mind, I thought.

"Aunt Charlotte—what is she? A ghost or something? You talk to her as if she's a hant-something-or-other."

"She's a wandering spirit."

"A what?"

"She always claimed her people were buried back yonder." Cleo waved towards the Swamp Fox woods. I shivered yet again.

According to Mr. Mac, Francis Marion—the Swamp Fox—had camped out there during the Revolutionary War, had even dug a holding pen for prisoners. My grandfather and I and sometimes Will had poked the ground with sticks. The most anyone turned up were pieces of broken glass caked with rooty dirt—that is, until a month ago when I had talked Margot and Stephanie into excavating the site with me. But that was a day I kept trying to erase from my memory. Had Cleo forgotten? She never did tell my parents—I would have known if she had. How I hoped she had forgotten!

"Nobody buried there I know of," Cleo continued. "Aunt Charlotte was already steep up in years, when next thing you know she had a stroke. Her granddaughter came down from New York and took her to live up North. She was pitiful. 'Bout all she could get out her mouth that wasn't mixed up by the stroke was 'Don't take me off. Don't bury me in strange ground.' But they buried her up yonder where she didn't know nobody. She's been a wandering spirit ever since. She found her way back down here, but she's not settled."

The bamboo rattled. It couldn't be Troy, unless he was a ghost for real.

Aunt Charlotte it must be—but why would any colored person want to come back here? Here wasn't any Promised Land. Why would she come South, where even at the doctor's office colored people had to sit in a separate waiting room with hard folding chairs, as if their skin was contagious—or so it seemed to me when I went with my mother to take Cleo to Dr. Monroe's. Mama and I, who were with Cleo all the time, who'd driven her to town, got to wait in the white one where the chairs were soft and a golden-framed painting of a boy in blue old-timey clothes, with bows on his shoes and a plumed hat in his hand, gazed down at us. Once, after we got Cleo's prescription filled at Whaley's Drug Store, my mother had to drive to the Sinclair Service Station for a colored women's bathroom, since the one at Whaley's had a sign: "White Ladies Only."

On TV and in magazines, I had seen pictures of fire hoses aimed at young colored people, ripping off their shirts, sending girls toppling over cars. I'd seen photographs of policemen with German Shepherds trained to attack; one of those policemen held a boy by his shirt front. What were those colored people doing that was so bad they had to be punished? Aunt Charlotte would be wise to keep away, even if that sort of violence wasn't happening right here, even if she was a spirit.

Cleo, beating the ground in front of her with her stick, began walking towards the pines and the screaming tree frogs and the path to her house. I hung back. Cleo knew things, I had to admit; my parents never talked about spirits, much less to them. Cleo lived as though the world was two places at once: the one you saw with your eyes and another that…well, it was hard to explain—a place you had to imagine, though it was different from stories you read or made up yourself. But smart as Cleo was, she couldn't be trusted to act when you needed her to. Troy could have killed Trudy, and there was Cleo—I could see her still—stopped dead in her tracks.

Now, walking behind her, I watched as Cleo trudged ahead, dragging her shadow. Suddenly that shadow became a ghost, flat on the ground for now, but stalking Cleo. Any minute, it would rise up behind her on its own two feet and snatch her off. But the sun sank into the trees; Cleo's shadow vanished.

If Aunt Charlotte's cabin had been standing since slavery days, it could be hiding something special. This was an ideal site to excavate. But everything around the place seemed haunted. Aunt Charlotte—she was *here*.

But why should spirits faze me? They didn't faze Mr. Mac. After all, though he never said as much, Miss Lila haunted the shuttered bedroom where she died. Still there, the walnut four-poster bed where she'd suffered, a horsehair blanket folded at its foot. There too, the marble-topped table and dainty desk. Once, sliding open Miss Lila's dresser drawer, snooping without permission, I had felt on the back of my neck the brush of fingers light as feathers. My own fingers had found a photograph of a thin, handsome young soldier in a pale dress uniform—Mr. Mac, my grandfather, hardly recognizable, as otherworldly as a spirit himself.

"Whether you're here or not," I said aloud to Aunt Charlotte, "I'm coming back with a shovel."

4: Shell-Shock

July 9, 1964

"Got your nose in that book again." Mr. Mac nudged my foot with his work boot.

It was morning. I'd been sitting on the front porch steps waiting. But lost amid the Sphinx and pyramids of Egypt, I didn't even hear him drive up.

"You know I'm going to be an archaeologist." I had told him this over and over, but he always seemed surprised. "Can we go hunt for Indian stuff? After the chores?"

"We'll see."

Mr. Mac's truck jounced along the dirt road that divided the tobacco fields. Dust blew in so hard I had to squint. Still, since Mr. Mac's shirt was already soaked through with sweat from loading hay in the bed of the truck, we kept the windows rolled down. I was just grateful to have the seat to myself for a change, and not be touching my brother's sticky knees.

Mr. Mac pushed his wide-brimmed hat back off his forehead. He was chewing on his cigar. "We need to find Will a present for when he comes back after his operation. I'm thinking he needs a fishing pole. When he feels up to it, we'll take the boat and go creek fishing."

Fishing was something that Mr. Mac and Will could enjoy doing together. Without me. "*I* don't have a fishing pole."

Mr. Mac looked at me over his glasses, which had slipped halfway down his nose. The frames were brown across the top but clear on the sides. His ice-blue eyes, eyes that were always startling, seemed to stab at me. "Didn't know you cared anything about fishing."

"Well, I do." My face went hot. He knows I don't, I thought. I turned away and stared at the field, a green leafy sea that met the far wall of trees.

So far as I knew, my family—like every other farming family in the South Carolina Lowcountry—had always grown tobacco. For all I knew, the ritual of growing Bright Leaf was the same now as it had been forever, except that around the time I was born, tractors began replacing the mules whose barn was now Troy's. I could remember standing with Mr. Mac near a barn in the fog of early morning and watching a mule drag a pile of cropped tobacco towards us. I couldn't have been older than three. Was it the last mule they owned? Was it my first memory? Will didn't remember any mules at all.

The entire year seemed like a patchwork quilt whose pattern told the story of tobacco. Christmas was no sooner over than Mr. Mac and Papa were preparing and planting the beds. In April, when the azaleas and redbuds exploded into bloom, they set the baby plants out in the fields. When school let out for summer, the long weeks of fieldwork began—weeding, fertilizing, irrigating, breaking off the blooms and little shoots called suckers that made the leaves puny if left on the stalk. Midsummer with its heat and bugs and frog-songs brought the frenzy of cropping, when the workers followed the tractor and gradually stripped the plants of their leaves, and curing, when the leaves were heated until they turned yellow-gold. Then in early August—sometimes sooner, sometimes later—came the grand finale. The market opened with the toasty smells of cured tobacco, the taste of boiled peanuts, the singsong speed-talk of the auctioneer. The work of the entire year would end with relief or disappointment, depending on the prices set by the buyers who came from Winston-Salem in chauffeured Cadillacs.

Mr. Mac and I checked three barns that were curing before we stopped at one that was "putting in." It was surrounded by workers hauling tobacco or tying the cropped leaves onto sticks to be hung inside.

"When you coming to work with us?" Evelyn asked. Cleo's niece was eighteen and pretty, but she always paid attention to me. I couldn't keep my eyes away from her. "You plenty big enough," she said. Her little sister Juney and a boy no older than Will stood "handing"—fitting together bunches of leaves for Evelyn to string and tie by their stem ends onto long, thin sticks. The children's little fingers were quick and sure, their eyes wide and serious.

"Why, Evelyn, you know Etta's got to help her old granddaddy." I was his number one assistant, he added. I stared at the ground, embarrassed. My grandfather was speaking of me as if I were a tiny child. I knew good and well that I never helped at all, not really.

"Now who's this over here?" Mr. Mac went to shake hands with a young colored man who sprang to his feet from the narrow bench against the wall of the barn. "That your fine keeyar?" he nodded towards the black convertible parked beside the barn.

"Roscoe Hawkins, nice to meet you, and yes, sir, that's my set of wheels." He had shiny curls and a tight t-shirt that showed off his muscles.

"Need some work, Roscoe? We could use another good set of hands."

"No, sir, I'm here to say hi to Evelyn." Evelyn looked down and smiled. Her mother, Starry, looked up and frowned. "Matter of fact," Roscoe continued, "I'm—"

A tractor backfired. Everyone jumped, but Mr. Mac staggered to the bench, his legs seeming to give way. His face turned pasty, and his mouth twitched. He grabbed his hands together, to make them stop shaking. Roscoe sat on one side of him, and Starry sat on the other. She told him to take a deep breath, another. "It going to pass, Mr. Mac." Starry was tall and thin, the opposite of her sister Cleo.

"The war-fits," Evelyn whispered in my ear. I nodded. I knew about them; Mr. Mac had been shell-shocked in the First World War.

It was okay for Starry to help Mr. Mac, but not Roscoe. He was a swaggering sort of boy, who grinned a suspicious toothy grin. A boy who came just to flirt with Evelyn—and who had overheard the baby way Mr. Mac had talked about *me*. I wished Mr. Mac would tell him to leave and not come back. But he seemed not to mind this Roscoe.

"How is Aunt Cleo doing?" Evelyn whispered, following me to Mr. Mac's truck. "She said at church she's not been feeling well."

"She's fine."

"She has high blood pressure, you know."

I nodded in what I thought was a knowing way.

Mr. Mac had to drive down through Boggy Swamp to reach the Island Pasture where the cows were grazing. Normally that meant sloshing the pickup through mud or even a shallow stream, where the black-green water ran from one side of the swamp to the other. But the road was bone dry. Buzzards clutched the craggy tops of the cypress trees hung with Spanish moss. Those trees reminded Will of witches, witches who could snatch you up, put a spell on you, and turn you into one of those buzzards who ate only dead things that stank to high heaven. He'd gone on so long about the witch-trees, I couldn't look at them any longer without seeing towering hunched figures with bony arms and gray hair—a childish thing to think, I scolded myself.

Since he was old enough to go out on the farm with Mr. Mac and me, Will was the one to have all the bad luck, all the accidents. If a shard of broken glass lurked anywhere in a field, it found its way into his foot. Stinging insects sought him out. And once, under the tractor shed, he sat in a pool of spilt gasoline and had to go to the emergency room. With a blistered bottom, he couldn't sit down for three days.

"Remember how Will used to cry when we got stuck out here in the mud?" I asked out loud. Mr. Mac, who was again his steady self, had just climbed back into the truck after opening the gate to the pasture.

"Wish we did have some mud. We sure need rain." He eased the truck forward.

"But remember how he'd act like a baby when we got bogged down? I'd tell him we could walk home, but he'd holler for Mama."

"I remember the snapping turtle that got his toe," Mr. Mac replied, defending him. "He acted braver than I'd have done."

I felt my cheeks redden. I remembered Will's foot and the turtle, its neck stretched out, attached to it. I remembered Mr. Mac on hands and knees in the mud.

"Hold the shell," Mr. Mac had ordered me. "Hold it tight."

My hands had clutched the sharp-edged, slippery shell. It was almost the size of a football. A scaly tail stuck out at me.

Mr. Mac tugged from his pants pocket the knife he used to cut the twine off hay bales. Pinching the head of the turtle between his thumb and forefinger, he opened the knife with his teeth. Two strokes and he'd sawed through the turtle's leathery neck. He hadn't hesitated. How could that be? I still didn't understand. Mr. Mac was a man who refused to hunt, who instead of slapping a horsefly buzzing against the windshield of his truck cupped his hand around it and tossed it back outside. He

wouldn't even kill a spider; he'd merely brush it aside. Blood—
the turtle's—had spattered all of us.

Will, who was whimpering in pain, had his eyes shut tight.
But I saw everything that happened next. Staggering to his feet,
Mr. Mac dropped his knife into the pasture. "Be all right," he
whispered, "in a minute." He jammed his hands into his pockets
and closed his eyes. He clenched his teeth, bit his cigar in two,
then spit it out into the mud. It seemed longer than any minute
before Mr. Mac opened his eyes again and wiped his face with
his handkerchief. "The war, Etta. Wants to come back now and
again."

That was the first time; I'd seen maybe a half-dozen spells
since. They unnerved me, these war-fits. I hated it when they
took him wherever they took him—away from me. But I always
pretended not to be bothered.

"Will's not scared of much that I can see. Not even spiders."
Mr. Mac was needling me now. He knew I hated spiders with
their invisible webs, their scurrying too-many legs, their fangs. I
thought of lashing out; his war-fits must show *he* was scared of
something. But I held my tongue.

Mr. Mac drove across the parched ground to where the
cows had clustered at the farthest end of the pasture near the
border of trees. I scanned the open pasture from one end to the
other but saw no strange figure, no Troy. Most summers, the
cows had plenty of grass for grazing; only in the winter did Mr.
Mac have to deliver hay. But this summer the cows would starve
if they had to depend on grass. It was so dry turtles were aban-
doning the swamp for the fields, where they died. Buzzards
made quick work of them, scattering their empty shells, shells
that brought to my mind old helmets or skulls.

It occurred to me that I could climb up onto the bed of the
truck and help by pushing out the hay. I set my weight against
the bales and tipped them towards Mr. Mac, who stood in the

pasture. He grabbed the twine and swung them down. The two of us made a team. Grasshoppers flew up as, one after the other, the bales hit the ground. I sneezed from the dust and wiped my hands on my shorts. "Need any more help?" I pulled out the hand-me-down knife.

Mr. Mac was cutting the twine, then kicking at the hay to scatter it. Next time, he said, I could use his sharp knife to cut the bales loose.

I had just now proved something, proved that I could work hard, like Evelyn. It was a loony notion, yes, but I was sure that Troy would know—he had ways of knowing.

We'd finished. Mr. Mac had wheeled the truck around and nearly reached the gate, when—I couldn't help it—I gripped his arm.

"How long has that been here—the trough?" The cows' water trough was a hollowed-out log fed by a flowing well. I'd seen the ancient-looking thing all my life, but I'd never before *thought* about it.

Mr. Mac gave me that half-smile of his. Far back as he could remember, he reckoned.

The old men at Walter's Store recently had told tales about the strange places Southerners hid their valuables during what they called "the War of Yankee Aggression."

"They hid silver and good jewelry in pig troughs, can you believe that?" Mr. Sneed had said, his eyes narrowing behind his thick square glasses. "Where they slop pigs. Ain't nobody—not even some fool Yankee—going to wade in no hog waller." He winked at Mr. Oliver, whose family had been plantation owners. "Your rich granddaddy keep hogs, Bud?"

I gripped the truck's door handle. "Things might be down there in the bottom—old things, from the Civil War even."

"I can't say it's that old, now."

But I wasn't really listening. I was imagining that somehow Troy, wherever he was, had seen me as worthy. He'd guided me to the trough where the water was clear and cold, and green algae carpeted the bottom—or was it the green cud-foam that slobbered from the mouths of the cows? The perfect camouflage for diamonds or emeralds.

"Five minutes? Please?" I was already kicking off my shoes.

Mr. Mac shrugged. "Least you got on your high-water pants. You've got too big for me to lift you, though."

I hoisted myself over, an awkward move, even with my long legs.

My toes sank into the layer of slime. Sludge oozed up between them. My calves knotted up in the frigid knee-deep water.

Mr. Mac began coughing and kept on coughing. Coughing and coughing. It was a bad spell, but I had witnessed worse. Besides getting shell-shocked, he'd breathed mustard gas during the war—which had something to do with why he didn't smoke cigarettes.

I tried to be patient. I needed his shoulder to hang on to while I searched with my feet; the bottom was slick as glass.

Perhaps it was Mr. Mac's coughing that caught the cows' attention, drew their eyes towards the trough, made the dumb things realize that in this heat they were thirsty. Whatever the reason, all of the cows at once began trotting towards us. All except one. One hung back, its head twisted and its back swayed. Not a cow at all: Troy. Shaking now as though *I* was shell-shocked, I slid one foot forward, feeling only the slippery bottom of the trough.

Two steps and down I went, my feet flying out in front of me—down on my back, hard, into the slime-green, ice-cold water. I tried to use my hands and elbows to scramble up, but algae slicked the sides of the trough as well. I slipped back; my head slammed against the bottom. I swallowed water, kept sliding under.

Between coughs, somehow Mr. Mac managed to grab my arms and haul me out. I coughed myself, and spit and stomped. The back of my head pounded. Mr. Mac was still hacking. A rash had risen up his neck all the way to his face.

"Now," he finally said, breathing hard, "we got to go home and get you some new britches."

"Did you see...?"

"What?" Mr. Mac had had enough of my foolishness.

"Nothing."

This was the sort of thing that happened to Will. Never to me. I scanned the pasture. But Troy had disappeared. Surely this time I'd been seeing things. Mr. Mac and Jesse had walked the entire fence line and made it secure. Yet Troy was there—he was—and jinxed me. But why? I'd helped Mr. Mac; I'd proved myself. It didn't make sense, his acting this way. Nothing the old horse did made sense.

Before he took me home, Mr. Mac had to check on the temperature of two more barns that were curing, the progress of cropping at three fields, and the putting-in of the strung tobacco at the barns that belonged to those fields. He had to arrange for the shifting of irrigation pipes. Then Jesse came driving up; he needed Mr. Mac back at the equipment shed to fix a broken tractor. By now, my clothes were practically dry.

Troy was right there, standing on the shady side of the mule barn. While Mr. Mac tended to the tractor under the shed, I stomped across the pasture. Several feet away from the horse, I stopped. He lifted his head in a disinterested way, flicked an ear, and fastened his good eye on me.

"It's a long way from here to the Island Pasture. You'd have to jump the fence and go through a tobacco field and the swamp somehow to get there. You're not even sweaty. Maybe that wasn't you out there. But if it was, then it's true: you really do have powers. Look here, Troy—" I slapped the wall of the barn and felt a splinter enter my palm, the kind that was half-rotten and would break off when Cleo tried to gouge it out with a needle.

"Mr. Mac made me out to be a little kid—in front of Evelyn and them. But I'm not, and I proved it, helping him with the hay. I know you saw me, somehow. But then you turn me into a fool, making me fall in the trough. Just like you made me lose those races to Will—made my feet stick in the mud. I don't know what you're after, what it is I have to prove. But one thing's for sure—you're not going to keep me from being an archaeologist. You're going to help me. You're Troy—get it? I named you after a famous find, and one of these days I'm going to be famous for finding something, and you'll be my trusty mascot. The second-most famous horse that ever was." After, of course, the Trojan horse!

I stepped towards him, and Troy nodded his lopsided head as if in agreement, while showing his square brown teeth, which always made me nervous. Still, I pulled a few soggy raisins from my pocket and held them out. "You want 'em?" Troy staggered a step towards me. I snapped my fingers closed around them. "I'm the boss. Not you." Troy moved forward again, still showing his teeth. I turned. I ran and didn't stop until I was over the gate and back into Mr. Mac's truck.

5: Walter's Store

July 9, 1964

Mr. Mac and I were late morning getting to the store, which meant I would spoil my appetite for Cleo's dinner. She'd fuss, but so what. Troy had ruined my day; it could hardly get worse.

I rifled through the red cooler until I found what I was looking for, a Coke with slushy ice in its green throat. I chose a Mars Bar to go with it and sat down with my grandfather on the wooden bench that stuck out from Walter's candy counter.

Mr. Hamm, Mr. Sneed, and Mr. Oliver, all three old and leathery, were sitting in sagging cane-bottom chairs around the pot-bellied stove. The stove was cold and black now, but when the weather turned, sometime in October, it would glow a hot orange. The men were murmuring about the drought and whose tractor had broken down and the quality of the North Carolina leaf and something going on in that place I had heard President Johnson talk about on TV—Veet Nam. My mind was still back with Troy. For all I knew, and for whatever reason, he'd found a way to bring both the drought and the far-off fighting the old men were referring to.

A rock sat next to me on the bench. It was large and round and had never been there before. With a smooth, hollowed-out middle, it was different from any rock I'd ever seen. To lift it, I had to use both hands.

"Heavy, ain't it?" Mr. Walter came out from behind the counter. He was a pinkish man with lots of white hair and a soft, baby-like look to his face. Since he wasn't a farmer, his hands were also soft and white. "John Henry ran across this over at that Injun field belongs to Grady Vickers."

I balanced the rock on my lap.

"He brought it to me yesterday evening. First one of these I know of been found around here."

Walter was a collector. There were two big frames on the wall behind the cash register. In one of them there were arrowheads of various shapes and sizes all together, arranged in the shape of one huge arrowhead. In the other, arrowheads and spear points and stained grayish tubes—they looked to me like cigarettes; I didn't know what they were—lay in neat rows. He limped over to me—one leg was shorter than the other—lifted the stone, and took it over to the other men to show them.

"What is it?" I asked.

"I'm pretty sure it's a grinding bowl. When Cass comes in, we'll know for sure." Cassandra Bearclaw, who had been married to a real Indian chief, was the acknowledged expert.

It must have been because Miss Cass had moved back down here from up North after her Mohawk husband died that Mr. Hamm thought to say, "Talked to my brother last night."

Mr. Hamm, who farmed some ten miles away near Horry County, had a brother in Mississippi. "They still ain't found them two Jew Yankees and that colored boy what disappeared two, three weeks ago. Got everybody, even Navy sailors, even the FBI, out digging and hunting." Mr. Hamm had lost both a ring and pinkie finger in a combine accident years ago. I always had to try not to stare.

"Klan probably got 'em. They got a big Klan over in Mississippi." Mr. Oliver didn't talk much, but when he did his enormous ears, ears bigger than my father's, moved at the same time. His head was bald as a baby bird's. He acted just like any other farmer, but his family had been rich before the Civil War, and he still lived next door to the ruined plantation house.

Puny by Charleston standards but impressive for our neck of the woods, the once-white two-story mansion, separated from the road by a pecan orchard, had two porches, upstairs and down, that stretched the length of the house. The upper porch was gradually falling down, both sides towards the middle. Mr. Oliver kept trying to prop it up with poles.

"Louis—that's my brother—he thinks the whole thing's a hoax to make the state look bad. Hoax or not, they got themselves a mess, that's what. Everybody locking their doors at night, white and colored." Mr. Hamm made a locking gesture with his three-fingered hand. I looked at the floor. The hand reminded me of a buzzard's talon.

"Yankees got no business coming down there interfering," said Mr. Sneed, whose black-rimmed glasses were so thick and heavy-looking on his big veiny nose I thought he must be almost blind, "even if they think they doing right, helping the niggers pass that literacy test. You want them to vote?"

"Verne…" Mr. Mac nodded towards me. My face grew warm. No one in my family used that word. But what I felt was not shock or even embarrassment. It was guilt.

"She might as well get used to it, Mac. She's going to hear that and worse, the way things are headed."

Mr. Mac sighed. "Getting as bad there as Alabama."

I remembered what had happened in Alabama, right after school started last September. A bomb went off in a Baptist church and four colored girls were killed. The TV said the Klan had planted it, and showed blurry footage of the KKK, white-robed grownups in pointed hoods swarming around a tall flaming cross.

Over a week or so, the nightly news portrayed first the church in rubble, then—pulled from a ruined basement—stretchers with white cloths draped over them. Finally the funerals with their small coffins. I could still see the expression on my mother's face. She'd bit her bottom lip and touched her forehead as though it hurt. "A church. Just children! Little girls."

I had studied their pictures in the *Time* magazine that came to our house. They wore nice Sunday clothes. One was my age, eleven. I remembered lying in bed, making up a story that had a happy ending. Instead of dying, they'd been turned by magic into birds, had flown off just as the church exploded. Nesting now in a high tree, they would return to their parents once the spell wore off, once they ate the last of the Klansmen whom the fire changed into white worms....

Only a fairy tale—now that I was almost twelve, I couldn't even halfway believe such a thing. Still, I wished it were true.

"At least our nigras..." Mr. Sneed slapped at his knee and winked at Mr. Mac. "Our *Ne*-groes don't cause trouble like them ones. Not yet, anyway—just you keep your Yankee kin in line." Now he narrowed his eyes at Mr. Oliver. "Having sit-ins at lunch counters, kneel-ins in decent white churches, marches and all the rest."

I pictured the colored families who were working right now in the fields and barns—Cleo's relatives and friends, faces I'd known all my life. They didn't seem unhappy. Whenever I was with them on the farm, they'd be singing or humming hymns, as Cleo did while she worked, or tunes that maybe sounded sad but hardly could be when so many voices were singing at once. Why, sometimes my arms would prickle; I could feel the fine hair stand up—yes, that was pleasure. Or else they'd be "carrying on," as my grandfather put it, teasing each other about something I couldn't figure out and laughing "fit to kill." And yet almost every night the grainy TV in our den showed colored people marching and getting arrested. For what? Why weren't they happy? Weren't there farms like ours in Mississippi, Alabama? What did they want?

For some time now, mostly at school, I had begun to feel that the outside world was coming closer and growing larger and more puzzling. There was talk of mushroom clouds; there were "duck and cover" drills, a blaring alarm that sent me diving under my desk and kept me there, my classmates and me crouching under our desks until the alarm shut off. Then, too, there were astronauts rocketing into space—hadn't we watched a liftoff in class on a small TV with rabbit ears?

These events were far away—what had they to do with me? When I left school and was home on the farm, I quickly forgot about them.

Until Troy came. And it seemed he not only changed my life with Will, Mr. Mac, and Cleo but also brought the changing outside world right into our house. The bombing in Alabama was just the start. With my family I had watched the President's funeral on television, his little son, younger even than Will, saluting the horse-drawn coffin. And then, though none of us had seen it live, the killer shot dead on TV. Every night at supper-time, or so it seemed, the charred and smoldering remains of other churches, houses and buses too, and angry faces, white as well as black, peaceful marchers and onlookers merged into a fighting mob—that world invading mine, even here at Walter's Store with talk of Negroes making trouble and Yankees coming down South where they didn't belong.

It made sense, I thought: if the Klan would bomb a church and kill little girls, it probably did something terrible to those interfering Northerners. I had learned in history this year about Sherman's Yankee army, how it swept eastward through the state burning everything it came across. Now, instead of Yankees, I pictured the Klan marching closer and closer, their torches raised.

The front screened door slammed shut. "Speak of the devil," Mr. Sneed murmured.

"I've got to have some twine, Walter." Miss Cass came in talking. "You'd better not be out....Morning, gentlemen; morning, Etta. How's that miracle-horse of yours? Troy, that right?

Good name for him—he's turned himself into a myth, don't you know?"

As put out as I was with Troy, I couldn't help feeling some pride. I grinned. Troy, my Troy, a myth! Miss Cass and I thought alike.

"Struck by lightning and lived to tell the tale." Miss Cass looked at the men as if she were telling them something they didn't already know.

Miss Cass always dressed like a man, except for her big dusty black pocketbook. She wore a fringed leather belt around the waist of her khaki pants and a wide straw hat over the loose yellowish-white braid that went down her back. She was old, but not as old as Mr. Mac. Her face was lean and angular, and her nose was sharp. Her green eyes, set far apart as they were and slanting up a little, gave her a foreign look, and her accent, which wasn't Southern—perhaps it was Yankee; I couldn't say—added to her mystery. She was always out of breath, as though she ran wherever she went. "Mac! When're you going to bring me some hay? How about tomorrow? My critters 're going hungry."

When Mr. Walter showed her the stone, she sat beside me on the bench. She turned it this way and that; she ran her hands all over it. "Indeed it is a grinding bowl. The Indians put corn in the hollow here and used another rock to grind it down to meal. These are rare. Gabriel left me a couple, but I've never found one out in a field. The Vickers field, you say? I wonder what else is out there. Be worth exploring after a rain. If we ever get another one, don't you know."

The old men nodded politely. Feeling fidgety, I started to pick at a hangnail. Rain? No telling when rain would ever come again, coaxing relics to the surface of the field. Mr. Walter had an impressive collection of arrowheads, now a grinding bowl. Surely more artifacts, even better ones, were waiting for someone to find them. Why not me?

Miss Cass paid for her twine, then turned back to Mr. Mac. "Hay? Tomorrow?"

"Yes'm," he promised. "Etta can help me."

"I'm sorry to say this," Mr. Sneed began as soon as Miss Cass was out the door, "but she is not, repeat not, one of us." She was a Yankee, he continued, and she was stirring up trouble, talking to the nigger—*Negro*—preachers, even driving all the way to that big march in Washington last summer.

She was all right, Mr. Mac said. She wasn't a troublemaker, just an "odd duck."

Abruptly he turned to Mr. Oliver and asked about his cotton. Mr. Oliver and Miss Cass were related somehow; she'd even grown up around here. This was common knowledge, but I still found it hard to believe. Miss Cass was different from any woman I had ever met. She made her own rules and didn't seem to care what anybody thought of her.

"You've got to promise to take me to the Vickers field. Please, Mr. Mac," I begged as we got into the truck to head home. No other field would do now. There, with or without Troy's help, I might discover what no one else had found: evidence of a whole Pee Dee Indian village—hatchets and spear points, pipes and figurines. Whole pots instead of just pieces of pottery. A grinding bowl filled with beads.

I was trying to forget about the Klan. Thinking about it made me feel sick to my stomach—almost like I'd felt last summer when I'd tried to follow Will across the Mile High Swinging Bridge in the Great Smoky Mountains, where our family had gone on vacation. Right in the middle I'd frozen, my hand stuck fast to the railing. I would fall to my death, I was sure. My father had to loosen my fingers and pull me the rest of the way.

Making a find would put my feet on solid ground. It would make me more than special; I'd be famous. And like magic it would erase everything that was wrong between Cleo and me. I pictured myself as I used to be, in Cleo's arms, breathing in her smoky spiced-peach smell as we swayed from side to side in a slow sort of dance.

I was quiet for a few minutes.

"How come Mr. Sneed hates colored people so much? And how come they all seem so scared—those men?"

Mr. Mac shook his head. "They're used to life being one way, and now they see it changing. Old folks aren't good at having their ideas turned inside out."

I nodded.

"But he was ugly, Mr. Sneed was. He was mean."

"He's set in his ways."

"Mr. Frank called on the telephone." Cleo met us at the back door, which opened into the kitchen. "Long distance. Will had all his tests and he's having his operation tomorrow morning. They all settled at the Holiday Inn."

While Mr. Mac and I ate at the kitchen table, Cleo cleared the stove and washed dishes.

"Let me tell you," I said loudly enough for Cleo to hear. I speared a piece of pork chop with my fork and waved it around for emphasis. "The water in that trough was cold! Cold as snow. I felt like I was drowning, drowning in a wood *coffin*." I put the bite in my mouth and chewed for a while. Somehow telling about the incident this way transformed it from humiliation to adventure. Though I'd done nothing heroic—I'd found nothing—I at least sounded like a hero. Plus, if I kept talking, I could postpone having to take another bite. I'd spoiled my appetite, exactly as Cleo suspected I'd do. "There was slime on the bottom five inches thick. At least. I wouldn't have slipped if..." I didn't want to mention Troy.

"My," Cleo said. I stiffened. I sensed what Cleo was thinking: What's a big girl like you doing wading in a trough? But instead of commenting, Cleo refilled Mr. Mac's iced tea glass. She brought him a warm biscuit in a napkin. And I, instead of feeling relieved, felt pushed aside.

"You planning to plant cabbage this year?" Mr. Mac asked her. "Turnips?"

I ate one more bite of pork chop, two green beans, and one forkful of rice.

"I believe," I interrupted, sounding reckless even to myself, "that I'll find treasure this week, maybe today. Mr. Mac is going to take me to the Vickers field, and I *know* I'll find something there. I can feel it in my bones."

"The treasure you find," Cleo said, "may not be the treasure you seek." She picked up my plate and looked at it. "You been eating candy, ain't you?" She frowned first at me, then at Mr. Mac.

It wasn't the first time Cleo had said that about the treasure, but what did it mean? Cleo was always repeating things that sounded like the Bible, whether they were or not. And half the time I couldn't make sense of them.

"I'll have to give old man Vickers a call first. Get his permission."

"I think that devil-horse still getting out of the pasture. I could have swore I saw him in the orchard when I was snapping these beans on the porch this morning."

"You were just seeing things, Cleo. They fixed the fence yesterday. And that old Troy, he can hardly walk at all." I gave a fake laugh. I didn't want anything to come between me and the Vickers field, especially Troy. "Besides, that gate is locked, unless one of you forgot to lock it." I couldn't believe they ever forgot, or would think they did.

Even so, Mr. Mac said, "Reckon I'd better take Jesse out and go back around the fence this afternoon. That horse is nothing but trouble."

I chewed my bottom lip. I knew from his tone he'd made up his mind. As much as I wanted to believe that Troy was special, a miracle-horse, as Miss Cass said, I had to admit my grandfather was right. From the get-go the old horse had been nothing but trouble.

6: Trojan Horse

"Yes, yes, I'll feed him," I had sworn to my parents, begging for months before my eleventh birthday for a horse of my own. "I'll groom him," I promised. "I'll share with *Will*," I even said, all the while picturing a magnificent Palomino who was devoted to me, upon whose back my friends and I could roam the farm. A horse so special that even Joyce Ann Richardson—a popular girl who looked the other way if I was with Will—would want to visit way out here in the country, miles from town.

Papa had taken movies of my first ride on the old horse who wasn't yet Troy but still Jim Dandy, a ridiculous name. I watched myself bigger than life on the projection screen in the den—wearing shorts, hanging on to the saddle horn, joggling up and down, trying not to look nervous. Close-up to my stuck-on smile. The camera panning from my back down to the horse's broad rear end. My feet kicking like crazy and Jim Dandy barely shuffling, head down, his red-brown mane swinging as though he were shaking his head at the insult of being ridden.

I couldn't blame my parents. They knew nothing about horses and had believed an old worn-out horse would be safer and easier to care for than a young one. Or maybe the truth was they'd been so caught up with Will, as usual, that they never really heard me when I specified "Palomino." At any rate, instead of a sleek and docile, brave and beautiful Palomino like the ones I'd murmured to in picture books, or even a Chestnut with devoted eyes like those I'd seen in movies—like the one my friend Stephanie had gotten—I'd been given this cranky hand-me-down whose coat was the color of dried blood. Instead of a mane that felt like silk and waved in the breeze like the American flag, his felt like an old string mop. Instead of a glistening coat you'd want to put your face against, Jim Dandy's—even when I got up the nerve to brush it—remained dusty and smelly, a magnet for flies.

Troy. At first I'd thought it was the name of the gigantic horse in *Ancient Wonders of the World*, a book that Will had taken to be a collection of fairy tales, what with its illustrations of gold and jewels, gardens and palaces. Such a name, I thought, would have to improve the old animal. Too late I read the story of the Trojan horse—how the Greeks, who had fought the Trojans for ten years on the plains surrounding Troy, made the Trojans a gift of a wooden horse. But in its belly, big as the hold of a ship, they'd hidden their fiercest warriors, and once inside the walls of Troy, the Greeks laid waste to the fortress. At least, I told myself, Troy was where Schliemann found Priam's gold, a buried treasure like no other.

Bribing him with sugar cubes, carrots, raisins, and apples, I did my best to make the horse my own. But saddling him up filled me with the same cold dread of failure that preceded piano recitals. As though he smelled my dread, every day he grew more defiant, until—click my tongue and shake the reins and kick his sides though I might—he would scarcely budge from the barn or its shade in the pasture. But Will, before he lost interest—Will in his Roy Rogers hat, toy pistol waving—got Troy to canter all the way to the fence.

My longtime best friends, Stephanie and Margot, came out to the farm to try their hands with Troy. Stephanie, who took riding lessons on her handsome Chestnut, looked impressive in her beige riding pants and tall black boots. She managed to get Troy to shuffle halfway across the pasture before he wheeled around and galloped back to the barn. Margot, who was pale-skinned and taller even than me, couldn't make him budge. I swung myself up.

"Please, Troy," I whispered. Pretend I'm Will, I silently pleaded. He trotted right out of the barn. I got him to skirt along the fence back towards the fields. Elated, I waved to my friends.

Then Troy slowed down. Stopped. Wheeled around. Now he was galloping fast. The saddle loosened. Slid to one side. "Whoa!" I shouted. I yanked the reins and gripped a clump of Troy's mane; I tightened my knees against the lopsided saddle. Crouching low, I closed my eyes and held on. Once I'd cleared the doorway to the barn, I was able to roll off without falling— stumbling, though, against the cobwebby ladder to the loft. "Devil," I hissed, swiping at the awful sticky webs clinging to my arm.

❧

I began to find one excuse after another to avoid riding Troy: homework in the fall, cold weather in the winter, and then, as spring began, rain. Of course I'd complained to everyone at home and at school about not being able to ride. But I was relieved beyond the telling. I dreaded the blue skies to come. Then I'd be expected not only to ride him but also to want to. "Just had to have a horse," I could hear my parents saying. "Just *had* to"— rubbing my nose in it.

The day of the accident, a Saturday afternoon in early March, Trudy Drummer had just finished her piano lesson with my mother, who taught from home on the Baldwin upright in our living room. Her parents and mine played bridge together. It wasn't unusual that Trudy's family, her brother and her parents, were there to stay for dinner.

Trudy was only seven, but she was what my mother called a firecracker. After her lesson, when the grownups gathered for martinis, Trudy glommed onto me and wouldn't let go. She wanted me to show her *everything.* I didn't mind. Trudy was all giggles and high kicks and cartwheels. She could do the splits. And she had a head of hair I would have given a little toe for. It was bad enough that I was stuck with the name Henrietta, which teachers loved to pronounce when calling roll. But kids at school called me "Henny Penny" because of my coppery hair. Or worse, "Henry." Unlike mine, which was so unruly I kept it in braids, Trudy's hair was long and straight and pale blonde—*platinum* blonde. She wore it in a ponytail that swung from side to side like the shiny tail of the Palomino I hadn't gotten.

We were all in the back yard: Trudy and I, Will and Trudy's older brother who was nine, like Will—and Cleo. Our parents were no doubt in the living room with their drinks and salted nuts.

The boys were monopolizing the tree house, and Trudy got tired of swinging.

"I want to go out *there.*" She nodded towards the pecan orchard, muddy from a recent rain.

"I gots to watch these boys up yonder." Cleo raised her eyes towards the gruff voices of pretend pirates.

"It's okay, Cleo. I'll watch her."

She frowned.

"I promise. I'm eleven-and-a-half years old."

"Don't you be climbing no trees; Trudy's too little. And don't you go anywhere near that horse. You know the rules. You hear me?"

I nodded. I had no intention of going anywhere near Troy, who had taken to wandering wherever he pleased. The minute the pasture gate was accidentally left unlatched, he roamed the surrounding fields or the pecan orchard that separated our house from Mr. Mac's.

I spotted a fallen pecan limb we could walk on like a tight-rope. When that got boring, we ran through Mr. Mac's yard to the black walnut tree just inside the gate to the pasture. I hammered nuts open between two bricks and picked out the meat with my pocketknife. Troy was nowhere to be seen. We followed Jasmine, an orange-striped tabby, out of the pasture to Mr. Mac's garage, behind it to the equipment shed, then over to the packhouse, empty now but full of cured tobacco in the summer before the market opened. We were hoping for kittens—the cat had a sneaky way of having them when no one suspected any-thing—but no luck.

Trudy and I were almost back to our yard when Troy came ambling past. I was sure I'd latched the gate.

"Troy!" I said in an affectionate way, pretending to like him and forgetting that I was absolutely forbidden to take another child near him without an adult present. I was showing off.

He had evidently found a tasty bunch of weeds and cut his eyes as though to tell me not to bother him.

"Let's pet him!"

I caught Trudy by the arm and pulled her back.

"You have to be careful. Gentle. Just pat his neck. Like this." I stretched out my arm and barely touched his coarse old neck. He ignored me, since I didn't have an apple.

"Etta! You get that child away from there. Right now!" It was Cleo. She was half-running towards us, her skirts raised—I could see where her stockings made rolls under her knees. Her round face was shining. "I told you...Oh my Lord!"

I looked back around. There was Jasmine, racing past. Running after what? A field mouse? But where was Trudy? She'd vanished, but how could she have? No, she was on the ground, beneath—right underneath—the horse. And covered with mud.

"Lord. Oh Lord." Cleo had stopped a dozen or so yards from us. She just stood there, breathing hard.

Troy, his eyes bulging, was rearing, stomping the ground with his hooves. I had never seen him act like this, as though suddenly overtaken by an evil spirit.

"Roll out! Roll out! Trudy, listen to me. Roll out, over this way. Roll to me!"

I heard the words come out of my mouth, but I felt as if I were watching someone else say them.

Trudy did roll out. It was like something in a dream, in slow motion. But thank God, she did.

She lay there and didn't move, a red stream soaking her pale hair, mud all over her face, arms, legs. She opened her eyes once, then her eyelids fluttered and shut tight.

Cleo had her apron pulled up to her chest. Her shoulders were shaking. She was wheezing as if she couldn't get her breath. She looked almost gray.

"Go get Mama and Papa," I screamed. "Go get her parents. Go!"

Finally Cleo's legs began to move. She limped back to the house.

So much blood. I was sure Trudy would die. In my mind, Trudy was dead. For hours and hours, after Trudy was rushed to the emergency room, I believed she was dead.

Somehow, she wasn't. The next day, Dr. Monroe gave special permission for me to visit Trudy in the hospital, even though you were supposed to be twelve to walk through those heavy hall doors. I wasn't prepared for what I saw. In order to sew up her wound, the doctor had shaved off a patch of Trudy's beautiful hair. Her mother had cut the rest short as a boy's, so it wouldn't look so strange growing out. I didn't know what to say; my breath was coming fast. Maybe Trudy's hair would grow back wavy, Trudy's mother said, like mine. Could she be teasing? I wondered. But it wasn't like an adult to make fun of how I looked.

I was grateful that my own mother and Trudy's had so much to talk about at the hospital. I was grateful that Trudy just kept sleeping. Because something terrible was happening inside me. I didn't know what it was—this voiceless growing thing inside. My chest ached, as if there were breath in my lungs that I couldn't blow out, now pressing with ever more force against my ribs; it was that, yes, and my ribs were aching, the bones themselves and all the muscles in my neck and throat—aching and seeming to have swelled, clogging my throat so I couldn't swallow.

The minute I got back home, I went into my room and shut the door. I cried like a crazy person. I huddled into a ball in the narrow space on the floor between my bed and the wall and cried until my throat was raw and my stomach cramped up. My mother came in and pulled me up onto the bed. She frowned. Enough was enough, she said.

"You're going to make yourself sick."

"But Trudy could have died. She was asleep in the hospital, but she could have been dead."

"What's done is done," she said. "Trudy's going to be fine. But Troy, well, your father and I think it might be better to let him go live someplace else. Jesse has a pen…"

I nodded, snuffling. I tried to hug my mother, pressing my hot cheeks against the cool white blouse.

"Now, no more of this." Mama was not much of a hugger, and she had little patience for comforting sweet talk. "You know, Etta, you weren't supposed to let Trudy anywhere near that horse. But since you did—well—you may have saved Trudy's life, telling her to roll out. You can take some comfort in that."

"Cleo didn't do anything."

In a flash, my grief hardened into anger. Because Cleo *had* done something—she had hollered, distracting me and startling Troy. I had known what I was doing. As I had told Cleo, I was eleven-and-a-half—I knew how to act around Troy, how to make sure a friend did too. Everything was going just fine till Cleo butted in. And the moment I turned to find out what in the world she wanted, Trudy fell. She stood there, Cleo did, as though suddenly she were another person—not herself at all—swaying and moaning.

"But you kept your head, Etta. Now come set the table."

7: Spells

July 9, 1964

Troy. Nothing but trouble. I stabbed at the food still sitting on my plate. Nothing. But. Trouble. Cleo stood at the sink, her back turned. Mr. Mac had left to find Jesse and walk the pasture fence all over again. Why couldn't they see—Cleo and Mr. Mac—how important it was for me to get to the Vickers field? The two of them had practically raised me, and now they seemed not even to know me. If Troy had been different, if he'd been the faithful Palomino he should have been, I'd have jumped on his back and ridden him to the field.

"The storm is passing," Cleo sang as she washed the dishes. "Mm-mm, mm-mm."

She hummed, then sang, hummed, sang.

"Getting on my every last nerve," I whispered under my breath. This was what my mother said whenever anything annoyed her—Will and I running in the house, one of her piano students who hadn't practiced, the Scurlocks at the front door.

In truth, Cleo's singing wasn't getting on my nerves, at least not in the way my mother meant; it was making my throat tighten and my eyes want to fill up. Her singing came from deep down in her chest and seemed to hold in its notes layers of meaning far beyond the simple words. And right now, it not only made me feel more and more frustrated over being stuck at home but also reminded me of the talk at Walter's Store about the missing workers and the Klan, the demonstrations and arrests—violence that suddenly seemed close to home. Was Cleo happy? Is that why she sang? Or was she sad—and scared? Was I to blame, even partly?

"Why do you do that all the time?" I asked.

"What you mean?"

"Hum and sing, sing and hum."

"Been doing it most my life and all yours. Why you just now making comment?"

Wiping her hands down the front of her apron, Cleo walked to the table and sat across from me. She pulled her skirt up over her knees, stretched out her legs and sighed. She pulled out matches and a tiny square of paper from her apron pocket, then the packet of loose tobacco from somewhere down the front of her dress. Cleo kept her cigarette makings in a variety of places: an apron pocket or waistband, her bosom, the rolled sleeve of the dark dress she always wore, the knotted top of one stocking or the other.

I tried to focus on my plate, on anything but Cleo, but it was no use. I wanted—I needed—to straighten things out with her. But I couldn't find the words to start. I'd waited and waited for Cleo to explain why she'd gone feeble like she had when Troy kicked Trudy, leaving me to try to save her. But she'd never said a word.

Wrinkling her forehead, Cleo smoothed the paper flat on the table. Positioning it between her thumb and forefinger, she made a little furrow lengthwise. Next, without spilling so much as a crumb, she shook the tobacco from the packet, evened it out, then rolled the paper and licked the edge. She lit the end and took a long drag.

Cleo often picked through my parents' ashtrays for smokable butts, no matter that they might be red with my mother's lipstick. It occurred to me, feeling cross as I was, to ask if it wouldn't be easier for her to do that now. But I'd stuffed a corner of biscuit into my mouth and before I could swallow, Cleo blew out a stream of smoke and looked down towards her shoes. "My feets—they already swole. And here it is hardly past morning."

It wasn't like Cleo ever to say she wasn't feeling well—she was talking more to herself than to me. "My chest sore too. Got to see Dr. Monroe just as soon as your papa and mama gets back." She shook her head. "Something's not right."

Cleo's feet did look too fat for her thin-soled flat shoes. The coin on its wire, loose just the day before, squeezed tightly against her ankle.

Cleo usually bragged on her good health, grinning and showing her dimples and her gold upper molar. But here she was complaining—complaining to me. She was angling for sympathy—that was it. She wanted me to worry and feel sorry for her—feel sorry and take all the blame for…for everything.

Suddenly Cleo pinched out her cigarette and put it into her apron pocket.

She breathed, breathed hard, as if at first she couldn't—as if a breath that hard was the only kind of breath she could take, and it took a huge effort, which she was able to make only by pressing both hands against the middle of her chest and closing her eyes. As Cleo tightened her mouth, I found myself sweating.

I tensed, gripping the seat of my chair. I would have been prepared for a coughing spell like one of Mr. Mac's—or even a shaking fit, which everyone blamed on the war. But this spell of Cleo's, if not so dramatic as either of those, was somehow scarier. Spells didn't have to mean anything bad, I told myself. Still, I'd never seen Cleo have one.

Opening her eyes, Cleo took, with ease this time, a deep breath. She nodded at my plate. "Cold rice and gravy. Not worth eating now."

I didn't answer. I blinked, blinked hard. Sprung up in front of me was the memory of last summer, when my parents had taken Will to Columbia for his first operation, a memory I'd pushed away until now. The Etta of last summer couldn't wait to race at daybreak out of bed and into the kitchen where Cleo, the old before-Troy Cleo, turned her back on the gray sink water. She wrapped her strong plump arms around me, that other Etta, and pressed me close for a long time. Then she proceeded to fix whatever I wanted to eat: bacon and three scrambled eggs, French toast, warmed-over blackberry cobbler with ice cream, anything. I had been to the Great Smoky Mountains to see real Cherokee Indians and waterfalls and ride on the Tweetsie Railroad. I'd been twice to Myrtle Beach and ridden on all the rides except the roller coaster. But last summer when I stayed with Cleo and Mr. Mac—that was as good as any vacation I'd had. There were card games to play and teacakes to make with Cleo, beehives and caged raccoons on nearby farms to see with Mr. Mac. I had been the center of their attention—never had I felt more special. And never had I felt less special than I did now.

It doesn't matter, I thought, shoving Cleo's spell from my mind and kicking the leg of the table. I'll spend the rest of the week with just Mr. Mac, and that will be all right. Surely he'd go back to being *his* old self now that Will was gone—surely he'd look at me the way he used to and give me his undivided attention.

For the moment, though, I felt abandoned by Mr. Mac, right when he'd promised to take me treasure-hunting, and as resentful as ever of Troy—mythical horse or not.

I took my book to the screened-in porch, where there was a warm breeze. I rubbed—as though it had the power to grant wishes—the glossy dust jacket that gleamed with King Tut's solid gold death mask.

Archaeologists saw into the past, which was almost like looking into the future. In *Ancient Wonders of the World*, they found such things as the Minotaur's Labyrinth, the gold and silver of ancient Troy, the tombs of the pharaohs in their colorful sarcophagi. The mummy's curse? It may have frightened some people, but it didn't faze the archaeologist who found King Tut.

Archaeologists dug for the truth; they brought buried secrets into the open.

I pictured a jigsaw puzzle, like those my mother set up in the den on a folding table at Christmas—all those tiny, scattered pieces assembled to form…I pictured pyramids, green palms, and golden sand; or better, a walled acropolis (I knew the word; it meant "high-up city") above a golden plain and there a wooden horse on wheels. Somehow the puzzle of the past, when pieced together, would set my world to rights. My world in the present had turned into a puzzle, a hundred scattered pieces. Only it lacked a box with a picture of the puzzle put together. And I couldn't come up with an image in my mind; I couldn't make the pieces fit. The only pictures that came to me whole, like puzzles with the last piece in, belonged to long-ago, legendary pasts.

My book—I hugged it to my chest—had changed into legend people and places I'd heard of all my life and taken for granted. These things were now full of promise, full of possibility, as once were the ruined palaces of Knossos and Mycenae, the tomb of King Tut, the plains of Troy.

There were a half-dozen Indian fields nearby—not even counting the Vickers field—that I had so far only played at exploring. I knew of several ruined mansions that had belonged to once-wealthy planters who likely hid their silver and jewels from the Union Army and the carpetbaggers. A couple of blacksmith's shops still stood, overgrown with vines, their windows too dusty to see through. Perhaps no one had thought to search them for tools and fittings worth at least a month's allowance. And surely, *surely* Francis Marion, who had given the nearby town its name, had left behind relics—a piece of musket, a knife, a tin cup. And now there was Aunt Charlotte's house, where something beyond imagining was waiting to be found. Finding real treasure—not just the pottery fragments that half-filled a shoebox in my closet—would place me in the center of a world that once again *had* a center.

✍

"Come on outside and hold the bucket for me while I pick some figs." Cleo was in the back yard. She opened the screened door for me. "That tree is plumb full. They all got ripe at the same time, looks like."

"I hate figs." I followed Cleo to the tree at the far edge of the carport.

"You sure do like them in preserves," she said, tossing the fat yellow-green fruit into the tin bucket.

Cleo climbed a stepstool and strained to reach the upper-most figs. Her arms glistened with perspiration.

"Don't you think we have enough?" The bucket was nearly full. And I was remembering Cleo's spell in the kitchen.

"Let's move around to the back, here. Birds sure to get them if we don't."

She stood on the stool, and I leaned against the woodpile—we were at the back corner of the carport.

"Don't be getting too close to that old wood, Etta. Remember that black widow you carried off with you when you weren't but two or three?"

"What on earth are you talking about?"

Cleo was breathing heavily. Another handful of figs went into the bucket.

"I was out here trying to watch you and pull weeds out of your mama's petunias at the same time, and you got off to the woodpile and found this spider. You come waddling over to me, your hand wide open, and that black widow crawling all around. Hourglass orange as a hunting vest.

"I slapped it off. Hit your little hand so hard it turned red. You cried and cried. Cleo never slapped her Etta before. You didn't understand a thing. You wouldn't forget, either. 'Cleo slap me,' you said, over and over. I hated that thing."

Somehow I had forgotten. Now the thought of myself holding any spider, much less a black widow, seemed incredible. It must be Cleo's fault—my fear of spiders. And yet, maybe it wasn't such a bad thing to be afraid of them, when there were black widows around. Back then, Cleo had acted quickly, though not quickly enough to keep me out of the woodpile.

Cleo reached up to pick near the top, then she began to sway. "My Lord." She grabbed a fig branch with one hand.

I dropped the bucket and threw my arms around Cleo's legs. Then I reached up and grabbed her free arm.

"Back down now. Slow. One step. That's it. One more... Good, just take your time." Cleo leaned her weight against me—which wasn't as substantial as I expected.

"Got spots in front my eyes. Can't see straight." She was stumbling.

"I have you. You won't fall." There was a glider swing under the carport. When I got Cleo seated, I went inside and poured us both some ice water from the Frigidaire. How many spells was she going to have?

Cleo wiped her face with her apron. "Sun got me." She looked as gray as she had the afternoon when Troy injured Trudy.

I sat quietly for a few minutes and waited for Cleo to stop breathing so hard. "That day in the orchard," I said, in almost a whisper. "When Troy kicked Trudy. Were you having a spell?"

Cleo shook a line of tobacco into a paper. But her hand wavered and she spilt some into her lap. It took two matches for the flame to find the end of her cigarette.

"I reckon maybe so," she finally answered.

I didn't know what to think. These spells were bad. But Cleo could be exaggerating. I exaggerated feeling sick sometimes, when I didn't want to go to school. Will did it all the time.

I gathered the spilt figs. I was tired of holding a grudge against Cleo. And I was scared, and I felt guilty. Cleo couldn't help it if she'd had a spell in the orchard. What was more, she might have saved my life years ago, knocking a black widow out of my hand. I wanted to show her that I wasn't always stubborn, that I didn't have *such* a bad temperament.

Instead, I began to brag. "I'm turning into a real rescuer." I gave Cleo a sideways look. "Back in March, I saved Trudy. And now, well, I bet you would have fallen without me here."

"You growing up," Cleo said with a sigh.

"Did you ever rescue anybody besides me, Cleo? With the spider?"

This was her chance. Right then she could have had it out with me about how I'd behaved towards her—how ugly I'd been—the day I took Margot and Stephanie into the Swamp Fox woods. And how, even still, she'd come to our rescue.

"Baby, I don't keep score of that. There was the time your brother got stuck in that pecan tree out to the road, yonder. Couldn't go up or down. So I climbed up myself and unstuck him. And I recall when Evelyn were little, she sat down in a pile of fire ants. We was both of us crying by the time I finished slapping off all those ants."

I knew good and well that there were a thousand times when Cleo had kept Will and me out of danger, or taken up for us so we didn't get spanked. She had come to my defense when I least deserved it. I felt more and more ashamed. Cleo hadn't startled the horse into kicking Trudy, as I'd had the nerve to accuse her of doing. Jasmine had spooked him, and I knew it. Troy never paid attention to anyone's hollering.

I gazed out towards the weed-covered spot in the orchard where the accident had happened: Troy rearing, his eyes wild, Trudy smeared with mud and blood. "Roll out! Roll out!" Over and over I had called. Not knowing if that was the right thing to do. Not knowing *what* to do. Cleo was there; she was supposed to do *something*.

"You feeling all right now, Cleo? Evelyn says you have—I forgot—something about blood."

She nodded.

"You know Evelyn's got this boy coming to see her— Roscoe. Starry doesn't like him. I can tell."

"Evelyn's a good girl. She just got growing pains. Like you. Sometimes you just got to let the young ones learn for themselfs. Even if you have to watch them step in a brier patch and then pick their way out all scratched and stuck up with stickers like a pin cushion."

"Did you ever have a boyfriend, Cleo? Is Jesse your boy-friend?"

Cleo cocked her head at me. The color rushed back into her face, and she broke into a smile. Cleo's dimple, just beneath her right cheekbone, got as deep as I had ever seen it. I could even see her gold tooth.

"You might say that Jesse is my boyfriend. The best kind. Comes and helps out at the house, doing whatever needs doing. Whether it be washing the dishes or building me a table…Time was, though—oh, honey—time was I had a boyfriend for every day of the week. I even married one of them."

"What? Who? Wait a minute, Cleo. You're teasing."

"It's the gospel truth. Been years and years back. He came to Marion with the fair. Took pictures in a tent. He had a big piece of cardboard painted to look like a old-time wagon, anoth-er one to look like a right fancy house. He had bonnets and jewry and things you could put on to have your picture took. Well, we got married and it was fine for a while. Mmm-mm fine." Cleo waved at her face with her apron. Sweat put a polished shine on it.

I felt the glider swing tilt and try to spill me. Cleo had a life, a past, that I knew nothing about. A husband!

"Why didn't you ever tell anybody?"

"You mean *you*. Your mama and papa knows. My fambly knows. It's not a secret. The subject just never came up with you before right now."

"What happened to…?"

"Davis R. Boston. That's his name. I just got tired of driving all over the Car'linas and Georgia and Florida going from fair to fair. Simple as that. The wearier I got, the readier I was to come back here where I belong. I *missed* Starry and my friends and my church. Oh, there was the fair people. Turns out they folks just like you and me. Even the freak show freaks—normal as can be—'cept for being too fat or too skinny or too tall or too short or too hairy—no-account things like that. We played a lot of card games. That's where I learned how to shuffle. I saw a right good bit of the world, and I'm glad. I just didn't belong to stay out there, 'specially when…"

"When what?"

Cleo looked at me as though I had just said something in another language.

"When what?" Cleo repeated my question.

"You just said you didn't belong to stay gone when…but you didn't finish."

She looked out at the orchard. "That could have been you out yonder kicked under that horse. Could have been worse than a 'cussion. I never did trust that old horse and his juju eyes. But it wasn't my place to say."

"I know how to handle him." Had Troy overheard me? Sensing his presence, I scanned the orchard. "I wonder where he is now. This Davis R. Boston."

Now that Cleo was feeling better, I was pushing the glider swing forward and back, faster and faster. I wanted to believe that Cleo had made it all up, the business about a husband.

"I suppose he's still taking pictures all over creation. He didn't want to bring me back home. He gave me all kinds of jewry from his picture-taking business, trying to make me change my mind. But I couldn't. I tried, but I couldn't change my mind. Finally, he understood. He used to come see me once or twice a year, but then he stopped." Cleo looked mildly surprised, as though she was only now realizing this fact.

She put her hand down hard on my knee. "Stop pushing this swing like a lunatic. You flipping my stomach like a pancake."

I closed my eyes. Though the swing was still, I could feel it moving under me like the Mile High Bridge sometimes did. My fired-up curiosity about Cleo's past was similar to the way I felt about Troy—pulled in and pushed away at the same time. I hated knowing about Davis R. Boston, and yet I wanted to know more. I no longer cared about Cleo's necklaces, surely cheap costume jewelry, but I wanted to study the photographs. They told a story of a secret world, like a chapter in my archaeology book. The young man in the framed pictures had to be Cleo's husband. And the strange picture of Cleo with the cloth on her head— that could be her wedding portrait. Cleo—a bride? And who was the baby holding the flower?

How many other mysteries were buried in Cleo's past? I felt as though I no longer understood the first thing about this woman I'd known all my life.

"Cleo," I asked as if out of nowhere, "do colored people want to take over?"

"Take what over?"

I shrugged.

"Well, if you don't know, I sure don't. Where you come up with that?"

Again I shrugged. I didn't want to name names.

"Colored folk just wants the same thing white folk wants. That's all. Things like eating when you're hungry, drinking when you're thirsty. A school that's got books. A job that pays enough to live on. Things like voting for the President."

Cleo and I both took long swallows of the cold water.

"Do you vote?"

"I gots a mind to next time around."

8: Ghost-Horse

July 9, 1964

It was one of those summer nights that wouldn't let go of the heavy heat of day. Even with my fan sitting on a chair at the foot of the bed and pointed straight at me, I was sweating. Whichever side of me was against the mattress got soaking wet. Over and over I turned my pillow to feel the momentary cool. Outside my windows the crickets and tree frogs cranked themselves into a frenzy, died down, started again.

In the old days, when Cleo had stayed with me, we sat up late into the night playing card games. While moths tapped and tree frogs stuck themselves to the windows, we sat at the kitchen table and had Crazy-8 and Gin Rummy tournaments. Cleo showed off her shuffling. She'd spill the cards like a waterfall from one hand down to the other, never dropping a one. Now I pictured Cleo studying the furry hands of the bearded lady, learning the skill from a sideshow freak. Cleo, married.

In the old days, Cleo sat with me until I fell asleep. She'd pull a rocking chair from the den, sit next to the fan and hum in the dark. She hummed until it became part of the nature sounds outside and the whirring of the fan. The sounds knitted themselves into a lap for me to sink into.

This evening, maybe because of her spells, Cleo went to bed even before I did, in the rollaway cot in Will's room. Was she really asleep? Sometimes when Cleo stayed over, I would wake up in the middle of the night to find her in the den, rocking with her eyes closed, or outside smoking a cigarette and looking at the stars.

Different things kept startling me. Beneath the moon, just past full, the shadows of the trees played on my walls. From time to time, headlights swept across my ceiling to the wall opposite me and made me think of the Klan with their torches, then of ghosts, of Aunt Charlotte and Miss Lila. The cars behind those lights screeched around the curve, then sped on the highway past our house. Something rattled the bushes beneath my windows. Stray dog, I told myself. Maybe cats. Cleo had once mentioned convicts who escaped from the chain gang and roamed the countryside. Was there any way to get her to come to my room without asking? A mosquito whined past my ear. I was biting my nails; there was little left to gnaw on.

I sat straight up. Something was scratching against the brick outside my room, as though it was trying to get in. Troy. He had never come right up to our house before, but he was there; I knew it. I'd seen him that evening in the orchard. Against the darkening blue of dusk, I'd recognized his silhouette. I didn't dare mention this to Cleo, or she'd have Mr. Mac out checking the fence yet again.

I went to my window. The yard was silvery bright. "Leave me alone!" I whispered, although I saw only the play of shadows on the lawn.

What did Troy want from me anyway? No matter that I'd tried my best to win him over, to heal him. No matter, too, that I was behaving myself—it was easier to do with Will away—even helping out on the farm as a grownup might. Maybe Cleo was right; he was possessed by the Devil and nothing more.

But there had to be more. Struck by lightning, Troy had journeyed into the spirit world and come back again. But suppose he wasn't all the way back. Suppose Troy was here in the flesh, but half of his body still felt the pull of the underworld. His left legs, streaked by lightning, did seem to want to tread underground, while the right ones held him up. And his blind eye, its pupil stuck way in the corner—I could imagine it glued to the *other side* where secrets were kept.

Not just the Devil.

He was a wanderer all right, but not like Aunt Charlotte. He didn't want to rest. Half in the spirit world and half in the world of the living, he found some way to fit his misshapen body through fences, to track me from barn lot to distant field to my own bedroom. Here, in the night, I sensed that Troy had his own plan, and it had nothing to do with helping me find treasure.

I headed for the kitchen to get some milk. A dim light came from the den: the TV. It was on, but not tuned in to any show. Only oatmeal static and black bars. Cleo hadn't gone to sleep. Wearing a loose white nightgown, she was sitting in the maple rocker she liked, her eyes closed. She was working her hands, one over the other.

"I've been changed," she sang, "mmm hmm. Yes, I've been changed." She opened her eyes and grabbed at her chest. "Lord, you started me! You have a bad dream?"

"No. I heard something. Outside my window."

Cleo didn't seem to be surprised. "Lightningstruck in your head now. Not no gimpy leg nor fence going to keep him out. Look like he's your cross to bear."

I sat on the sofa and stared at Cleo across the gray room. Suddenly I, myself, felt possessed. "I heard a noise. I didn't imagine it; I'm not a freak. But he is—a real one; he belongs in the freak show. And here I am stuck with him."

"What's done is done. Can't be undone. You need me to come sit with you?"

"I'm not Will. I'm not a baby. And when we move away—to Columbia—you won't be there. You won't be able to treat me like a baby."

I went back to my room and slammed my door. I both did and didn't want to care about Cleo anymore. If I could move to the city tomorrow, I'd go and not look back.

Why couldn't I fix things with Cleo? And why had she kept a secret from me—that she'd had a husband? She was more and more a stranger to me. I wanted to blame Troy. He'd caused the rift between us when he kicked Trudy. But I couldn't blame him for Davis R. Boston. The distance between us, Cleo and me—had it always existed?

Again I heard scraping against the brick outside my room. Again I pressed my nose to my screened window. This time I saw—not close but out at the edge of the yard, in the moon-shadows near the orchard—a shadowy shape that was Troy. It wasn't my imagination.

With the palms of my hands, I pressed back tears. Cleo had come to my rescue many times. But I had never been her child.

I had forgotten about the milk, but I couldn't go back out. And now I'd never get to sleep. I turned on the light over my bed and stared at my bookshelf. *D'Aulaires' Book of Greek Myths, The Jungle Book, Treasure Island, Pollyanna,* fourteen Nancy Drews, *Grimm's Fairy Tales*, a stack of comic books, and the half-dozen horse books I ought to give away. Besides *Ancient Wonders of the World*, which I slept with, only the book of myths held any interest for me.

Elsie Dinsmore. There it was, stuck in the middle of the Nancy Drews. My hand went towards it. I'd read out of obligation the book that had belonged to my grandmother Henrietta, and I had no intention of reading it ever again. I detested the simple-minded goody-goody who was Elsie. It had taken little effort, the pages being thin and brittle, to gouge a hole with my pocketknife right in the middle of the book, and there I'd hidden the small clay sphere. Now I plucked it out—a secret I'd shared with no one—and rolled it between my palms.

"I had everything under control," I said to myself, recalling when my fingers had found it. We'd been facedown, my friends and I, in the Swamp Fox pit. "Everything was under control. Cleo didn't have to follow us. We were fine. Fine."

A huffing. It sounded so close it could be in the room with me. Springing up, I put my eye to the screen. Right against Troy's wild rolling eye. My hand clapped over my mouth, stifling a scream. "Go home!" I said in a hoarse whisper. "Leave!"

But Troy seemed determined to be a real Trojan horse, barging if he could into my room and bringing with him all the awfulness of that day in the woods, spilling it out of his scarred side, forcing me to remember what I wanted desperately to forget.

Trudy's accident in March had made the rest of my school year even worse than it normally would have been: the popular girls in my class ganged up on me. Joyce Ann and her clique whispered about me behind my back. Trudy might not have held a grudge, but rumor spread that my old, lunatic horse almost killed the little girl. And it was *my* fault. My horse—it should have been shot. Joyce Ann and her friends hovered around Trudy when she returned to school; making a show of adopting her as a little sister, they brought her hats and scarves in every color to cover her bandage.

By late May when Troy was struck by lightning and lived, school was almost out for summer. Too late for my classmates to come around to thinking Troy was special—and that I, Etta, by association was special too.

At least Margot and Stephanie, the only friends I felt sure I would ever have, wanted to see Troy's wound. As soon as school let out in June, they came to the farm to visit. At the barn,

Margot, who found all animals fascinating, couldn't stop staring at Troy's side. Her parents, who worried all the time, didn't approve of even dogs and cats—or much of anything. They'd built a fallout shelter in their back yard in case the Russians dropped an atomic bomb. Margot, her dark hair tied back in a blue ribbon, edged as closely as she dared. She wanted to see every inch of the wound. The horse *was* a miracle, she whispered. Stephanie, on the other hand, took one look at the scorched and slimy gash and gagged. "Should have put him out of his misery," she said.

All the while, Troy stared at me with his one eye that, now that it could see again, looked feverish, even wild. Cleo right away had thought it was evil. But it didn't scare me.

"Let's dig for treasure." I made it sound as though the idea had suddenly come to me. In fact, reading and rereading my archaeology book, I'd planned this for days. If my friends and I could not ride horses together, perhaps we could be archaeologists together. I pointed towards the woods near Boggy Swamp. Just down the road—we could walk—was the Swamp Fox pit.

"You know the Swamp Fox used to hunt redcoats out this way. Right back in the woods here there's a kind of hole in the ground he dug for his prisoners. I bet we'll find something."

"Like what?" Stephanie asked.

"He didn't have any money," Margot said. "Remember the TV show? He and his men wore rags and ate possum."

All children with a TV set had seen Walt Disney's series *The Swamp Fox*. It had run several years earlier, but in the town of Marion where Will and I went to school—and where our friends lived—people still talked about it, still knew the theme song by heart.

"They had rich friends." I was talking fast. "Remember the episode when the Swamp Fox went to Charleston to warn everybody there about the British?...But even if we don't find coins, we might find a sword. Or brass buttons or musket balls…or silver buckles. Those things would be valuable."

"I don't know if I want to dig in the woods and get dirty for some old rusty something," Stephanie said, blinking. She'd sneaked her mother's mascara; it had run and was stinging her eyes.

"Sounds like fun to me," Margo said, to my relief. "A buckle would be neat. Or buttons. We could polish them up."

Soon the three of us were climbing over the gate. We'd found a shovel, a hoe, and something like a trowel in the dusty corners of the barn. And there was Cleo, coming straight towards us.

"What you fixing to do with those things?" She stopped to catch her breath. The key to the gate was in her hand. "Something told me I ought to come check on you all."

I had barely spoken to Cleo since Trudy's accident. I was shunned at school, and it was her fault as much as Troy's. "We're going to dig for treasure." I nodded in the direction of the Swamp Fox woods.

"Not in those woods, you ain't."

I told Margot and Stephanie to follow the dirt road. I'd catch up.

"Mr. Mac done heard gunshots back there. Those woods is off-limits until he gets a chance to find out who's doing that shooting."

"We're going to do what we want to do, Cleo. And you can't stop us."

"Well, I'm going to turn right 'round and tell your mama."

"She's in town, so I reckon you're not." She'd taken Will to the doctor. Papa, of course, was at work, and Mr. Mac's truck was gone.

Cleo put her hands on her hips and gave me a sad and disappointed look. Her mouth tightened. "Meanness. I never thought I'd see mean get into you, top of that bad temper'ment, but there it is. Staring right out your eyes. Just like that horse yonder."

"Well, I never thought I'd see—see dumb in you! It was your fault Trudy got hurt. She could have gotten killed, and it was your fault. You shouldn't have hollered—you scared Troy. That's what happened. And then—then you just stood there. You wouldn't *move*," I went on. "Just like a dumb…" Tears had risen in my eyes.

Now in my bedroom, with Troy breathing hard outside my window and scraping—with hoof, hide?—at the bricks, my eyes filled once again. Troy was forcing back to me my own words to Cleo. Words that could not be excused or taken back. I rolled the clay sphere between my palms.

"Like a dumb…" I saw myself as Cleo must have seen me, my face flushed and ashamed. My parents didn't allow the word that wanted to come from my mouth. Cleo raised her hand. It was poised to slap my cheek. Then slowly, slowly, her hand moved down to her side. *Nigger.* Had my lips moved to form the two syllables? Surely not. I *hadn't* said them. I wouldn't.

"Blind." Cleo had frowned and shaken her head. "Oh that the blind may see and the lame walk and the wicked repent their wickedness. Go on ahead. Get your girlfriends and yourself shot dead. That's not dumb. Not one bit."

When I caught up to my friends, Margo seemed troubled. "Maybe we shouldn't go. Cleo looked upset."

I walked fast, leading them past the tobacco field with its half-grown plants. "She was checking on us, that's all. I explained what we were doing, and she said—all she said was to be back before dark." Lying meant nothing to me now.

"Swamp Fox! Swamp Fox! Tail on his hat," I sang in a loud voice, to kill the sick feeling inside. The other girls joined in.

"Nobody knows where the Swamp Fox's at. Swamp Fox! Swamp Fox! Hiding in the glen. He runs away to fight again."

The road that forked to the right went to Jesse's house. But we bore left and walked past two barns. Aunt Charlotte's house stood in the distance, beyond the tobacco. To reach the pit, we'd go almost to Boggy Swamp, then make a sharp left and enter the woods.

I stopped. I looked back and listened hard. No gunshots. And no Cleo following us. Only the sick feeling tightening its grip.

The trees were a mixture of pine and hardwood and scrub. Briers and weeds caught our legs. I was used to this, but my friends complained about getting scratched up. They didn't say a word, though, about wanting to go back. I spotted a rectangular rise of dirt that framed what was barely a depression in the ground. I tapped my hoe. "This is it!"

"Are you sure?" asked Margot, leaning on the shovel. "How do you know it's not over there?" She nodded at another depression, five or so feet away.

"Mr. Mac said it was here, that's why. He should know."

"It's not very deep," Stephanie said.

"This is what happens over time," I explained. "Dirt and plants come in and fill up everything. But you can tell this was a pit."

I walked around it, tugging at my chin. I directed Stephanie to an area in the corner of the depression. I ground my heel into the opposite corner and told Margot to dig there. I struck the blade of my hoe into the center.

The ground was full of tough roots. None of us made much progress. Margot, who with a shovel had managed to dig down a foot or so, suggested we work on the same spot. Sure enough, hacking together at the roots and packed dirt, we doubled the size of Margot's hole. "Got no blankets, got no beds." We began another verse. "Got no roof above our heads. Got no shelter when it rains… Something something something brains."

Then we forgot about singing. The hole slowly grew bigger, but the deeper we went the harder it was to dig. My neck prickled. Someone—some*thing*—was watching us. I stood straight up and squinted hard into the trees. Nothing there. Nothing visible.

We'd hit a layer of packed clay. I scraped with the hoe; Margot stomped her foot on the blade of the shovel; Stephanie, on hands and knees, hacked with the trowel. Then she stopped and tugged at something with her fingers. It was hard and shiny: a piece of porcelain. "Old china," Stephanie breathed.

"I guess it *could* have belonged to the Swamp Fox," I said.

"Doubtful." Stephanie tossed it back down.

Margot leaned on the shovel. "How much longer are we going to dig, anyway?" Suddenly she stiffened. "Look!"

I jumped. Troy? Somehow even then he had sprung into my head. No. Only a young deer, a doe, grazing a few yards away. There was a gunshot, and the deer vanished, her tail a flash of white. Another shot followed. Another.

"My gosh," Stephanie cried. Her eyes were huge. "They're going to shoot us. We have to run!"

"No!" I grabbed Stephanie's arm, then Margot's. Her upper arm slipped from my grip, but I managed to find her wrist. "Lie down. Now!" We fell flat on our stomachs. The gunshots came closer.

"They shouldn't be here. It's private property," I said. My fingers rested on something round and hard. Without looking, I pried it from the ground and shoved it into my pocket.

"It's not even hunting season," Margot whispered.

"They're breaking the law," Stephanie said.

A distant rustling grew louder, turned into footsteps. I heard the rumbling of men's voices. Cleo's convicts…convicts on the chain gang that picked up trash or cut the tough grass by the side of the highway—Cleo had said that sometimes they broke free and hid in the woods and swamps and survived by eating mudfish and possum. If they had escaped, they could have stolen guns. Or maybe it was the Klan. I racked my brain. Did they use guns? My chest felt so tight I was dizzy even lying down.

"What if it's colored people?" Margot whispered.

"Colored people?" I didn't understand.

"Daddy says colored people got no business with guns. He says they want to kill white people and take over the country."

"I know I seen something over here, Roy. Pretty sure it was a doe."

Scurlocks. I took a deep breath. They might be no-accounts. They might be drunkards. But at least they weren't the chain gang. Or the Klan. Or the kind of colored people Margot's father was scared of.

"I ain't seen nothing. You seen anything, Ray?"

"No, not nothing."

"I swear I seen…Oh shee-it. It's girls. Oh shee-it. I think it's the McDaniels gal."

A head came down next to mine. It smelled like whiskey and onions.

I opened my eyes. The head belonged to Aubrey, the youngest. "Jesus!" He jumped to his feet.

"We aren't dead. We're just trying not to get shot." I sat up. My heart was pounding, but I was determined not to seem afraid.

One of the tall skinny twins stepped forward and poked my thigh with his boot. "I reckon you know you fools could have got yourselves kilt. Or worse than kilt—three little girls all alone out in the woods." He winked and elbowed his twin. "Ain't that right, Roy?"

Roy crouched down in front of Stephanie. "Hey, Sugar," he said.

Stephanie hugged her knees and stiffened. She stared off to one side, mascara smeared beneath her eyes.

"Hey, I'm talking to you, Sugar." Roy nudged her shoulder with his gun.

"Point that gun somewhere else, I mean it," I said.

"You jealous, Miss McDaniel? You want some attention? What about your other friend? She want some attention?"

Margot shook her head.

"Three of you and three of us. We could have us a party in the woods." Roy and Ray moved their hips in a sort of ugly dance.

I gripped the handle of my hoe. I wanted to pull out my pocketknife, but I couldn't make my arm move.

"I think y'all are scaring the girls," Aubrey said. He was a foot shorter than his brothers, and pudgy. People said he was a little bit slow. "Cut it out."

Ray rammed the butt of his rifle into Aubrey's side. Aubrey bent over and staggered backwards.

"Get your sorry selves out these woods right now." It was Cleo. She was out of breath.

"Miz Cleo, we wasn't doing nothing," Aubrey wheezed. His brother had knocked the wind out of him. "Just..."

"Just hunting deer out of season, in woods you not supposed to be in anyhow."

"We was wanting to surprise our pa." Aubrey looked like he was about to cry. "We didn't mean to shoot at no girls." He *was* crying. Tears came plopping out. I had never seen a boy that old crying.

"These here chirren play back here. It's the McDaniel property and it's posted no trespassing. Roy and Ray, you two knows better. Now take Aubrey on home."

Roy squeezed Aubrey's arm and shook it hard. "Shut up, idjit. Quit bawling."

Ray lifted his gun and aimed it at Cleo. "Ain't no mammy going to boss us." He tossed his head and gave a snorting laugh.

Cleo stepped forward until her bosom touched the gun. "Roy, Ray, whichever one you is, you full of wicked. Wicked and whiskey mixed. I'll say it one more time. You trespassing. Use what little sense you got. Who is it bails you out of jail every other Sunday morning? Mr. McDaniel, that's who. Now take Aubrey, go home, and don't come back in these woods."

"Yes, Mammy." The twins turned and walked away. "Pow! Pow-pow!" they yelled, then snickered, pretending to shoot. Aubrey limped after them, holding on to his side.

"I gots to sit down," Cleo said. Chest heaving, she sat with us in the dirt.

Margot and Stephanie hugged each other. "Those Scurlocks, they're just trash," I said in a big voice, although I couldn't keep my bottom lip from trembling.

"You got no business calling nobody trash," Cleo snapped. "And they got no business with guns, half-drunk on last night's whiskey. Oh, Lord, they could have shot you as easy as not."

"Etta said we'd find Swamp Fox treasure," Stephanie said, sniffling. "She said this is where he kept his redcoat prisoners."

"Some say that," Cleo said.

Margot and Stephanie forgave me. They didn't even tell their parents what had happened. And Cleo didn't tell mine. That had been the old Cleo there in the woods, giving those Scurlock boys what for, taking charge, protecting *me*. It would have served me right if Cleo had told—more than right, after my lying...and worse. I almost wished she had. Any punishment would have been better than what I'd put my own self through, pretending that I hadn't hurt Cleo's feelings while knowing deep inside that I had.

After my friends had gone home, I fished the sphere from my pocket. I first thought it was a musket ball. But no, it was made of clay, bits of paint clinging to the surface. I had no way of knowing whether it was a relic or not. Ordinarily I'd have showed it to everyone, bragging on myself. Instead I'd buried it in my book, as though to bury my shame.

Now I spoke through my window to the horse who had gone silent, who might be nearby or might be off somewhere in the moon-dappled night. "You were there. That day with my friends, when Cleo came to the pasture gate. I didn't say the— word, did I?"

As I sat on my bed, pressing the gritty sphere between my sweaty palms, I told myself that I had not. I had never used that word. "Please, God," I prayed. "Don't let me have said it."

Whether I had or hadn't said it, the word had been in my head and on my tongue. Why, I'd as good as betrayed Cleo. I was no better than Mr. Whaley the druggist, who wouldn't serve "coloreds" at his soda fountain. No better than Mr. Sneed, the heavy-spectacled farmer from Walter's Store, whose ugly words had shaken me. And now I saw clearly what I'd tried to forget— Cleo's eyes hard with disappointment, her mouth sad, her shoulders slumped.

In truth, I had been terrified that day at the Swamp Fox pit. That was real danger—not something imaginary, out of a fairy tale, but real men with real guns making real threats that I didn't quite understand. Even if they had been just Scurlocks. Once again, I'd had to think fast. But I didn't have everything under control, and my friends and I were far from fine. What a relief when Cleo appeared and sent the Scurlock boys home! I wanted to think Cleo would always come to my defense, that her one failure to act—the time with Trudy—was due to her spells. But I wasn't ready—not yet—to excuse her these spells; I wanted her not to have them. Anyhow, she'd rescued us in the woods, and I hadn't deserved it—that was for sure.

The chorus of insects rose and fell outside in the darkness; my fan shoved the heavy July heat from one side of my room to the other.

"You still out there, Troy?" The scraping sound had not returned. But I had a feeling the old horse would hang around, he with his visible scar, and me with my hidden one.

I opened my hands that had been praying all by themselves. Dirt had rubbed off the sphere and stuck to my sweaty palms and fingers. Again I pressed my hands together, hard, until the center of my palms felt bruised. The word that hung between Cleo and me at the pasture gate—it, too, was like a bruise.

How many weeks had it been since that day? Four? All that time, I'd tried to tell myself that Cleo—if she hadn't forgotten my meanness—surely placed the blame on my childish bad "temper'ment." But I was no longer a child, to be excused for saying, or nearly saying, something I knew was wrong. And words could never be unsaid. They couldn't be prayed away.

9: The Ranch

July 10, 1964

At dawn the next morning, I made two jelly sandwiches—one for my breakfast and one for Troy's. Cleo would have made scrambled eggs for me. All I had to do was ask. But how could I after last night, when Troy—how else to explain it?—had made me face the truth about that wretched day with my friends and Cleo? How could I even meet her eyes?

I'd have to hurry with Troy. Mr. Mac would be leaving soon to deliver hay to Miss Cass's ranch. He was counting on my help; he'd said so.

As I crossed the orchard, the heavy dew was already steaming. Like a big sad hound dog, a train whistle howled from Eulonia; I heard it every morning and every evening. Today it sounded sadder than ever. I pictured the train moving west through the stand of tall longleaf pines Mr. Mac and I sometimes walked in. West through Georgia, Alabama, Mississippi. Mississippi. I wondered if the searchers had found those three missing men. Maybe they were hiding in the woods like the Swamp Fox and would come out mosquito-bit and hungry, but alive.

Troy's empty bucket was on its side. As I bent over to set it right, Troy nosed my hand—the one with the sandwich. I stepped back. "That's right. I brought your favorite. But we need to talk first. You were in my yard most of last night, weren't you? Maybe—maybe you do want to show me something buried. And maybe you're like me with Cleo. You want things to be right, but you have trouble figuring out the first move. I think that's what you were up to—coming to my house—part of it anyway.

"I think"—I tried to sound upbeat—"what we need to do is start over. Like Cleo and I need to start over."

I sighed. "I wish I knew how to make up with Cleo. I want to say I'm sorry. How I acted out there at the gate was worse than anything. I'm worried about these spells she's having. I care about her—I do. But now there's this *husband*. And there was that picture of her as a *bride*." Again I felt stung, remembering that there had been no photograph of me—not even one of Will and me together—on Cleo's table.

I held up the sandwich. "First, let me pet you, just a rub. Then you can have it. Understand?"

In a crooked sort of way, Troy appeared to nod. With my left hand, I held the sandwich behind my back. With the other, I reached to stroke his right jawbone, then the side of his neck. He stiffened and seemed to grow taller; his good eye widened. I stroked along his bony right flank. It shivered. "You don't need any more fixing. You're getting around fine when you want to. I just want us to be friends."

Troy stank, and my hand was turning gray from the dust that clung to his coat. "There, that's not so hard, is it?"

Then I sneezed, turning just enough to make it possible for Troy to swoop down with his head and snatch the sandwich. He backed away, showing his ugly brown teeth as he chewed, standing so that his hideous scar, crawling with flies where it still oozed, was right in front of me.

Cassandra Bearclaw, in her wide-brimmed straw hat, was out by the road with her arms folded when Mr. Mac and I drove up in the pickup stacked with hay. Mr. Mac had promised that afterwards we'd visit the Vickers field. I didn't dare reveal that Troy was still getting where he shouldn't be—that he had been in my yard last night.

"Welcome to the ranch!" With one fluffy white dog under her arm, two others identical to it running circles around her dusty cowboy boots, Miss Cass swung open her wide wooden gate. Nobody else had "ranches," and I had yet to figure out what made it a ranch, which sounded fancy, and not just an ordinary farm.

"Drive her around to the back," Miss Cass hollered. She put the dog down with the others, hoisted herself up onto the bed of the truck, and sat on top of a bale. The three creatures had to run as fast as their stubby little legs would go in order to keep up. The rutted, dusty drive passed a trailer with all sorts of porches and extensions built off of it. Mr. Mac had told me that Miss Cass kept hedgehogs in there somewhere. I had never seen a hedgehog.

When we came to the next gate, Miss Cass ran around to open and then close it behind us. She led us to a barn, and as Mr. Mac drove slowly toward it a mule, three burros, and four miniature horses the size of big dogs ambled out. From somewhere behind it came two goats. Then some pot-bellied pigs. The tiny dogs were yapping up a storm. Miss Cass walked up to the truck window. "Let's dump four bales here and four across the stream. Then we'll come back and toss the rest inside the barn where it'll stay dry—not that rain's coming any time soon."

I joined Miss Cass in the bed of the pickup. Together we pushed, and in no time the first bales were out. Mr. Mac arranged them, then pulled out his pocketknife. He stopped, grinned, and held the knife up to me. I leapt down and sawed through the twine while he and Miss Cass scattered the hay.

"What are their names?" I nodded at the three dogs, who kept jumping around Miss Cass and nipping at each other.

"Wynken, Blynken, and Nod. Spoiled rotten. Especially Nod. They're Bichon Frises. Won't mind. Yap all the time. I had a pair of Saint Bernards, but they died, poor things. First one, then the other. They don't live all that long, don't you know. Now these little fellows, they ought to outlast me."

The burros and goats had begun to nibble the hay. A goose came waddling up. Three more followed.

Mr. Mac's truck could hardly squeeze itself onto the narrow wooden bridge over the drought-low stream that divided the ranch. On the other side were another family of pot-bellied pigs, ducks, geese, chickens, and four sheep—two white and two black.

"Cows?" I asked. Miss Cass nodded towards her back fence. Four brown-and-white cows were trotting towards us.

"It's a menagerie," she said in her quick, breathy way. "I'm virtually self-sufficient here, don't you know. I grow my own veggies, milk my own cows, gather my own eggs."

"Do you grind your own grain, Miss Cass?"

"Perhaps I should. I do have a grinding bowl or two around here.…Shut *up*, Wynky, Blynky, Nod. Shut *up*!" she scolded.

Back across the bridge and inside the barn, all three of us—Mr. Mac, Miss Cass, and I—stood in the bed of the truck and shoved down the remaining eight bales. I had never before helped this much. I felt grown up and necessary. I really *was* Mr. Mac's assistant. If only the dogs would quit yapping! Once all the hay was down, Miss Cass clapped. I joined in.

Then I stopped. Something was wrong. Two, not three, dogs were barking. I jumped down and pressed the side of my head against the hay. Sure enough, there was a muffled whine coming from beneath it. I threw all of my strength into shoving aside one of the bales. "Mr. Mac! Miss Cass! He's under here—the dog!"

Together we pushed the bales aside and set Nod free. He seemed fine, but Miss Cass was done in. She sat and cuddled all three panting dogs in her lap. "What a fright! What a fright! I must have some tea. Etta, you saved the day. You and Mac must have tea with me. You must."

"I don't reckon we have time…"

"Please? Please, Mr. Mac?" I whispered, forgetting for the moment the Vickers field.

We entered Miss Cass's fortress through one of the built-on screened porches. It was more like a covered walkway, long and narrow, lined with six cages that held balls of what looked like overgrown cockle burrs.

"My babies," said Miss Cass, in the doting way she used for her dogs.

"Are they…?"

"Hedgehogs, darling one. Nature's own pest control. They sleep all day, don't make a peep. But at night, when I let them out, they catch crickets and roaches all night long. They even eat the big ones, the watta bugs. But do you know what they like to eat more than anything?" She put her face down close to mine.

"Spiders?" I whispered.

"Mealworms. So easy to grow. I save them for special occasions, don't you know. Christmas, Easter, my birthday…They'll bite off your finger for a mealworm."

My hands curled themselves into fists.

The porch smelled like nothing I had ever smelled before, an odd combination of sawdust and sour milk. Hedgehogs.

Inside the trailer, the smell was different but equally pungent. The windows were open, and five floor fans stirred up the smells of overripe fruit and tin cans that needed to go out in the trash and a smell I would later identify as herbal—mint and lavender and rosemary. Miss Cass scooped up an armload of the newspapers that covered the stove and set them atop one of the stacks on the floor. She put her kettle on to boil, then crossed her arms and stared at me. "Looks just like her papa. Just like him."

I looked at the floor. Always my father. I wished that just once someone would say that I resembled my mother.

White dog hair drifted across the yellowish linoleum. Wherever Mr. Mac and I took a step, it flew up like feathers or dry, dry snow. *Life* and *Time* magazines and newspapers were stacked on every chair and in every corner and were spreading. Miss Cass nodded at a pile of *Life*s; the cover on top featured bandaged soldiers from the First World War. "I saved that series for you, Mac. All about the war. Take it home with you."

I knew he'd leave the magazines. My grandfather, whenever I asked about it, dismissed the war as though it wasn't important.

Empty bottles of all sorts—green soda pop bottles, brown medicine bottles, clear ketchup bottles—stood about in rows, the way Will arranged his toy soldiers. If a grinding bowl was here anywhere, it was camouflaged.

"Shall we have tea in the library?"

Miss Cass, balancing a tray, led us into the next room. On the floor, helter-skelter, were egg cartons full of seedlings. "I've got to make some shelves one of these days," she said. Books, most of them yellowed and tattered paperbacks, rose in crooked towers along three walls.

We sat on a dusty sofa pushed up underneath a row of windows. On a small table right next to me was a black-and-white picture of an Indian chief on horseback. He wore a beaded tunic and a feathered cap with three tall black-tipped feathers in a row front to back. Two rattles made from turtle shells lay beside it.

"My husband, Gabriel. He was a chief, you know, in the Ohkwari—that means Bear—Clan. He died in '51, before you were born I suspect."

"Klan. The Klan?"

"No, not that Klan, Etta—not the KKK. *Clan* with a *c*. It just means *tribe*."

I pointed to the picture. "That a Palomino?"

"Indeed it is."

"That's what I wanted." It slipped out before I could stop myself.

"But you have a mythic horse, one that was struck by lightning and lived."

You don't have to look at him, I thought. Or deal with his spitefulness. Still, if I could get through to him—if he led me to buried treasure, then he'd deserve to be famous.

She pulled a picture off the wall, a color photograph, and dusted it with her sleeve. "Now *this* was one fine horse."

Miss Cass was much younger in the picture. Her braid was a rich golden-red color, and her lips were bright red. She was sitting bareback astride a tall and gorgeous black horse. "Beauty," she murmured. Her husband sat beside her on a dappled gray horse, also bareback. They both wore tunics and leggings.

"Bet you can't guess where this was taken."

I squinted.

"The Great Wall of China! See the wall right here?" Miss Cass sighed. "Early Kodachrome. That color cost us a pretty penny....Gabriel and I, we had some life together. You have to grab the good when it's here, don't you know. Nothing lasts forever. Don't reckon you've met too many other folks who've ridden a horse on the Great Wall of China."

I tried to picture myself, like Miss Cass, astride a fine horse on the other side of the world. But only Troy with his lopsided head and shambling hooves came to mind.

"Like my tea, Mac?"

My grandfather answered by blowing on his cup and taking a sip.

The tea was strange. In the first place, it wasn't iced. I sipped and tried not to make a face. It looked like dirty water and tasted exactly as I imagined boiled hay might taste. Not terrible, but a long way from being even halfway good.

"I learned about healing teas from Mother Orenda. She was the clan mother, don't you know. And president of the Bear Medicine Society."

It was odd, but I began to feel calmer, more relaxed. Unlike Mr. Mac, who was fidgeting and seemed ready to go.

"I make it myself with herbs right out there in the yard. This one's my Calm Down Formula. And I tell you the truth, I need a lot of calming down these days, with the world in such a state. Those boys in Mississippi, the car they were driving—the one that turned up burnt—was just like mine, a Ford Fairlane station wagon. Only mine is red, not baby blue. I bought it last summer so I could take some of my Negro friends up to Washington for the march. But not one soul would go with me." She shook her head. "Not one. I picked up hitch-hikers, though, folks trying to get to the march however they could."

"What? Their car got burned?"

But Miss Cass, not hearing me, continued with her story. "That was an experience, let me tell you—the march. I've never seen so many people in my life. There were movie stars, Etta. Marlon Brando. Charlton Heston. And famous singers. Mahalia Jackson. Sammy Davis, Junior. And of course Dr. Martin Luther King." She reached down to a stack of pages on the floor by her chair and handed one to me. It was the Reverend King in his jail cell.

"Cleo has this same picture on her wall," I said.

"Turn it over," Miss Cass said. "I tried to talk Cleo and Starry into going with me. They looked at me like I was crazy. Isn't that a shame?"

Under the title, "Excerpts: Letter from Birmingham Jail," were several long paragraphs. I tried to skim them, but the language was complicated. "Wait," I read out loud, "has almost always meant Never." I nodded.

"I gave these out to the Negro churches, don't you know."

"Is Dr. King really dangerous?" I was remembering Margot's parents' warning.

"Anything but. He organizes peaceful protests. His followers don't engage in violence. The violence comes from the other side."

"I hope you're watching your step, Cassandra," my grandfather said.

Miss Cass tilted her head and looked at him as though he had said something incomprehensible. "I am worried about those boys. Look at this." She opened a new *Life* magazine to a photograph. It showed Navy men in boats with nets, others wading in high boots, searching a swamp for the three boys. From a nearby bridge a group of young white men in crew cuts and ironed-stiff shirts stood watching. Their ugly, sneering expressions reminded me of the children at school who bullied Will.

"Do you think the Klan—the Klan spelled with a *K*—got them?" I asked.

"You ought not be thinking about any Klan—or any of that mess going on," my grandfather said, stumbling to his feet.

"We got to go now, Miz Cass. Cleo'll have our hides if we're late for dinner."

I had noticed the beads peeking out from the open collar of Miss Cass's work shirt. I couldn't help staring when she bent forward to rise from her chair. She winked and pulled out a strand of tiny whitish cylinders interspersed with several deep purple ones. At the center hung an animal claw.

"Gabriel gave me these when we got married. They're the real thing—Iroquois wampum. Mohawk, to be specific. Back in the old days, only the families of the chiefs were allowed to wear them. The white ones stand for wisdom and purity, the dark for the imperfections that make us human. This"—she fingered the claw—"this is a bear's, naturally. Here…" She lifted the strand of beads and put them over my head. "See how they feel."

Going out, we passed the row of hedgehogs. "Are they tame?" I asked. "I mean, will they come back to their cages in the morning on their own?"

Miss Cass stopped. "Here's how smart they are. The minute the sun goes down, their little heads are moving this way and that. Their little black eyes are darting all around, and their tongues are going to town. I open the cages and out they scamper. I go to bed, and they go to work. When I get up at five, they're back in their cages rolling themselves up for the day. Hedgehogs. Highly recommended. Highly."

I had been running my fingers along the beads, pressing the tip of the claw.

"Can you feel Gabriel's spirit?" asked Miss Cass. "He's there. He speaks to me through the beads, through the totem." She gently removed the strand from my neck.

Yet another kind of spirit, I thought. How many were there?

"Totem," I repeated. "Like totem pole?"

"Exactly. Years ago, the bear sought out Gabriel's clan and claimed it. That's what totem animals do. If you're lucky, one will find you. It will come at just the right time. It will teach, and you will learn."

I didn't see the connection. The animals carved on the totem poles at Cherokee (fake totem poles for the tourists, I later learned) weren't like any animals I'd ever seen. Nightmarish things. I wouldn't want one of them to find me.

Miss Cass put the beads back around her neck and tucked them down her shirt. "I wore them all the way to Washington and back, and I knew I was safe."

∽

"Dog*gone*, that was nasty stuff." Mr. Mac had to stop at Legette's Grocery, the first store we came to. He got us both a Coca-Cola for the ride back. "Like drinking bath water, that tea of hers. Miz Cassandra is one piece of work. She's got gumption, you can say that much for her. I just hope she doesn't land herself in trouble."

But all I could think about was finding beads like Miss Cass's at the Vickers field—Jewels of Helen.

∽

"Your baby brother doing well, you just might want to know."

Cleo was standing on the front porch waiting for us. She had her hands on her hips.

"Good." I looked past her to a green lizard sprawled against the red brick wall. "I've been worrying about him."

She raised her eyebrows. I had forgotten all about Will, and Cleo knew it. Talk about a third eye! Whether I liked it or not, she could see straight into my insides. I was glad Mr. Mac was there, so I didn't have to be alone with Cleo just yet.

She continued when Mr. Mac and I sat down to eat. "Mr. Frank called thirty minutes ago. Will just now waking up from the operation. They all fine and say not to worry, praise God."

There were chicken and dumplings, fresh stewed corn and butterbeans, and the apple, banana, and marshmallow salad that I liked.

"Did they say how he looks? Is his mouth put together the right way now?"

"I didn't axe that question." Cleo was busy scrubbing out a pot. "But I suspect that since they did some more cutting and sewing and Lord knows what else, he's pretty swolled up."

I hoped beyond hope that Will would look normal once school started. What good were these operations if they couldn't make him look normal? Not Cleo, not Mr. Mac, not anybody knew how often I stood up for Will.

"Cleo, how come you didn't go to the march? Miss Cass invited you, didn't she? In Washington, last year. She said she did. You could have seen Dr. King."

Cleo turned, drying her hands on her apron. She glanced at Mr. Mac, who was busy helping himself to more corn, then at me. "Am I the same person as Miss Cass? Am I the same as you? The Lord make us every one different. But we all parts of the Body. Miss Cass—she's the foot, going that long distance; I's the hand, doing what I can do for you and Will. You too young yet to know what's your part. But we all gots our work laid out for us."

"I'm the eye," I said without missing a beat. "That's what I am. I'm going to see things at that Indian field nobody else can see."

And I would get through to Troy yet—I could picture him stomping and scraping the ground with his spastic front hoof right where the treasure lay beneath.

10: Handing

July 10, 1964

Pottery shards. Despite my new resolve, despite my new optimism, all I found as I stirred the loose dirt with my dull pocketknife were pottery shards. Not even good ones, just little pieces so worn I could hardly make out the patterns. Mr. Mac spotted a couple of arrowheads, but that was all. Not only had it not rained a drop, but Mr. Vickers hadn't even disked over last summer's crop. Dried cornstalks littered the ground. Mr. Mac kicked at the sand with his boots. "Seemed like the fields were full of pottery when I was a boy plowing behind a mule. I'd be tossing pieces big as my hand out the way."

"I wish you'd saved them. I bet they were valuable."

"Not when you're stepping on them with your bare feet, no choice but to keep going, bleeding or not. I was cussing the tar out of those Injuns."

"I wonder what happened to them, why they just left—and left behind only arrowheads, broken pottery, and *one* grinding bowl, I reckon. Where are the beads? Up at Cherokee, you can buy stuff with beads all over it—moccasins, belts, headdresses. And look at what Miss Cass has."

"That Cherokee junk, they make that for the tourists. Now Miz Cass, she's got the real thing." My grandfather pressed the points he'd found into my hand.

"And why don't skeletons ever turn up? Didn't the Pee Dee Indians get buried?"

"Bones don't last in the dirt around here. Acid eats everything up right fast. Good for growing crops, though. Makes for rich soil."

I stared at a dead dragonfly with striped wings, its body an iridescent blue. Tiny black ants were swarming all over it. Dead things everywhere, I thought, looking up at a trio of buzzards gliding overhead. No matter where you went out here in the country, the buzzards were a constant presence, riding the air. Again I thought of the three boys lost somewhere in Mississippi—why couldn't I keep them out of my mind? If the Klan had buried them, they could be turning into black dirt this very minute.

What was left of the Vickers family's antebellum house stood on a rise off Catfish Creek. Here, at the Indian field, we were almost there. Once when I was younger, I had roamed the ruined shell—it was far worse off than the Oliver homestead—with my parents and Will. I begged to go now, but Mr. Mac refused. He wouldn't enter it without permission. Besides, thanks to this detour, we were behind on checking the fields.

With Troy's help, I might have found something worth finding in the Vickers field. At least another grinding bowl. Then, together, we'd have trotted straight up to the old mansion with perhaps its stash of coins beneath loose floorboards, a box of jewels in the attic, a secret cupboard full of silver. With a find such as that, I wouldn't have to apologize to Cleo. She and everyone else would know how special I was. Whatever mistakes I'd made in the past would be forgiven, forgotten.

"I'm not giving up on you." In my mind I spoke to the old horse. "You may think you can keep your secrets, but I'll pry them out of you. I'm as stubborn as you are. Mr. Mac says I'm a hard rock, and he's right."

Heading back towards the highway, we passed the fork in the road—there was the Morning Star Holiness Church where I had gone with Cleo last summer. Today the church looked drab, its white paint peeling, cardboard taped over two of the windows. But a year ago, with Cleo and her sister Starry's family, all

I had seen were the reds, purples, and yellows of the women's dresses, the bright ribbons in the girls' braids, the white starched shirts of the men and boys. Inside, the birds' chattering came right through the open windows. Every hand held a fan to move the heat around. The choir had paraded to the front, clapping and singing: "I'm gonna sit at the welcome table, one of these days, Hallelujah! And have supper, have supper with the Lord!" Evelyn had sung one verse all by herself.

"There is a train, Brothers and Sisters." The preacher, a big man slick with perspiration, had seemed to be singing when he spoke in his booming voice. "And it's coming soon. That's right. Already carrying Job. Ha! And Daniel. Ha! All the saints. Yes! All the prophets. Yes! And there's Moses. Standing at the door. And next to him, the Reverend Dr. King. They reaching out their hands—let freedom ring!—to pull you on board. All you got to do is step up, Brothers and Sisters. Step up on that *sanctified* train. Ha! That's right. You know where it's going?" He'd put his hand to his ear. "What's that? Promised Land? Say it louder."

Everyone sang out, "Promised Land!"

"That's right! The Promised Land! The Lord is that train, Brothers and Sisters. Out of His mouth come fire and smoke. It brings joy," he sang—now he was really singing—"It brings joy to my soul." The choir joined in. Cleo, all in purple—hat, dress, even shoes—had stood close beside me, showing me when it was time to stand, when to sit, when to sing along, when to hum.

I turned to Mr. Mac. "Cleo had two spells yesterday. She got dizzy. Couldn't catch her breath. And her feet swelled up."

"She seemed fine at dinner. It could just be the heat. I'll give Dr. Monroe a call, maybe run to town and pick up something at Whaley's."

Cleo. If I went home anytime soon, we would be alone together. There would be time for talking.

"How about you drop me off at the barn with Evelyn and Starry and Juney? I'll hand with them." There would be plenty of time to talk later. Later, once I had found the right words to say.

Mr. Mac nodded. He grinned around his cigar. "They might could use you. You're helping a lot these days."

"I'm getting big," I added.

Past the church, where the dirt road turned to gravel, was a long stretch of land belonging to our family: a stand of pine trees, then Esau and Starry's house, then White Horse field, which was full of hay this year. The gravel road met the highway where Lamar Scurlock and his three sons lived in a trailer at the back of a deep lot. No trees stood, or bushes, or grass. But in the vast front yard there sat a rusting pickup truck, scattered farm machinery—an old plow, a mower—and several rolls of chicken wire. Mr. Scurlock owned this property himself as well as the small tobacco field next to it and—fenced off from that—a pasture with three handsome horses the Scurlock boys got to ride whenever they wanted: a Paint, a Gray, and a Chestnut with a white diamond on its nose. The Scurlock boys didn't deserve them.

Starry and her daughters were still working at the barn near the entrance to Boggy Swamp. "Etta!" Evelyn said. "Good! We need you." Beneath the overhang she stood stringing at a long table two feet deep in green leaves. A friend of hers from town, a thin light-brown girl with horn-rimmed glasses, was handing along with Juney.

"Etta, this Sandra. Sandra, this Etta."

I put out my hand. "Pleased to meet you."

Sandra's hand was limp in mine. She didn't even try to smile.

"You hand to me, Etta," Evelyn said. "We'll have us a good time."

"I'll look after her. You go on, Mr. Mac," Starry said.

I didn't want to tell anyone I didn't know how to hand, but it turned out I didn't have to. "Just grab three leaves—like this." A skinny wrinkled hand grabbed mine and put the tobacco in it. "Hold them at the stalk—ends got to be even—and hand them to Evelyn. Look out for hornworms, though!"

"Look out for what?" Everyone laughed at me. I felt my face redden. If Mr. Mac was still here, they wouldn't be laughing like this.

Miss Pity was so old her hair was white. She had one gold tooth, right in the front. She dipped Peach Sweet Snuff, "Sweet as a Peach." Will believed it was candy she and the other workers didn't want to share, and no one could convince him otherwise.

"Hornworms?" I tried to keep my voice steady.

"They fat and green and got a horn," Miss Pity said. "You have to pick 'em off and squash 'em. With your feets."

Although I was careful not to react, the group laughed all over again—except for Evelyn's friend Sandra, who just kept scowling. Since everyone else was barefooted, I had taken off my too-tight shoes first thing.

The work was easy—even fun, though I kept sensing that the others were watching me, waiting for me to make a mistake. I pictured myself telling Will about it; he'd insist on working, too, but I doubted our mother would let him. Evelyn and Juney, who was a year younger than me, sang "Pass Me Not, O Gentle Savior" and "Jesus, Keep Me Near the Cross." Then Starry and Viola and Miss Pity started gossiping. They told stories about people I halfway knew, or knew only by name. And all the while everyone's hands moved quickly, sorting, handing, tying, arranging the green tobacco.

"That Miller boy at the Baker Farm, you know he stole a pickup truck and gone clear to Big Pee Dee to fish. Him and his friend Derek and the beers they took from the store at the fork…"

"Poor Vinnia—her baby girl China, she done gone bad."

"Mm, mm, mm." They all shook their heads.

"She goes with whoever comes knockin' on the door, and they can't do nothing about it. Can't even get her to church, can't get her to do nothing." Miss Pity sounded disgusted. "Her poor mama is heartbroke."

I was learning the sorts of things my parents never discussed in front of Will and me. It was odd, though. I had expected they'd talk about the missing civil rights workers in Mississippi. I'd thought they might at least mention the protests going on everywhere, it seemed, except here. But then perhaps they wouldn't, in front of me. Just like Cleo and Starry wouldn't go with Miss Cass up to Washington.

Roscoe—again—came driving up fast in his black convertible, covering us all in a cloud of dust. He jumped over the door instead of opening it and marched up to Evelyn like he was somebody. Maybe Starry would run him off.

"Roscoe, what you doing here?" Evelyn asked in a high voice.

He whispered something in her ear. Evelyn grinned and nodded and batted her eyes. I studied them. It was clear they were making a date. I frowned; Evelyn was too good for this swaggering boy. And too pretty, with her long eyelashes and dimples, her hair smoothed into a pageboy.

Sandra, a sour look on her face like she had indigestion, took over Evelyn's spot stringing so that Evelyn and Roscoe could talk beneath the far corner of the overhang. I had to strain to hear what they were saying.

They were planning something. Something about Marion. And Saturday, which was tomorrow. I hoped they weren't scheming to get married. Then Evelyn said *no* in a loud voice. Then *why*, she asked. *Why not*, Roscoe said. Soon the two of them came back and Evelyn, her mouth tight, went back to stringing. Roscoe picked up Juney and swung her around.

"I'm joining the Army, Miss Juney Bug. And your sister don't like it. I told her I'm just going to be over at Fort Jackson—that's in Columbia—at first. Then I'll get to see the world like my cousin. He ended up stationed in Germany for three years. Germany, where they make cuckoo clocks! I'll bring one back to you, how about that?"

"And what if they send you off to that jungle? Then what?" Evelyn was mad.

"Then I'll just stop those Communists before they come to get you." He put Juney down and tickled Evelyn's neck.

She started to smile, but stopped herself. "It makes me worried, that's all."

I screamed. I hadn't meant to—it just happened. My hand had closed over something that felt like a soft sticky sausage. I wiped my hand, hard, on my shirt.

"Pick it off!" everyone shouted. "Throw it down and step on it!"

I tried to make my hand work. I tried, but I couldn't make it touch the worm again, much less pick it off the tobacco and step on it with my bare foot. "Go on, go on!" everyone urged. The older women bent over laughing. The little children danced in circles. Roscoe was laughing loudest of all. He had a wide mouth and white, white teeth—whiter even than Dr. Fowler's. Only Sandra kept a straight face, and that was almost worse—as if to her I wasn't even worth a laugh.

I grabbed the leaf and shook it, but the worm held fast. Finally Miss Pity grabbed it from me, picked off the worm, and threw it into the dirt. She ground it to a paste with her heel and spit out a brown stream of tobacco juice. I stuck my hands into my pockets and pressed the tip of one of the two arrowheads into my palm. They were pristine. But Mr. Mac had been the one to find them, not me. And now I was even more of a failure. Evelyn, still giggling, smoothed my hair and patted my shoulder. I tensed. I would not cry.

"I don't like touching hornworms either," Evelyn whispered. "They nasty."

I squinted out at the fields, half-expecting to see Troy somewhere in the distance.

Roscoe gave Evelyn a little kiss on her cheek. "Tomorrow," he said in a low voice. He gunned his motor, wheeling his car around to leave. Another dust cloud.

So there *was* some kind of sneaky date planned. Roscoe wasn't just talking about the Army after all.

Starry shook her head at Evelyn. "Don't you go getting into trouble with that Roscoe, you hear me?"

If she hadn't gotten into trouble so far, Evelyn told her mother, she wasn't likely to.

Sweat stung my eyes and soaked my shirt. Every inch of me was covered with dust. My legs were tired. My hands were black and gluey with tobacco juice and dirt. What if I found another worm—or, worse, touched it before I saw it? They were the exact bright green of the tobacco, and they had a curved spike on their heads.

I was thirstier than I could remember being. I felt like I could drink down the whole cooler from Walter's Store. I looked out towards the field, at the steadily moving tractor, the croppers following. I wished Mr. Mac would come back to get me. Surely Juney and the other children were tired and thirsty too, but they didn't complain, so I wasn't about to. I concentrated on handing and on scrutinizing every leaf.

"You-all still got that horse was lightning-struck? I used to see you and Will a-riding in the pasture over there." Evelyn was trying to change the subject.

"Still got him. But he's all crippled up. We don't ride him."

"That right?"

"I take care of him, though," I bragged. "I practically had to teach him to walk again. Every day I give him carrots and apples, lead him out in the pasture. Poor old thing, I don't know what he'd do without me."

"That right?" Evelyn said. She started singing again. "I'll fly away…" The others joined in, even Miss Pity. Even Sandra.

"You ought to come work when there's no old folks here," Evelyn whispered to me. "We sure can sing some blues. You ever heard 'Driving Nails in My Coffin'? That's a good one." She nodded at Miss Pity. "She makes us hush." I nodded and smiled as though I knew what Evelyn was talking about.

The tractor came pulling another drag piled high with tobacco. The men and boys who'd been cropping began to cluster under the shed.

The sticks of strung tobacco had to be hung just right inside the barn, and Lamar Scurlock was in charge. He had the same dark wavy hair as his sons, except his was shot through with silver. He was skinny as a tobacco stick and was famous for mumbling and cussing.

"Damnation! S'hotter 'n forty acres o' hell stew-down t'a quart."

Starry scolded him for using curse words in front of Juney and me.

"Me-uss Etta! Bless my bony a-a-a soul. What you durn out chur?"

"She's working and you'd better watch your mouth," said Evelyn.

He turned his attention to his sons. Their greasy black hair was mostly hidden by yellow and green John Deere caps. Even before the confrontation in the Swamp Fox woods, I had disliked being near them. Now, when Roy and Ray climbed up onto the rafters in the barn, they reminded me of buzzards. Mr. Scurlock and Aubrey lifted the sticks of tobacco up to them.

There was still a good hour before quitting when Mr. Mac drove up.

"Etta did good," Starry bragged. "She's a good worker!"

Miss Pity spat out another brown stream of Sweet Peach. "She don't like hornworms much. And she might not like working like we does, from can't see to can't see."

11: Trouble

Mr. Mac and I always went to Marion early on Saturdays. This morning, from the beginning, something about the town felt wrong. At first I blamed myself: I hadn't been able to gather the nerve to talk to Cleo, as I'd promised myself I'd do. This put me in an anxious, self-critical frame of mind. But there was more to it. The town seemed too quiet for a Saturday, as though it was holding its breath, waiting for something—a parade or a thunderstorm. People seemed to be talking in whispers, or maybe it was my imagination; maybe it was the heat.

Farmers and Merchants Bank, open on Saturday morning during tobacco season, was dark and cool—a serious, grownup place. All the surfaces were so shiny they might have worn a layer of glass. Everywhere you looked was polished dark wood. Behind a heavy door, behind another door with bars, there was a steel vault that I longed to enter. No telling what treasures it held.

Mr. Mac took care of some business at the teller's window, then he led me past the vault to the office of Mr. Turnage, the bank president. A square man with wavy silver hair, he sat behind a wide desk made of the same dark shiny wood that was everywhere. Mr. Turnage acted glad to see me, but his toothy grin was too set to be convincing.

The two men talked for a little while over some ledgers, both of them overly polite with one another. Then, as he always did, Mr. Turnage opened his upper right-hand drawer and pulled out a pack of candy cigarettes. Sometimes they were made of chocolate wrapped in paper, waxy as crayons, not worth eating. But these were the good kind—cool sugary wintergreen, white with painted red tips.

"Many coloreds out today?" It was understood that Saturday was the day Negroes shopped downtown.

"Too hot even for them, I reckon. I sure hope our nigras don't get ideas from those Northern Jews and the Communists. Heck," Mr. Turnage laughed, showing all his teeth, "they got it good! I wish I had a whole race of people taking care of *me*. Us white Southerners—we're the best friends the coloreds have got."

Mr. Turnage loved to talk about colored people, how they had it made. Grownups certainly could be strange, the way they sometimes made pronouncements that anybody who had eyes could see weren't true. Maybe some whites and coloreds were friends—Cleo and I used to be more than friends; Miss Cass spoke of Negro friends—but the Klan wasn't friendly with any colored people. And there were a lot of other whites besides the Klan who wanted to keep Negroes "in their place." Negroes like Cleo and Jesse, who always rode in the back seat of my mother's station wagon and would have had to sit in the balcony of the Rainbow Theatre, if they ever even went to a movie. Of course I'd heard the men at Walter's Store holding forth: it wasn't the business of any "Jew Yankee" to help the "nigra" to vote; besides, the "nigras" were too ignorant to vote. Even in sixth grade, I knew the colored school wasn't as good as mine.

I didn't nibble like I used to, like Will still did, but instead I "smoked" my cigarette while walking across Main Street and towards the barbershop. Feeling more cheerful—confident that I would fix things with Cleo as soon as I got home, or at least before my parents and Will returned tomorrow—I blew out make-believe smoke and waved to Mr. Ajax, who was directing traffic. He gave me a military salute and blew his whistle. Mr. Ajax wasn't really a policeman, but when he came back confused from

World War II, the town let him wear a uniform and pretend. Only the meanest kids and teenagers made fun of him.

The same was not true of the owners of the new record store. The couple, the Khourys, had come from another country, Lebanon. They spoke with an accent no one had ever heard before. Mr. Khoury sported a mustache and a floppy fisherman's cap. His wife outlined her brown eyes in thick black pencil, like King Tut. I often went there with my mother to buy sheet music. But some people—adults as well as children, both white and colored—called them A-rabs and Mooslims and refused to buy from them.

In Treadwell's Barber Shop, all the barbers were Negro cousins with skin the exact shade of Kraft caramel. They wore starched white shirts with the sleeves rolled up. With the penny Mr. Mac gave me for the bubblegum machine, I got orange, my third favorite, then sat down to wait. *Progressive Farmer* was the only magazine there. I put it in my lap, but as usual I never got around to opening it. There was too much to take in. The barbers, four in a row, sharpened their razors on strops—shreep, shreep, shreep. They wrapped steaming towels around men's faces, lathered them up with a brush, whipped out long blades to shave them, then slap-slapped a spicy-smelling tonic onto the newly smooth cheeks. They used electric buzzing shavers for the haircuts. In the background, the conversation circled around tobacco and corn, cows and hogs.

Mr. Vance Treadwell, with his flattop haircut and thick-rimmed glasses, was the owner and Evelyn's friend Sandra's father. Once he had given me a haircut—Will and me both. I had watched the whole operation in that wall of mirrors. It was exciting. There were so many mirrors it was hard to decide where to look. But Mama had words with Mr. Mac. It was okay for Will, but not for me. This unfairness made me jealous, even though I did enjoy Miss Bonnie's Beauty Parlor, with its *Look* magazines and Nehi grape sodas and the ladies—everyone working there was white—who made a fuss over me.

I watched Mr. Treadwell snip at the horseshoe of gray hair around the bottom of Mr. Mac's head. I watched the steam rising from his turbaned face, then the fluffy beard of shaving cream. When Mr. Treadwell took his straight razor to my grandfather's throat, I got goose bumps. But as usual, Mr. Mac never suffered so much as a scratch. At home he nicked himself almost every time.

Whenever I was downtown with my mother, we'd follow Khoury's music store with Belk's, the department store with its wide staircase to the second floor; then Woolworth's dime store, with its popcorn and roasting peanut smells, its bins of pop guns and jacks and little plastic soldiers, the parakeets in cages, the turtles the size of half-dollars—some with painted shells—in fish bowls near the cash register. But Mr. Mac hated those stores.

He and I went straight from the barber shop to Whaley's Drug Store, where we both veered to the book display against the left wall: he to fish for a Perry Mason mystery he hadn't yet read, and I to find a comic book. Mr. Mac found one at once, but I had to look through everything all over again. Stephanie and Margot had discovered Archie comics, though Margot's mother didn't let her buy them since they pictured teenagers who flirted and sometimes wore bathing suits. I liked Archie okay, but I could choose only one, and the Classics Illustrateds were my favorites. I was torn. *The House of the Seven Gables*? Or *Robinson Crusoe*? Aha. Peeking from behind *The Last Days of Pompeii*, which I'd bought last time: *The Iliad*, which I'd never seen. I snatched it up. The cover showed a prancing horse pulling a chariot, several warriors with spears.

The bell jangled above the door. My back was turned to the newcomers. I noticed nothing until the ladies behind me shopping for perfumy soap and hand lotion stopped their soft chattering. The sudden silence made me turn. The ladies were staring at the soda fountain, where four young people were sitting on the stools that twirled around. Three were colored, and one was white. They were sitting there together. The two white girls who worked the fountain looked like they were going to cry. Then I recognized the white boy's cap, green and dirty yellow. Aubrey Scurlock—sitting next to Sandra Treadwell. Evelyn sat beside her, with Roscoe on the end. I started to go speak to them, but something stopped me—the faces of the fountain workers, the silence. I ran to the back of the store where Mr. Mac was now having a prescription filled. "Come quick," I couldn't help gasping. "I think it's a sit-in!"

In a flash, Mr. Whaley came around the prescription counter. As though they had witnessed a terrible accident, all the customers stood in a group off to the side. Mr. Whaley went behind the soda fountain and rubbed his hands up and down the front of his white jacket.

"Now look," he begged, "this is not the way we do things. I don't want trouble here, and I know you four well enough to know you don't want trouble either. Roscoe, you worked for me last year, you know better. And Sandra, your daddy will lock you in the house if he finds out what you're up to."

"Evelyn." Mr. Mac tapped her shoulder. "Starry know where you are?"

She shook her head, looking scared. She and Roscoe were squeezing each other's hand. So this is what the two of them had been scheming yesterday at the barn.

"Mr. Mac!" Aubrey was flushed, he was so excited. "We having a sit-in." He patted the stool beside him. "Y'all sit-in, too."

I stepped towards the stool. Mr. Mac grabbed my shoulder and pulled me back.

"Aubrey, you going to end up back in jail." Mr. Mac then looked at Evelyn. "You-all got no business bringing Aubrey into this."

"I want to, Mr. Mac!" Aubrey said.

"You want to spend the night in jail?"

"No, sir." His face sank into a pout.

Aubrey made a move to rise, but Sandra gripped his arm and pulled him back down. She whispered something in his ear.

"All we asking for is a fountain drink," Roscoe said. "I'm leaving for Fort Jackson next week to fight—if I'm asked to—for everybody in this country. I just think I ought to have the same rights as the folks I'm fighting for and be a first-class citizen."

"I appreciate that, young man," said Mr. Whaley, brightening. "Tell you what. If you come around to the back door, I'll give you and all your friends here ice cream sodas free of charge."

"No thank you, sir," Roscoe said. "But I'll be happy to pay good money for Coca-Colas right where we sitting."

Evelyn cut her eyes at me. She smiled a little and gave a secret below-the-counter wave. I half-waved back. Roscoe winked at me. But I felt sick. Where were they—the firemen with hoses, the policemen with attack dogs? My eyes kept moving to the front window.

First the ladies who'd been looking at the lotions quietly left. Then the colored family with a toddler and a little baby. Then the old couple who was colored, then the old couple who was white. Mr. Whaley kept rubbing the front of his jacket. He whispered something to the two girls behind the soda fountain, and they left to sit in one of the booths.

The front door jingled as a pair of teenagers came in, talking and laughing. They stopped, their mouths open. I recognized Brenda Richardson, homecoming queen and older sister of Joyce Ann. She was with the older brother of the Boatwright twins who were in Will's grade. Pretty little blond girls who picked on him. Brad wore a blonde crew cut, and his face looked sun-burned. He stood behind Roscoe and Evelyn. "Look what we have here," he said, "three niggers and a retard. That the best y'all can do for a sit-in?"

Brenda giggled. Aubrey grinned until Sandra pinched his arm.

"Fun's over. You all got to move now. Brenda and me, we want to sit here, and we ain't sitting with niggers."

But the four didn't move.

What happened next took only minutes, but when I later recalled it, I saw every detail in slow motion.

Brad put a Camel cigarette in his mouth. He struck a match and held it in front of Roscoe's face. "Hear me, nigger-boy?" He lit his cigarette, shook the flame from the match, then pressed it into Roscoe's forearm. Roscoe didn't flinch.

Turning to Sandra, Brad pulled off her glasses, smeared ketchup on them from the bottle on the counter, and slipped them back on her face. "Here's some rose-colored glasses for you. You need 'em if you think you're going to get yourself a Co'Cola, sitting here."

"Brad!" Brenda said. "Look at this colored girl's nice straight white-girl hair." She'd pulled a pair of manicure scissors from her handbag. "I think I'll just snip myself a little keepsake." Evelyn shut her eyes tight like she was praying.

Roscoe grabbed Brenda's wrist, and Brad pressed the lit end of his cigarette into the back of Roscoe's shirt, burning a hole right through it. "Keep your hands to yourself, coon."

I opened my mouth. I tried to protest, but whatever I start-ed to say made a catching sound in my throat.

Whether he heard the sound or not and took the hint, my grandfather grabbed Brad's arm. "That's enough, son," he said.

Brad grinned and pulled a long drag on his Camel. "Looks to me like you old fellas need some help. We'll be back, won't we, Brenda? We going to bring y'all lots of help."

As soon as the couple left, Mr. Mac, his neck flushed, told Mr. Whaley that if he didn't want worse trouble, he'd have to call the police. Sure as anything, that boy was going to round up some of his friends.

"No!" My throat was dry. I pulled on Mr. Mac's arm. "Not the police! What if they bring clubs and dogs?"

Again Mr. Whaley pled with the foursome to leave. They were giving him no choice, he said. He would have to call the law. Aubrey squirmed, but the other three sat stone still.

Mr. Ajax walked in first, followed by two officers with guns attached to their belts. Had Mr. Ajax been watching from the sidewalk? Aubrey started trembling. Mr. Mac was shaking as well. He took my arm and led me over to a booth. Beads of sweat had risen on his forehead and rolled down his cheeks. He held his hands beneath the table to stop their jerking.

I hated missing the conversation at the soda fountain. The police were pointing, Roscoe was waving his arms, Mr. Whaley was wiping the front of his jacket.

Suddenly, Aubrey came over and sat down with us. "Police making me nervous, Mr. Mac."

"I'll ride you home."

Sandra, wiping her glasses with a napkin, turned and glared at Aubrey. She shook her head in disgust.

Finally, the policemen, Mr. Ajax, and Mr. Whaley stood off to one side and talked among themselves. One officer left, one posted himself just inside the door, and Mr. Ajax sat two stools over from the group. One of the fountain workers brought him a cup of coffee. The three young colored people still sat without being served.

❧

After we drove up into the Scurlocks' yard, Mr. Mac walked with Aubrey to the front door of the trailer. I stayed in the truck. Mr. Scurlock came out and stood with his arms folded across his skinny chest. He wasn't wearing a shirt. Mr. Mac gestured with one hand; the other rested on Aubrey's shoulder. Quick as a snake, the older man grabbed his son's arm and slapped him hard on the side of his face. He slapped the other side. He shoved Aubrey inside, then shut the door.

"Why'd he do that?" I couldn't take in what I'd seen. My own cheeks felt slapped. "Why'd he hit Aubrey like that?"

"He don't know any better. Lamar's a good worker, but he's got his faults. He's one of those people still fighting the War Between the States. He'd about rather see his boy dead than see him socializing with the coloreds—and worse, taking their side against the whites. Don't matter a flip they all work together in the fields."

I stared out the window as we passed long stretches of to-bacco, the kudzu-blanketed old schoolhouse, the tumbledown blacksmith's shop. I rubbed at my palms; they felt dirty, as though from the grease and dust of Troy's fly-bitten hide. I pictured the horrible scar. It seemed as if the things I'd witnessed—Brad and Brenda, those bullies, trying to pick a fight at the drugstore sit-in, the fear seizing the grownups' faces, Lamar Scurlock's scrawny hand slapping Aubrey—all that ugliness was seared into the horse. It was strange how Troy, even when he wasn't physically stalking me, tracked me down in my mind.

"I don't get it."

"Get what?"

"I don't get it why Mr. Whaley didn't just sell Evelyn and them their Cokes. He sells medicine, soap, everything else to colored people."

"It's not just the Cokes. Serving the coloreds sitting together with whites—well, that would have stood for something a whole lot more. If he'd done what they wanted, he'd have opened the door to…things we're just not ready for. I'm not saying we don't need change. People just don't like change forced down their throats. Around here folks aren't ready to eat in public with coloreds, send their children to school with coloreds. Pushing too hard, well, that just leads to fighting."

I sat quietly, trying to make sense of what Mr. Mac was saying. My grandfather was a smart man, a good man. Everyone said so. I'd always believed him to speak the truth. And he was right: fighting was bad. But Dr. King hated fighting, too…It was confusing. I was lucky to have been born with white skin. Immediately the thought made me feel guilty. Guilty the way I felt when I was glad that not I but Will was the one born with a cleft palate. Still, it would be awful to have to try to figure out what colored people had to figure out—how to become first-class citizens, as Roscoe put it, without pushing too hard and making people mad and getting thrown in jail or worse. I remembered the quote I'd read at Miss Cass's house: "Later almost always means Never."

"When *will* we be ready?" I whispered. But my grandfather was turning in to park at Walter's Store and didn't hear me.

Mr. Sneed, Mr. Hamm, and Mr. Oliver had already gotten wind of the sit-in in town. Mr. Walter said he'd pull out his shotgun if any of that foolishness happened at his store.

"That was Starry's Evelyn? What you going to do about that, Mac?" Mr. Oliver's ears wagged, as they did when he got worked up.

"You oughter kick that girl and her family off your land," said Mr. Sneed. "I halfway 'spect it's Cassandra got those young niggers, 'scuse me—*Ne*-groes, thinking about this protest business. You know she goes to the colored churches passing out stories about that Ne-gro preacher." He raised his eyebrows and looked at Mr. Oliver.

Mr. Hamm rubbed his knee with his good hand. "She's getting to be as bad as those Yankees coming down to Mississippi. Stirring things up when everybody is just fine with the way things are."

I looked at Mr. Mac. Not everyone, white as well as colored, was fine with the way things were—Miss Cass for one and Evelyn for another. Besides, Miss Cass had grown up here; she was his friend. And Evelyn was his best stringer, not to mention Cleo's niece. Why didn't he say something about their gumption? He just sat and chewed on his cigar and stared at the cold stove.

I suddenly remembered that no one had paid for the Classics Illustrated *Iliad*, which lay sweat-smudged and creased on the seat of my grandfather's truck.

PART TWO

12: Catfish Creek

August 1, 1964

For two entire weeks after his operation, Will was too weak and sore to go fishing. He slept late and sat around the house while everybody spoiled him rotten. Especially Cleo and Mr. Mac. Cleo, thanks to the medicine from Whaley's and a visit to Dr. Monroe, claimed she felt good as new. She marched back and forth toting trays of special food to Will's room: not just applesauce, but milkshakes and pudding, too. How could I try to make up with Cleo when Cleo had no time for me?

The sit-in the day before Will came home had thrown me off-kilter. Before it happened, I'd planned out most of what I was going to say to Cleo. I knew things now, I was going to say, that I didn't know before. Back when Troy kicked Trudy, she— Cleo—had a spell that kept her from thinking straight. I'd been hateful afterwards, and I was sorry. But I was more sorry than anything for what I'd said—almost said—and what I did that day I led my friends into the woods to the Swamp Fox pit. But there were other things I didn't know how to express: my tangled feelings about Cleo's life apart from mine, her secret life with a husband. And I was curious about even more things. What did Cleo think about the sit-in? Was Evelyn planning another? (Did Cleo know?) Or maybe a march down Main Street? Cleo might open up to me—once we'd sorted out our problems—even if no one else on the farm would. But Cleo no longer had a second to spare. Not for me alone.

Even if Will had been able to go, Mr. Mac was too busy, during those last two weeks of July, to take us fishing. It was all he could do to keep up with the tobacco, the fever pitch of gathering and curing. Most days, though Mama worried that I might get overheated, I handed with Evelyn. Still, despite my grown-up job, I stayed irritable—with Will, with Cleo who was always out of breath from babying Will, with my own failure to find real treasure, and with the old horse who still escaped the pasture to stalk me whenever he pleased. I didn't breathe a word to anyone about Troy's wandering—and strangely, no one else seemed to notice him. Often when I was handing, yes, doing honest work, I'd look up to see him standing at a distance, tilting to his left as if he might fall over, though he never did, head angled so that his good eye fixed its faultfinding gaze on me. In addition, I was disappointed in myself for not having the courage to say something—anything—to Evelyn about the sit-in. No one at the barn mentioned it; and I sensed that if the workers discussed it at all, they did so behind my back.

On top of everything, Mr. Mac kept letting me down. For days after the sit-in, the old men at Walter's Store couldn't get enough of expressing their opinions. They couldn't believe the police hadn't just jerked the protestors off those stools by their collars and dragged their behinds to jail. It set a bad example, they said—letting them sit there until closing time…If Roscoe wanted to join the army, he needed to follow the rules…They'd have to find somebody other than Sandra's daddy to cut their hair…Mr. Mac ought to fire Evelyn, or else he could expect more trouble from her. The conversation inevitably veered to Miss Cass, the old men calling her a "race mixer" or an "agitator." I kept thinking that Mr. Mac would set them straight. Instead, he just nodded. Then he asked about Mr. Oliver's cotton or Mr. Hamm's timber.

"Why don't you stand up for Miss Cass, and Evelyn too?" I finally asked, as we left the store to ride home.

Mr. Mac took his cigar out of his mouth. He wiped at the back of his neck. "Those old fellows don't mean any harm. They're just getting things off their chest."

Not hardly, I thought. Not when day after day those things are right back on their chests.

～

Normally, now that it was August, the market would have opened. But the dry weather had delayed the crop's maturing. It would be a week or two before the tobacco would sell. Everyone was holding his breath, praying that no fire would take a barn— or worse, a packhouse where cured tobacco from the barns was stored.

Mr. Mac came just after sunup to pick up Will and me. Greasy and stinking with the 6-12 bug repellent our mother had smeared over every inch of our bodies not covered by pants, long sleeves, socks, and shoes, we climbed up beside him. "Watch out for snakes and ticks," Mama had ordered. "And keep your life jackets on."

Mr. Mac wrinkled his nose and grinned around his cigar. "Maybe you'll keep the skeeters off *me*."

"We're going to burn up in all these clothes," I complained. Under them, my sour humor stuck to me along with the repellent. Now that he finally had a day free, Mr. Mac could have been taking me to hunt for treasure—to Aunt Charlotte's spooky, tumbledown house or at least the Swamp Fox pit, where I didn't want to go by myself.

"Won't be too bad." He was wearing long sleeves, too. And his straw hat. "How you doing this morning, Will?"

One corner of Will's swollen mouth turned up. "Good. Canna wai use new rod." He still couldn't talk very well; the swelling hadn't gone down much. But he would be fine by the time school started. That's what our mother had said.

Sure enough, Mr. Mac had bought two identical rods and reels and presented Will's to him right after he got home. Will had run his hands up and down the shiny pole. "Ow! Ow!" he repeated. He was trying to say "Wow."

Mr. Mac had kept mine at his house, propped up in a corner of Miss Lila's room: our secret. But no matter how I tried, I couldn't feel excited about it. I'd hoped at least that Will would be jealous that I had a fishing pole just like his. But he seemed not to notice.

Catfish Creek came off the Big Pee Dee River on the other side of Bull Swamp, so it took us a good twenty minutes past the turn-off at the Scurlocks' trailer to reach the landing. The boat made a racket in the back of the pickup. We passed the fork and Cleo's church. We passed the Vickers field—I knew better than to mention stopping to look for arrowheads—and then the old mansion. My heart sank: the roof had fallen in; an entire wall had collapsed. Unlike Mr. Oliver, who worked at keeping his family home standing, and the Richardsons, who, according to Joyce Ann, planned to restore theirs, the Vickerses had let theirs rot away. I'd never get to go back inside now.

On the landing, Will and I strapped ourselves into our puffy orange life jackets. Wearing life jackets was one rule Mr. Mac wouldn't let us break. But it made casting even more of a challenge, at least for me.

At first Mr. Mac used the motor, but only far enough to reach a narrow branch of the creek. Then he silenced it and paddled past the rotting black posts, all that remained of the docks for steamboats that transported cotton a hundred years ago. The Swamp Fox and his men had likely roamed these banks in still earlier days. I stared into the thick coffee-colored water, past the cypress knees and into the dense tangled green beneath the tall witch-trees, as Will called them, draped with Spanish moss.

If only I could see with Troy's special third eye….This was a place for buried treasure, and for wandering spirits.

It took a while before we reached a cove that Mr. Mac liked the looks of. Will reached into the bucket and grabbed a worm. Mr. Mac showed him where to cast, and his line zipped right to it.

I couldn't stand even looking at the swarm of squirming pinkish earthworms. I hadn't minded digging them up one at a time from the black mud of Boggy Swamp, but all together like this, they resembled something's insides. I thought about Miss Cass with her mealworms, about Miss Pity and the hornworm— *they* wouldn't hesitate. I shut my eyes and reached into the bucket. But the worm I picked writhed and refused to be hooked. After I dropped it twice, Mr. Mac wormed my hook for me, wincing. He didn't enjoy impaling worms any more than I did. He never even fished. He only guided the boat.

"Takes some practice," he said. "Since Will's line is over to the left, you cast yours to the right. See where that log's sticking up?"

I took my time. I aimed, then cast. But my line, instead of whizzing clean into the water, lassoed the low-hanging branches. I'd be more careful next time, I promised.

Mr. Mac was too busy untangling my line to reply.

Staring at the water, Will was in a world by himself. His swollen lips moved as if he were communicating with the catfish and bream in their own silent language.

I cast again. Again my line went into the branches. This time Mr. Mac had to stand up to fumble with the mess of twigs and Spanish moss. He hung on to a branch with one hand and waved at a horsefly with the other. The boat tilted and rocked. I grabbed the bench under me with one hand, the side of the boat with the other. Mr. Mac kept untangling. "Good Lord Almighty, what a rat's nest," he cursed under his breath. "Son of a sorry switch."

He guided my hands as I cast the next time, making me feel like a baby. Will cut his eyes at me. "Girl," he said—I thought he said—under his breath.

"What did you say?"

He ignored me.

Both Will and I caught a bream. Mine was bigger—a relief, though I pretended otherwise. "You'll get the big one next time, Will," I said, trying to sound sweet. I tried to catch Mr. Mac's eye to wink at him, but he was still wiping his face. He'd been coughing, doing his dead-level best, with his handkerchief over his mouth, to stifle the sounds so as not to scare off the fish.

Again we were on the move to try a different spot. Mr. Mac paddled around bend after bend, past cypresses and fallen logs where rows of turtles sunned themselves and then dove off, one after the other. "Coming to get you!" I pinched Will, a little harder than I should have, but he didn't react. He was studying his rod and reel, running his hands over it as though for good luck. There were dragonflies everywhere and little yellow butterflies and the faint rose-scent of some invisible flower. I started to hum, but Will and Mr. Mac both shushed me.

Mr. Mac found what appeared to be the narrowest channel in the creek. Low, moss-draped branches from each bank overhung the water, meeting in the middle. We eased to a stop. Will wormed his hook, then cast without being told where to aim it.

"Look at Will." Mr. Mac chuckled. A dragonfly landed on my grandfather's forearm. He blew it back into flight.

I breathed deeply the sharp creek smell, managed to get a worm on my hook, and cast. Again—*again*—my line tangled in the limbs.

"Ay to go, Etta."

"Shut up, Will."

"Look out, now," Mr. Mac warned.

Again he maneuvered the boat to allow him to reach the line. Again he had to stand up, steadying himself with a branch. Mosquitoes swarmed around his head and neck. He was taking a long time. The boat rocked so hard both Will and I gripped the edges, Will holding his rod between his knees. Finally Mr. Mac sat down and pushed his hat back from his forehead. He wasn't smiling. "I'm afraid you did it good this time." He pulled out his pocketknife. "Got to cut the son of a gun."

"But how am I going to fish?"

"Reckon you're not."

"Stupid life jacket. I can't move in this thing."

Will reeled in another bream. The biggest one yet. He did a little dance in his seat. Show-off.

The board I sat on was making my bottom sore. The life jacket was pinching and making me sweat; the thick layer of 6-12 ran as though it was melting, its waxy smell making me want to throw up. Will caught yet another fish, a bass.

Mr. Mac patted his shoulder, admiring the bass, ignoring me. It was plain that he favored Will over me. Nothing was like it used to be; I could see that now. Girl. I was sure Will had said it.

Nothing this summer was going the way I'd planned. I was no closer to finding treasure than I'd ever been. I'd gotten nowhere with Troy. Worst of all, I hadn't made up with Cleo. Now I couldn't even fish. My life was as murky as the creek water, as knotted up as my fishing line overhead in the branches.

And I had no gumption at all.

Often I had replayed in my head the day of the sit-in. Trying to make sense of it. Staring at the reflections of trees and moss across the surface of the dark water, I again pictured Mr. Whaley's soda fountain. I imagined myself, comic book in hand, sitting with Mr. Mac beside Aubrey, becoming a part of the group of protestors. That's what Miss Cass would have done. She'd have plopped herself down on one of those stools and her huge handbag on another and big as anything ordered five milkshakes all for herself. And when they came, she'd have passed them down to the others. Why hadn't Mr. Mac and I done just that?

Well, I for one had been scared. It embarrassed me to remember how scared I'd felt.

I hoped I'd have another chance to prove my gumption. Anything was possible. Look at Troy: it was impossible that he should be alive, much less roaming around. He was a crippled old horse that moved like a spirit, which had no age. Impossible. But not.

I imagined Troy somewhere behind the tangle of trees on the bank. I looked hard through the mossy branches. It would be just like him to figure out a way to follow me.

Maybe there would be a second chance, another sit-in at the drug store. I pictured myself, Miss Cass, Mr. Mac, even Mr. Whaley joining the protest. We would be on TV, the hot bright lights from the cameras making us sweat. Then soon, all over the country even, white and colored people would begin sitting together at soda fountains—and nothing terrible would happen. The Reverend Dr. King would come to town and shake my hand, posing with me for a big front-page picture in *The Daily Sentinel*. In a parade down Main Street, I'd sit astride Troy, transformed into the golden Palomino of my dreams, waving to Cleo and my family and friends. So many friends! Everyone clapping and cheering.

Will's cork dipped. "Hooee," he said. "You icked one good lace to ish, Ister Ack."

I didn't care that he'd just had an operation and could barely eat or talk. Enough was enough. I prayed that this fish would be

Will's last. I stared at the cork bobbing atop the nearly black water and willed it to stay afloat.

I pictured Troy as he really was, the same ornery old horse. But maybe, if I kept on with him, struggling against my fear of his weirdness and my disgust, I would learn gumption. How had Miss Cass learned it? I wished I knew. But maybe if I showed some, he'd be my horse for real and let me in on the secrets his blind, underground eye could see. And we would find treasure together after all.

A large gray heron rose with a clatter and slow-winged across the channel. Bullfrogs thrummed. A creature I couldn't identify chattered rapidly. I shivered and peered hard into the woods. I thought about those three missing civil rights workers. The search for them was still going on in the Mississippi swamps and fields. My eyes panning the trees, I pictured white robes looking at first like white birds flocking among the branches, then pointed hats parting the Spanish moss, dark eyes peering through the eyeholes of the white masks, searching me out right here in this swamp—hunting me because I was on Evelyn's side.

Another bass plopped into Will's bucket. "What if we can't find our way out?" I whispered. I pictured the maze that led to the Minotaur, the corridors of a pyramid. "What if we just keep going deeper and deeper into the creek?"

"You're not gonna ake e cry, Etta."

I wasn't trying to. I had read in my book of myths about the Medusa, and now I imagined strands of gray moss, like the Medusa's snaky hair, coiling around the head of one of the Klansmen, and felt my bones stiffen as if I were right on the verge of turning to stone. Others I could see taking flight, cawing like Harpies as they swarmed toward me, and I began to imagine their sharp claws tearing at me while I twisted in my seat, struggling to keep my balance, and swatted at them with my fishing rod.

"Look out now," Mr. Mac said.

"Mosquitoes." My voice was high-pitched and quavering. I tried to steady my breathing.

"She's having a fit," Will said, suddenly able to pronounce all of his consonants.

13: Evil Eye

August 2, 1964

I was stuck. Sweat was streaming down my face, rolling down my sides underneath my shirt. I had one foot on the bottom rung of the ladder to the loft in the mule barn. The ladder was netted top to bottom with cobwebs. I stepped away, furious with myself.

Just yesterday Jasmine, the orange tabby, had been so swollen she looked like she'd swallowed a big balloon. But earlier today, I had seen her looking as if all the air had escaped—her belly sagged almost to the ground. Will had noticed too, I suspected. But since my attempts to find artifacts had gone nowhere, since I hadn't even caught a fish on my own, I deserved to be the one to find the kittens, which had to be in the hayloft. Otherwise, all I had was one secret—that Cleo had a husband—which I was still keeping from Will.

This was the day after the fishing trip, and Will was feeling fine, well enough to ride along with Mr. Mac and me to check the tobacco barns and feed the cows. He copied me, as I knew he would, by helping push the hay bales off the truck. He wanted to hand tobacco as I'd been doing, but the handing was almost over for the season.

When Will and I were here at the mule barn early this morning with with Mr. Mac, I'd heard mewing. I started talking loudly so Will wouldn't hear it. My plan was to wait until our mother made him lie down after lunch. Then I'd sneak over to the barn—as I had now done—and find the kittens all by myself.

Where *was* Mr. Mac? Used to be even our thoughts could reach each other. When I needed him to swipe the cobwebs from the ladder to the mule barn loft, he'd simply appear.

I told myself that I could do it. If Will could learn to run fast, catch fish, hit baseballs, and maybe even not cry when we got stuck in mud, surely I could do this. Surely I could overcome my fear of spiders enough to get to the loft and find the kittens.

It was, I told myself, like climbing Jack's beanstalk or Jacob's ladder. There would be a reward at the top. But I'd never had to clear the webs myself and sweep away the spiders. Mr. Mac had always done those things.

The pocketknife pressing against my thigh gave me no courage at all. I could not for the life of me move higher than the bottom rung. I gazed up at the square that opened into the loft. Motes swirled in the golden sunlight. Between the spaces in the ladder hung tattered yellowish cobwebs that caught the slightest hot breeze like dirty gauze curtains; new silvery webs stretched tight as trampolines with black spiders sprawled in their centers; even single strands extended as though cast out like fishing line into the air. I could feel them sticking to my neck. I was afraid to put my hand there; if a spider was crawling on me, I might make it mad enough to bite. Mr. Mac *had* to be somewhere close by— fueling up a tractor or trying to fix one that broke down.

I fumbled through the litter of farm tools in the corner—a dust-coated wooden maul, some metal pipe, a harness and collar for a mule—until I found a decent tobacco stick. Again I placed one foot on the bottom rung. And stopped cold. An eye was looking at me. An eye that was white and brown and black and rolling around—Troy's. From outside, he was spying through a gap between the warped boards of the wall. He huffed and stomped. Then he repositioned his eye in the opening.

"Get on!" I whispered. Then, louder, "Unless you're going to do something to help for a change, you can just get on with your evil eye." The horse shuffled away from the wall. But instead of leaving, Troy came right inside and stood in front of his bucket.

I stepped back from the ladder. "Okay. I'll fill your bucket. But first, you have to do something for me. You've got one good leg in the front. Use it. Kick it up and clear those webs."

Troy sighed at my lack of gumption.

"You could do it, you *could*."

Troy lowered his head and nudged at his bucket.

I hit the ground with my stick. "I give up. I'm sick of you with your bony swayback and your ugly scar. You're never going to look right. You're never going to act right. You've never been anything but bad luck. You should see yourself, with that sideways head and that—that dead eye. I know where that dead eye is looking. Right where Cleo says it is—down to the Devil."

Troy's spastic hoof knocked his bucket on its side.

"I ought to feed you rat poison, that's what I ought to do. I tried to teach you to walk straight and see with that dead blind eye. And what do you do to thank me? Stalk me, that's what. Put curses on me. Even when I'm out there handing tobacco, you make me feel like I'm about to do something wrong. But you put up with Will, even though he never tried to help you. Well, I hope you're satisfied. Now everybody...*everybody* likes Will better than me."

Never before had it bothered me that Will commanded the attention of our parents: Papa, when he wasn't working in town or helping Mr. Mac on the farm, and Mama, when she wasn't teaching piano lessons or making dinner. That was the truth. Because I had Mr. Mac and Cleo. But there had been a shift, as though the invisible plates under the ground that I had learned about in science had begun to move apart. Mr. Mac was talking to Will as a boy—not as a baby or even a little boy, but a boy all fevered up about fishing and baseball. And Cleo—well, since

Will had come home, Cleo seemed to have forgotten all about me. I was special to no one, not even to this misfit of a horse.

"It could have been different." Again I hit the ground with my stick. "If you wanted to, you could have helped me find real treasure—under there, where you've been and come back from. We could have gone together to the Vickers field or Aunt Charlotte's house. Or the Swamp Fox pit—yes, I'd go there. You could have shown me where to dig, then we'd be famous by now." I shook my head. "Miss Cass calls you a miracle-horse—if only."

I pointed the stick towards Troy. "A hant-horse, Cleo says. A devil-horse." I stabbed the air near his scarred side. "Here's what I'm thinking. I wouldn't be surprised if you don't have something to do with the stuff going on out—out there." I waved the stick in a wide circle. "I don't know how, but I'll bet you do. Those three boys in Mississippi still haven't turned up. I'll bet they're dead, killed by the Klan. Are you a Klan horse? Is that what you are?"

From the loft came the shrill mewing of the newborn kittens. Hot tears rose in a hurry and nearly spilled out. "All I want to do is find the kittens. I deserve to find them. I haven't found anything else."

I turned back to the ladder. The sight of the webs made it hard for me to breathe. Some treasure hunter I was, when I couldn't even get myself up to the hayloft to find a litter of kittens. Some archaeologist I would become. I waved my stick in crazed, furious circles.

The webs that wound around the end of the stick were yellowed like old women's hair—like Miss Cass's. I pictured the way some spiders made themselves into little brown balls. Then, when a fly or moth got caught, out stretched their terrible legs. They moved fast. They could scale the stick to my hand in no time flat.

Something *was* crawling on my neck. I jumped back from the ladder and hurled the stick to the ground. In a panic, I slapped at myself. "Help!" I screamed.

"Help! Help!" It was Will, mimicking me in a high-pitched voice. He'd tickled the back of my neck with his pretend fishing pole—twine tied to the end of a tobacco stick. "You look like you're having a fit."

"Go away. I got here first." I gripped the splintery side rails to block his way.

For some reason Will wasn't scared of spiders.

"You're not up *there* first. I heard the kittens too, you know."

I was sweating more and more. "I'll clear the webs, then you can come up after me."

I reached for my stick, but Troy snorted and stomped. I hesitated; Will grabbed it.

"You're too scared. I'll clear the way, then you can come up after me."

"Give me the stick. It's mine."

I felt trapped. I saw in my head furry legs unfolding, fangs dripping poison. My sweaty arms, legs, and neck felt coated with sticky webs. Things were crawling up my overalls, inside my shirt, into my hair.

"Shhh! I hear 'em! Move outta the way." Will pointed the web-wound stick at me. I jumped back. He scrambled up, swiping at the webs as casually as Mr. Mac did.

"No! Wait!" I grabbed the stick with the twine—he'd let it fall—and jabbed at his feet.

He'd find the kittens first. He'd get to name them; that was our rule.

I hated him. I hated my brother as much as I hated Troy. He'd brought home enough fish for supper last night; Cleo and my parents and especially Mr. Mac had gone on and on. A natural fisherman, our grandfather claimed.

I forced myself to climb. I got halfway, but there was silence at the top. Maybe the kittens weren't there after all. Then Will let out a shrill scream. "Oh my gosh, Etta. Run. Run for your life! It's not kittens, it's spiders! They're huge and hairy, and they're screaming they're so hungry. They're going to get me!"

I was back down the ladder before I knew what I was doing. Then I looked up. I knew what I would see. My face burned.

"Ha ha ho ho hee hee," Will taunted. With his neck craning over the opening to the loft, he looked like a gargoyle. His red hair stood up in springs all over his head, and his ears stuck out bigger than ever. "Scaredy cat," he sang. "You're nothing but a slow-poke scaredy-cat…girl!"

Girl.

My mother had told me—when I finally asked about Will's operation—that he'd be able to breathe better and he wouldn't have so many ear infections. His appearance? One last surgery would correct that, she explained, in a few years. A few years! She seemed to think this meant nothing.

Girl.

"Fat lips! Goblin face!" I shrieked. The words were out before I could stop them.

There was a clang behind me. Troy was kicking at his bucket. And rolling his eye at me.

When I looked back up, Will had vanished.

At first, when I reached the loft, I couldn't find him. Then I saw his skinny back curled in the far right corner. He sat deep in the hay. His head was lowered.

"I'm sorry," I said. "I didn't mean that. What I said. I'm sorry."

Will was cradling three tiny kittens against his chest. He smelled like boy sweat and sour milk. He didn't look up.

"This is Tiger," he whispered, rubbing his dirty index finger on its tiny orange head. "This is Lily. And this is Peter Pan." Lily was gray and white. Peter Pan was orange, but paler—more golden—than Tiger. He laid them gently into their nest. Then he looked up at me, looked me in the eye. "It's your turn."

Without another word, he got up and walked off. I heard him climbing down the ladder.

The kittens were perfect. They felt soft as our mother's cashmere sweater. Their eyes were shut tight.

I couldn't unsay what I'd said. "Will," I whispered.

The kittens made a hot furry pile in my lap. My tears fell right onto them, and the feel of their tiny helpless bodies filled me with shame that had no bottom but just kept sinking. I put them back one by one into their warm bowl in the hay. Jasmine would wonder, when she licked them, why they were so salty.

I climbed over the hay to the opposite end, unlatched the loft door and swung it open. From here Mr. Mac pitched hay into the bed of his truck parked directly below. But the truck wasn't there. Only the ground, packed hard by tires. Will and I were never allowed to stand on the edge as I was doing. The ground looked far away.

"We're drunk!" Will and I had shouted with laughter, looking back to our parents following at a distance on the Mile High Swinging Bridge up on Grandfather Mountain. But I was secretly terrified. A large loud family in front of us kept lurching from one side to the other, pushing against the railings, making the bridge sway and my stomach do flips. I'd gripped the handrail tight and stepped on each board, hoping and praying it held. I forgot to breathe, then I forgot how to move. Beneath—a mile of air before the deep valley, the tops of trees, huge rocks. It looked like a mile, even though my father, when he loosened my fingers from the handrail, said it really wasn't.

My temperament was more wicked even than Cleo knew. I was no better than the trashy children who made Will's life a misery. I inched my feet forward until my toes stuck out past the edge of the loft. I didn't deserve to live. On the ground, the hard earth below me—merely a scattering of hay, nothing to break the fall. It would be like hitting rock. I swayed forward, staggered back. Troy was jogging lopsidedly—but, yes, jogging—across the pasture towards the trees that hid Cleo's house. Swishing his tail, he appeared pleased, as though he'd accomplished exactly what he'd set out to do. He looked almost spry, happy to be rid of me.

∾

I sneaked in through the back door. Will was at the kitchen table, sobbing. His head was in his arms. Mama had her hand on the back of his neck. There were tears even in her eyes. I just stood and waited. Whatever was coming to me I deserved. I deserved—I welcomed!—all of it and more.

But our mother left Will to give me a soft hug. She ran her hand over my sweat-matted hair. "It's Cleo," she said.

"Cleo fell down," Will sobbed.

"Yes," my mother said, "and Papa has driven her to the hospital."

"Did she break something? Her arm? Her leg? How did she fall?"

"She was washing dishes and dropped to the floor. I'm afraid she's had a stroke. A heart attack maybe."

"Will she be okay?"

My other grandfather, my mother's father, had died from a stroke when I was four. I couldn't remember him. I knew his face, with the high Cherokee cheekbones I'd inherited, only from the faded Olan Mills photograph on my mother's dresser.

14: Through a Keyhole Backwards

August 5, 1964

All that morning, the morning of Cleo's funeral, I tried to keep the ground from pitching out from under my feet. "I know about this," I told myself. "I know exactly what's going to happen."

It was not my first funeral. In December I'd gone to Great-Great-Aunt Sadie's in the big Victorian house that was the funeral home in the middle of the wide green lawn next to my school. I'd gone with my parents and Mr. Mac. Will, my mother said, was still too young. A stiff man in a stiff black suit showed us into a room that was dim and cold. Gold wallpaper covered the walls, and heavy crimson curtains fell nearly from ceiling to floor. The crowd was sparse. Great-Great-Aunt Sadie had been ninety-nine. Not many of her friends were left on the green side of the grass, according to Mr. Mac.

I had felt no sadness; I'd met the old woman only once. I couldn't stop looking around—at the crystal chandelier, the high windows whose velvet drapes shut out all daylight, the backs of heads, all white or silver or bald. Nobody there was anywhere near as young as even my parents. The preacher droned and droned, and nobody even sniffled. The casket, dark and shiny as the polished wood in the bank, was shut. A saddle of carnations rested on top of it.

"I know what to expect," I kept saying inside my head. But in truth, nothing since my father had come home from taking Cleo to the hospital—and told us Cleo had died—had been familiar.

This morning was worse than all the other days since Cleo's death. The fog that at first shielded me had burned off. Now, every single thing seemed so clear I could see inside it, all the way to its soul. The maple rocker in the den, the one Cleo dragged into my room those nights when my parents were out— the chair looked so sad that I couldn't bear to glance at it, though my eye went there on its own, like my tongue to the tender hole in my gum where a baby tooth had been. The kitchen seemed like a kitchen in another house. It smelled empty. Without Cleo's humming, it was a dead space. The clown-faced cookie jar with Cleo's stale teacakes inside grinned a dead grin. But the geraniums on the front porch that Cleo had watered every day were the opposite of dead. They were too red, too healthy, too full of themselves. I wanted to tear the petals off and grind them with my feet as Miss Pity did with the hornworms.

Even things that had nothing to do with Cleo seemed wrong. The sound of the lawn mower in the front yard grated on my nerves. "Stop!" I wanted to race outside and scream at my father. How could he be mowing the grass when Cleo's funeral was—again I glanced at the clock over the mantle—in only two hours?

I did something I couldn't remember ever doing: I took a bath in the morning. First I got out all the clothes I was going to wear to the funeral and laid them on my bed. Then I took the time to fill up the tub. I lay on my back and sank down until only my nose was above the water. Then I slid under. I held my breath until I had to give up. I tried again. My chest hurt, the hurt was sharp. Again I tried. Again.

I wanted to know what it was like to be where Cleo was, in a place of no breathing, no moving, no feeling. The three civil rights workers had finally turned up dead in Mississippi, murdered, the TV said, by the Klan. They felt nothing any longer. Cleo felt nothing. How was not feeling even possible?

The searchers had found the men's bodies buried deep in the earth someplace out in the country. And I couldn't get rid of the notion that somehow *I* had let them die, those workers. Worse, I had let Cleo die. No matter that I'd been told about her bad heart. I had never made up with Cleo. If I had, maybe she would still be alive.

This was agony far worse than I'd felt after Trudy's accident—Trudy, who kept on living. This was my insides twisted and wringing themselves out, as though they were rags in Cleo's hands. I took my washcloth and began scrubbing. I started at my toes and went up. When I got to my face I scrubbed until my skin burned. Still I didn't stop.

❧

Will and I had stayed up late the night after Cleo had fallen. We'd waited and waited for Papa to return from the hospital. But when ten o'clock came and he still wasn't home, our mother made us go to our rooms. Near midnight, his headlights hit my wall. Wide awake, I raced out to meet him.

"Cleo is gone," he said. "They couldn't bring her back."

I watched my mother cry, her slender shoulders shaking. But I couldn't cry. I was trying too hard to breathe.

I went back to bed and lay still. My chest ached with the effort of breathing. Was I awake or was I dreaming? The whole day, maybe it had been nothing but a terrible nightmare, from my hatefulness to Will in the barn to Cleo's dying. None of it had happened for real. I would wake up in the morning, and Cleo would be there like always.

But the next day, I was all tangled up in my head. I'd slept until noon—was I sick? Dull pain throbbed over my eyes. My eyelashes had crusted together, as though I'd wept in my sleep.

❧

Two days later, in deliberate slow motion, I pulled on my Sunday dress, a blue check with crinoline underneath. I would wait for my father to tie my wide blue sash. He was better at it, more patient, than my mother. He and Cleo took the time to make it perfect. Now only he would do that. I slipped on new ankle socks and buckled my white patent leather shoes. Instead of braiding my hair, I pulled on a blue hair band and let it fall in frizzy waves down my back. I looked in the mirror. I'd scrubbed my face raw-red. Cleo had ironed this dress; she was the last person who had touched it. I ran my hands down the front of it, smoothing the skirt, trying to feel it with Cleo's hands. I fastened my one necklace around my neck, the scarred gold cross from when I was baptized, the one I chewed on when I was bored in church, and I felt my insides twist all over again.

Will's room reeked of glue. On the floor, surrounded by green plastic soldiers, my brother was working on a model army jeep.

"Shouldn't you be getting ready for the funeral?"

"Why? It's only 9:30."

I sat on his bed. "When we go, you just stay right by me."

"Why?" He looked up at me.

"I've been to a funeral before, so I know what to do…And I've been to Cleo's church. You haven't. You might be scared." I pictured the swaying bodies with their loud *Praise God*s, the choir clapping while they sang. "It's different—at Cleo's church."

"What's the matter with your face?" Will squinted, wrinkling his nose. He went back to working on his model and sighed. "Poor Cleo. I wish she didn't leave us."

"She had a heart attack."

"I know," he said. "Mama told me, same as you."

I went back to my room and shut the door. I tried to read, but my mind couldn't hold a sentence. Near the toe of my Christmas stocking, long months back, had been a sky-blue leather diary with a key. I opened it now. All the pages were blank. At the top of the first page, I wrote, "Today is Cleo's funeral." I shut the little book and locked it.

At last it was time to go. I stepped outside; the sun hurt my eyes and stung my raw face. The smell of cut grass even burned my nostrils. Everything looked fake, as though an angry child had colored the sky blue, the geraniums red, the trees and the grass green—colored them hard with fat crayons.

I wanted to run. No, I wanted to be on Troy's back, of all things, Troy somehow running. Even if he wasn't transformed into a Palomino, even if he was just his old disfigured self—what I wouldn't give to be able to jump on his back and escape. Deep into the woods he'd take me, sure of his direction.

The day before, I had gone through the motions of giving Troy his feed and water. Numbness made a sort of cocoon around me; I felt no emotion towards him. After all, I'd given up on him for good that awful day of the webs and Will, the kittens mewing above us in the hayloft—the day Cleo died. But somehow, I couldn't pull myself away. I couldn't make myself turn around and leave. While the horse ate, his nose in his bucket, I inched closer and closer to his left side. I reached towards the red and purple flesh. My stomach tightened as I smelled in my memory the burning skin and hair. My hand trembled; I'd never before deliberately tried to touch the scar. It had not been oozy for some time, but it still attracted flies. And now it was drawing me, as though...what had I missed? If I put my hand where the lightning had been, then would I *see*?

"Lightning should have killed you, but it didn't—even as old as you were." I was talking, rambling, more to myself than to the horse. "But a heart attack took Cleo away."

I could picture lightning, but not a heart attack. I'd been too proud to ask what it meant. I imagined one side of a heart wrestling its twin and squeezing out the life.

My fingers kept stretching towards Troy's side. Almost—I was almost touching the hideous, hairless scar. "Lightning-struck," I whispered, hearing Cleo's voice.

Troy threw his head up, and I stepped back. We stared at each other. The old horse's eyelashes, I noticed for the first time, had gone frosty white. The pupil of his blind eye had managed to creep nearly all the way back into his head.

Now, steeling myself for Cleo's funeral, I balled my hands into fists and slid after Will into the back seat of the station wagon. We drove next door to pick up Mr. Mac. Like everything else, he too seemed changed. I rarely saw him dressed up in his pale gray coat and tie. My baptism, Great-Great-Aunt Sadie's funeral, Will's and my piano recitals—that was about it. He fingered his starched collar as he crouched in on the other side of Will. He looked at me over the brown top rim of his glasses and asked if I'd gotten sunburnt.

My eyes refused to adjust to the brilliant morning. As we turned off the highway, the Scurlocks' trailer reflected the sun. The too-bright light flashed in and out of the shadows of the pines. The fields shimmered. I couldn't bear to glance towards the graveyard when we neared the church.

As we walked towards the front door, groups of people standing outside stopped talking to stare at us. No one wore the bright yellows or reds I remembered from the previous summer. Nearly everyone was in white or black. The broad brim of Miss Pity's hat was covered with black feathers—a crow's? I fingered my blue checked skirt with one hand and reached for Will's hand with the other. He pulled away to walk between Mama and Papa.

Entering the church was like going into a tobacco barn. It was dark at first, and the heat made an oven of my lungs. Perspiration stung my scrubbed-sore face. The thick dusty-sweet smell of carnations made it hard to breathe.

The preacher, the big man I remembered, rushed up to greet us. He was wearing a white robe. "Reverend Benjamin Hughes," he introduced himself, shaking first Mr. Mac's hand, then my father's. So much sweat was running down his round, clean-shaven face, it looked slick as a seal's. "Our Sister Cleo is strolling up to the Heavenly path. Praise God!"

He escorted us into the sanctuary and directly to the front, to the pew behind Cleo's family's, which was marked by a white bow.

To the right of the pulpit and elevated so that it was just above my line of vision lay the polished casket surrounded by flowers. Again the urge to flee came over me. "Is Cleo *in* there?" Will whispered. He was sitting between our parents, while I was between my mother and Mr. Mac. The top half of the lid was open, but the casket was up too high for us to see inside.

Behind us the church began to fill quickly. It became so full that some of the men stood in the aisles and some of the women sat in folding chairs. In front of our family sat Starry, with her husband, Esau, and Juney. When Jesse walked down to speak to Starry, she whispered and pulled his sleeve until he sat beside her. Not one other person, however, would sit on the empty space left over on our family's pew. It felt like punishment to me, punishment for being white. Then, at the last minute, Miss Cass came rushing in and sat beside Mr. Mac. Out of breath, she leaned forward to nod hello to the rest of us. Her loose brown dress, cinched with a fringed leather belt, went all the way to the floor. For once, she wore her bear claw necklace outside of her clothes.

The funeral home had provided fans. I flipped mine back and forth. One side featured snow-capped mountains and a lake that reflected them. The other pictured the colored funeral director with his wife and three daughters all dressed up in matching white frilly dresses. The little girls' hair hung in ringlets. Little white purses dangled from their wrists. They wore white gloves. And white patent leather shoes.

A row of white-robed women filed in and began to sway and hum behind the pink carnation crosses. Evelyn was one of them. Her face looked wet. I shut my eyes tightly and tried to breathe. Wrong, wrong, wrong. I shouldn't be here. No one should be here. Cleo shouldn't be in that box. Not Cleo, who had loved me since I was a baby, and who had kept loving me even when I didn't deserve love, even when I refused it. No, my Cleo should be sitting on our screened porch humming and singing and shelling butterbeans. "If you come back," I bargained inside my head, "I'll help you every day. I'll have the best temperament in the world." I felt my hands lifting Cleo's feet onto a stool. I used to help Cleo that way, while she worked on the porch with a bowl in her lap. I saw the beige stockings tied in knots beneath Cleo's knees. I saw the coin pierced by wire around her right ankle.

This *was* a bad dream—again I tried to persuade myself— one of those nightmares that seemed realer than real life and didn't want to end. And if it wasn't a dream, I would make it one. I shut my eyes as tightly as I could. When I woke up, I told myself, I would not be here but at home with Cleo. One, two, three, I counted slowly. I pressed the pinpoints of crinoline into my thighs. But when I opened my eyes, there I still was, in the hot dim church.

Reverend Hughes gave a heavy man's skip and half-danced to the pulpit. His wide face glistened.

I made myself look to the left, towards him, and not straight ahead at the casket. He reached his arms out wide. "Brothers and sisters," he began, "we have come to praise God and sanctify the life of our beloved sister, Cleo Louise Calhoun Boston." *Louise*? I hadn't known that Cleo had a middle name.

"This is a joyful time, brothers and sisters, because Sister Cleo is no longer amid this world of misery and sin, of sickness and woe, of sorrow and sadness. Ha! Cleo is free, my brothers. Cleo is dancing, my sisters. She's dancing her way to the streets of Heaven. She'll be singing with the angels. And sleeping in the arms of the Lord."

All the people said "Hallelujah," and the choir started to sing. I kept my eyes on Evelyn. Everyone stood and clapped and swayed. I had loved this part when I came with Cleo. I'd swayed with such energy that Cleo gave me a warning look. But this time I couldn't move. Will was watching Juney and swaying along with her. He even sang "Hallelujah" in his high little voice. But all the rest of my family stood still.

"We mourn our own selfish loss, brothers and sisters." Reverend Hughes said this in a low voice, almost a whisper.

Everyone sat. "Yes, Jesus."

"But who among us," the preacher's voice rose, "can know the ways of the Lord?" I looked down at my hands gripped tightly together. I didn't care what Reverend Hughes said. God had made a mistake in giving Cleo her heart attack.

The preacher's voice wove in and out of my consciousness. My lips were moving. "I'm sorry, Cleo. I need to tell you I'm sorry...sorry."

What was he saying, the Reverend? Someone had been killed. Cleo's father? Reverend Hughes had been going on about the burdens Cleo carried.

"Joe Calhoun was murdered and that's the truth—by an escaped convict right on his doorstep, when Cleo was twelve years old. And her mama was taken to Heaven only two months later bringing a little sister into this world. Why, Cleo was the one named her Starry—little sister born on a starry night." He nodded towards Starry, who put her hands to her face.

He went on to describe how the girls' aunt (Aunt Charlotte—at least I knew this much) had taken them in and given them a home. When their aunt got on in years, he continued, Cleo nursed her. And until the old woman went to live with her granddaughter up North, he said, Cleo refused to get married.

"The heaviest of her heavy burdens"—he shook his head, his voice lowered to a whisper—"was when Sister Cleo's own baby boy passed on to the angels. Little Eugene Boston, not even one year old."

"Lord have mercy!" Was that Starry? She hung her head, shaking it from side to side. Esau fanned her with those snow-capped mountains and lake.

Behind me a woman shrieked. The shriek moved into my throat. I fought to stifle it. Cleo had had not only a husband but a baby of her own? And never *told* me? And Cleo's parents, her own papa and mama, had died when she was about my age. I never knew Cleo at all.

What else? I thought bitterly. Again I tried to focus on the Reverend's voice. What else was he going to say about Cleo, the Cleo I never really knew? All my life, Cleo had lived in a separate world where I had no place. I pictured a convict with a gun, a crazy red-eyed man, shooting Cleo's father, then running off into the night. I pictured blood spilling from the hole where her father's face had been, pooling on the porch. And there, the girl who was Cleo, stunned by the sight, unable to move; there, the pregnant mother on her knees. I then saw another Cleo, grown up but young like Evelyn, holding her dead baby—the one in the picture who was sleeping with a flower—to her chest, humming as though that would bring him back to life. I envisioned a tiny casket, a miniature of the one in front of me. Cleo had kept hidden from me everything important that had happened to her.

My skin prickled. Reverend Hughes was talking directly to me. Sister Cleo, he was saying, did not lay up for herself treasures on earth, where moth and rust corrupt and thieves steal.

"She laid up for herself a treasure in Heaven. For there, my brothers and sisters, is where her heart was. I see her going, I do. Climbing to meet her poor little baby, and her daddy and mama. And she is *full* of light! Ha! Full of the light of the Lord."

Reverend Hughes started soft then grew louder and louder. His face twisted as if shouting was painful. Then he closed his eyes and sang, and when the choir also began to sing, his voice was like a river's deepening current. The voices of the congregation surrounded me, swelled, and became a part of the flow and the pressing heat, the dense mix of carnations and perfume. Starry rocked back and forth. Jesse sat straight-backed and rigid. Everyone was working together—preacher, choir, congregation—to send Cleo to Heaven. To send her there good and proper, to lock the door so that she could never set foot on this earth again.

What if Cleo wasn't ready, despite what the Lord wanted, even if she had laid up her treasure in Heaven? Didn't Aunt Charlotte linger, earthbound even now? And Troy—Cleo herself had insisted that he'd died and come back.

Suddenly my mother was pulling me to my feet. Reverend Hughes, his face dripping, was gesturing towards the steps leading up to the platform and the casket. Cleo, he announced, had already said good-bye to her earthly body. Now it was time for her friends and family to do the same. Except for the humming of the choir, the church went quiet.

"Take your time, now," whispered the Reverend. "You folks take all the time you want."

"Precious Lord, take my hand," Evelyn began singing in her clear high voice. "Lead me on, help me stand…"

Starry stood at the casket for a long time. She put her fingers to her lips, then placed them down onto what must have been Cleo's cheek. Esau appeared to be helping her walk. Juney took one little peek and blinked hard. Jesse closed his eyes and seemed to pray. Then I was standing where they had stood.

Cleo was all wrong. She looked fake, even more fake than the dressed-up Cleo in her bride picture. Her head was uncovered. Someone had curled her hair into tight ringlets, glossy with oil, and arranged little bangs on her forehead. There was a strong, sweet dime-store perfume smell. Someone had played with her as if she were a doll. Those little girls on the funeral fan—had they done this to Cleo? Lying there, dressed in her shiny purple church dress against puffed ivory satin, a grayish tint to her plastic-smooth skin, she might have been a doll—a new one still in its box: a box that hid her legs. Anger rose inside me. I couldn't see if Cleo was wearing her stockings. Or the coin around her ankle.

I stood still and proper, my fingers laced at my waist. But I could see myself—clear as anything—reaching down, grasping Cleo's shoulders, and shaking her, jarring the poisoned apple from her mouth, pulling her out of her sick sleep.

"Take my hand, Precious Lord, lead me home…"

I wanted more than anything to take Cleo's hand and snatch her from her box. Together we would jump onto Troy's back, a Pegasus Troy, whose wings would fly us out of this stifling church and into the sunshine and home, where Cleo belonged.

My parents decided to forgo the burial. The funeral—well, that had been enough for Will and me. But I had glimpsed, on my way to the car, the open grave in the cemetery behind the church. Miss Cass, her long braid down her back, walked towards it along with the rest of the congregation.

"Did you all know?" I asked, my throat dry. "Did you know those things about Cleo? Those awful things."

Mama shook her head. "I knew she'd been married." She and Papa had lit cigarettes as soon as he started the car.

"I knew she'd taken care of Aunt Charlotte," my father added.

Instead of chewing on it, Mr. Mac actually lit his cigar and puffed, something he hardly ever did. My mother stiffened, but she held her tongue. "I knew," he said. "I knew all that. But Cleo kept it private. She wouldn't have wanted it let out like that, at her funeral. Reverend Hughes likes the sound of his own voice, that's for daggum sure."

Mr. Mac, coughing, stubbed out his cigar in the little ashtray in the car door. No one said another word until we pulled up under the carport.

"Well," Mama said, "I feel like I've been pulled through a keyhole backwards."

"Me too," I whispered, grateful for the words.

"Me three," Will piped up.

Hurrying to my room, I wrote in my diary: "The funeral is over. I've been pulled through a keyhole backwards."

There was nothing else to write. I opened *Ancient Wonders of the World* to the place where I'd stuck my comic book version of *The Iliad*—to the picture of a wooden Trojan horse with soldiers stacked in its belly, their spears sticking out in all directions. Staring at the page, trying to read, I felt in my own insides the sharp points of those hundred spears.

For the rest of the day and when I went to bed that night, I kept repeating "pulled through a keyhole backwards." Every time I said it was like hammering a board to a wall, and the wall was like a giant scab that covered, bit by bit, the raw wound inside me.

15: Miracle-Horse

August 6, 1964

The farm bell rang in my dream. I was outside Cleo's house, hoeing. I tore not at weeds but at the good plants, uprooting squash and collards and even the flowering bushes beside Cleo's porch. The bell was calling me indoors. "Dinner's ready," Cleo shouted. "Getting cold!"

Then sirens screamed my eyes wide open. Red lights hit my wall.

"I'm coming," I said in a hoarse voice, not knowing whether I was talking to Cleo or to myself. It was still dark outside, but lights were on in the hallway.

"Dammit! Dammit to hell." My father almost never cussed. A barn was on fire—had to be. The back door slammed.

I ran past my mother, who was making coffee in the kitchen. I was still in pajamas, but I didn't care.

Papa was already in his car, with the engine running.

"Please." I was panting. "I want to see."

"Get in." He backed out of the carport.

"Which one?"

"Barn just this side of the swamp." The barn where I had worked.

He drove his old Bel Air as though it was a truck, jarring my teeth as he raced over bumps and holes down the dirt road towards Boggy Swamp. He frowned, letting the ashes fall off his cigarette into his lap and onto the floorboard. I knew better than to ask any more questions. Heat lightning was putting on such a show, it was hard to distinguish one from the other—the sky's fire from the barn's. The scene was surreal, as dreamlike as my memory of Cleo's funeral the day before.

Papa jerked to a stop beside one of the two fire trucks. "You stay here by the car. I mean what I say."

The barn had become a huge orange bonfire that lit up the woods nearby, the patch of woods that led to the swamp. It gave off blasts of heat so harsh that I couldn't have gone near the fire even if I'd wanted to. It roared and groaned and cracked. Several of the firemen were working hoses that stretched from the trucks, but it was too late. It was always too late when a tobacco barn caught fire. Other firemen, Mr. Mac, and my father, walked in a wide circle around it, gesturing with their hands in a way that said there was no use. Mr. Mac kept taking off his hat and wiping his forehead. Papa stomped at the ground.

"The funeral of Hector," I whispered to myself...Hector, the son of Troy's King Priam, whom the Greek warrior Achilles had killed in battle. The words were fresh in my mind. Only hours ago I'd sat in bed with my archaeology book reading yet again about Schliemann and the Homeric legend of Troy. Between that and my Classics Illustrated version of *The Iliad*, I knew the brutal story. Achilles tied Hector's dead body to his chariot and dragged him around and around in the dirt. In the night, poor old Priam went alone to Achilles' tent. On his knees and offering a princely ransom, he begged Achilles to take pity and release to him his son's body.

The scene in front of me was like the pyre pictured in my book, with its licking flames. But I envisioned at the core of the fire not Hector but Cleo—Cleo's body turning to soot, gusting heavenward in smoke and sparks, flying away from me. No one, it suddenly seemed to me, had any real power over anything. The firemen couldn't rescue the barn. Surgeons couldn't really fix Will. The doctors couldn't save Cleo. And nothing I could do would keep Cleo's spirit from escaping.

I blinked—was the smoke affecting my vision? The fire, instead of dying down, was growing. The firemen, I realized, had turned their hoses away from the barn and towards the nearby woods. Flames leapt from tree to tree, filling them with light. One, then another, another, another…The fire hoses seemed to be fanning the fire rather than damping it down. I willed my burning eyes to stay open. What I now saw couldn't be real, for there was Troy in the middle of the flames, spears of lightning flying from his side as if he were Zeus in disguise, Zeus in the form of a horse. Though my eyes were stinging from the heat, I strained to keep them open, fixed on the scene. It couldn't be real. I staggered against the car; I was falling asleep on my feet. I'd rest for just a minute, I told myself, curling up on the front seat.

"Etta, Etta. Time to go home." Papa was shaking me awake.

I sat straight up. The entire sky seemed to be aflame. Streaks of pink and orange stretched overhead. *When rosy-fingered dawn appeared, the people assembled around the pyre of Hector, tamer of horses.* I'd memorized the caption beneath the illustration of the hero's funeral.

I stepped out of the car. The sun was rising bleary-red and angry-looking. The fire trucks were leaving, and all that remained of the barn were scattered bricks and the collapsed and crumpled tin roof.

The fire that leapt into the woods had not veered into the cropped tobacco field or reached Aunt Charlotte's house; I could see the roof taking shape through the smoke. Perhaps the firemen had saved something.

෴

As soon as my father, grandfather, and I had splashed the smoke and grime off our faces and eaten breakfast—and I had changed out of my pajamas—we returned to the site. Will was having trouble with his stitches. Mama, nervous that the inflammation meant infection, made him stay home. He was furious, especially since he'd slept through the night and missed the excitement.

The Swamp Fox woods, mostly pine and scrub wood, had burned like tinder because of the drought. Clear to the edge of the swamp a smoldering wasteland spread—charred limbs and fallen trunks. Everything else was ash, soggy as from a rainstorm.

I wandered about, wading through muck, kicking the blackened chunks. There was no telling anymore—no telling where the Swamp Fox pit was. It had been tricky to find before the fire, not much to see. But now...I tried to orient myself by sighting the barn's fallen roof and the cypress treetops of the swamp.

Mr. Mac and Papa were discussing options. "I can get some seedlings over at Conway," Mr. Mac said. He coughed. It sounded bad, as though he was choking. My father slapped his back.

"Smoke got me," Mr. Mac said, staggering. He took the cigar out of his mouth and put it into his pocket. His hand was shaking as it did when he had the war-fits. He mopped his face with his handkerchief.

My father pushed his hat to the back of his head. "Makes more sense to me," he said, nodding at the cropped tobacco, "to go ahead and expand the field."

I expected Mr. Mac to object. He and my father rarely agreed about changes to the farm.

But Mr. Mac nodded. "Have to call in a bulldozer."

"No!" I said. "The Swamp Fox pit. Remember? You can't bulldoze here. It's historical!"

He was sorry, Papa said, but they couldn't just leave it like this.

"Mr. Mac?" I pleaded. He put up his hand and turned, shaking his head as he coughed.

I wasn't sure whether my eyes burned from the heat of the fire or from the disappointment growing inside me. I walked away—if the tears had to come, no one would see them. I kicked at the soggy rubble, at the mounds of dirt. The day was heating up; steam was rising. Along with it rose the biting smell of wet burned wood.

I sensed Troy's presence even before I looked up and saw him. Beyond the leafless stalks of tobacco, across the hayfield, he stood between Aunt Charlotte's house and the stand of bamboo. When I had seen him last night, a fiery figure in middle of the burning woods, I told myself it was a dream. Now I believed it was true. He'd found a way to set the fire, Troy had. He escaped before the flames ate him alive. His scar—the way it caught the morning sun through the steam—his scar appeared to be giving off smoke. "Devil-horse," Cleo's voice repeated in my head. I began to walk towards him, in my anger kicking harder at the ground.

It seemed that Troy, though he hadn't exactly led me there, showed me where to kick, as if—as I later imagined—the old horse was like a god after all, presiding over my actions.

My toe caught what looked like a sooty turtle's shell half-buried in the dirt. Disoriented because of the drought and lured by the irrigation, turtles kept crawling out of the swamp. Once they died, the buzzards cleaned them good.

I couldn't say what made me take a second look, what made me kneel and loosen the object from the ground. But I did. And what I dislodged was a skull. Part of one at any rate, and it looked human.

"Where did you find this?" Papa was out of breath. He'd run, thinking from my hollering that I was hurt.

I pointed to my feet.

"Put it back," he said. "Right where you found it. Good Lord. Now we're going to have to have a survey. We can't touch the land before that's done." He searched his pockets, then asked Mr. Mac, who'd just reached the spot, if he had anything they could use to mark the skull's location. Wheezing, he shook his head. His neck had flushed bright red; the corners of his mouth twitched. I pulled off my belt, the beaded one with the red thunderbird and turquoise arrows I'd gotten at Cherokee. I curled it around the skull like a bright snake.

"I hope it's a redcoat," I said, feeling a little queasy.

"I'll have to call the experts at the university," my father said.

The skull had weighed almost nothing. It had felt in my hand like a fine, if dirty, antique—a china bowl.

16: Burying Ground

Next morning an archaeologist, the expert from the university, was drinking coffee in our kitchen. A living archaeologist! Who even picked my chair to sit in! I sat in Will's. While my father described the property and explained the fire, I memorized everything about our guest.

Dr. Raintree was young and blonde, with a pattern of freckles that resembled mine scattered across his nose. He laid upon the table a wide-brimmed straw hat with a red bandana tied around the crown. Beside it he placed old-fashioned-looking wire-rimmed sunglasses with round lenses. He wore baggy tan khakis and a pale blue shirt whose pockets were stuffed with pencils, pens, a little spiral notebook, a tape measure, several small brushes, and other things I couldn't make out. His hands were callused and freckled, just like a farmer's.

My father explained that he had to go to work in town, but Mr. Mac would take Dr. Raintree to where the skull lay. I would be going along, he added, if that was all right. His daughter was an aspiring archaeologist.

My face burned. But Dr. Raintree raised his eyebrows and nodded approvingly in my direction.

When Mr. Mac's truck pulled up, Papa drew me aside. "Stay out of his way, Etta. You understand?"

Tongue-tied, I led Dr. Raintree to the door. He would be following Mr. Mac in his own truck.

"Will not coming with us?" my grandfather asked.

"He's still got a fever. Mama's taking him to the doctor."

I could spot my belt all the way from the road. I ran ahead of the men and then turned and waved. When Dr. Raintree reached me, he grinned at the belt, then pointed to his hat. "You and I think alike. I never go anywhere without something bright on me. You can spot a red bandana a half-mile away."

He rolled up his shirtsleeves to his elbows and knelt. With a small brush, he flicked off the sand and soot. Then he measured the skull, this way and that. He made quick jabbing notes in the little spiral notebook. With the skull on the ground, he took several photographs with the camera that swung from a cord around his neck. He stood and turned around in a slow circle, as though absorbing everything around him.

"It—it is human, isn't it?"

"Oh. Yes. Indeed."

"Can you tell…if it's from a redcoat?" I widened my eyes towards my grandfather. Mr. Mac had taken his time joining us.

Dr. Raintree looked puzzled.

"Before the woods burned," Mr. Mac explained, "you could make out a depression. My pap always told me it was where Francis Marion had dug a holding pit for his prisoners."

"That so?" Dr. Raintree looked back at me. "I just need to do a little more work and I might have an answer for you."

Mr. Mac had to leave to check some barns. Was I coming along to help him?

I shook my head. "Papa said I could stay and watch Dr. Raintree if I kept out of the way."

"That's fine," said Dr. Raintree. "She can be my assistant."

Mr. Mac walked off. I could hear him coughing.

The one day of sun and heat had completely dried the ground and what remained of the trees. Everything had a dusty, bitter smell, like charcoal. Today would be another hot one. We were already sweating, and there was no longer one bit of shade.

Dr. Raintree crawled on his hands and knees, pausing every so often to scrutinize the blackened debris. Then he stopped. He'd found a broken piece of china. It looked like the one Stephanie had found. He recorded something in his notebook, laid the fragment back down, then took a picture of it. He continued crawling. He lifted a small sooty medicine bottle and scratched at it with his fingernail, wrote in his notebook, took a picture. These ordinary things seemed important.

Finally, he stood. The legs of his tan pants were smeared black. "Those fire hoses did us a favor. They acted like a hard rain, turning things to the surface."

He could use my help, he said, walking towards his truck. He pulled a shovel from the back of his pickup and handed it to me. Then he grabbed two other tools, a long metal probe and another metal stick with a cylindrical base. This he called an "auger." He hauled out a heavy leather bag with a long strap and hung it from his shoulder, then gathered from his front seat a larger writing pad, a longer tape measure, and a canteen, which he offered to me. An archaeologist's water: more delicious than any Coca-Cola.

Dr. Raintree seemed oblivious to the heat and to the soot that gradually coated his clothes. For the next hour he walked and measured, measured and walked, crisscrossing the area where I had found the skull. I held one end of the tape while he stretched it tight. He wrote often in the large notebook. Repeatedly he took the probe, plunged it into the ground, then jotted something down with his pencil. He seemed to be making a picture, or map, of small rectangles. He used the auger to harvest cylinders of dirt, which he then bagged and catalogued. Because of the tangle of roots, he frequently had to stab several times at the ground. I carried the shovel, which he used only to scrape gently here and there at the topmost layer of earth.

Despite the sweat rolling down my face and arms, I shivered. The pit was clearly more extensive than anyone had imagined. Dr. Raintree found and recorded still more broken pieces from plates and cups, a tin spoon, a dull olive-shaped shell—a cowrie "all the way from the Indian Sea"—and two small spheres like the one I had found and hidden inside *Elsie Dinsmore*. These were marbles, he explained. Made from clay.

So I *had* found something valuable after all. I wondered if Troy—just as yesterday he'd drawn me to the skull—had made the relic rise into my hand that day in the Swamp Fox woods, when the shooting started and my friends and I hit the ground. I knew he hadn't been there. Not in the flesh. But still, hadn't I felt his eerie presence?

From his shoulder bag Dr. Raintree pulled big nails—railroad spikes. He hammered them into the dirt, making a sort of pattern.

"Is that where you plan to dig? Where those spikes are?"

"Probably not. I don't like to disturb the dead."

"But there could be other stuff, right? Stuff the prisoners used, like that spoon?"

"I'll tell you the truth, Etta. What we have right here is a graveyard. And from what I've seen so far, I think it's a slave burying ground."

"Aunt Charlotte said an old graveyard was out here." I blinked. "Cleo told me."

"Cleo?"

"She died." My knees weakened, and I sat down in the dirt. Dr. Raintree's presence had pushed Cleo's death to the corner of my mind. Now it spread, like a wasteland of char and ash, and filled my whole body with a dull ache.

"These things we've turned up—the broken crockery, bottles, shells—they were used as grave decorations back in slavery times. Did your family own slaves back in—say—1840? 1850?"

I shook my head. Still focused on Cleo, I was shocked by the question. "Our family never had slaves. Not the McDaniels. I'm sure we didn't."

When Mr. Mac returned, he seemed as surprised as I had been. "A burying ground after all. Well I'll be…" He coughed, staggered, collected himself.

Dr. Raintree showed Mr. Mac the railroad spikes. "Can you see? From here to here, a slight depression in the ground. Six feet in length. And over here…and over here. I've been able to locate three graves so far. I'm betting there are more."

"Far back as I remember it was grown up in trees. I reckon the markers, if there were any, rotted pretty quick."

"Francis Marion did roam this area, no doubt about it," said Dr. Raintree. "He may even have dug a holding cell here. And before him the Indians likely had a settlement. They preferred this sort of site, an elevation near water." He showed us a few shards of pottery and an arrowhead. "The Pee Dee were here—no question. Did you know that despite all the relics common to this area, we have no identified sites attributed to the Pee Dee Indians? No way to know if this was a camp or a burial site or a trash dump.

"But back to the graves, here. Unfortunately—or perhaps it's fortunate—the law won't let me excavate in what is clearly a cemetery. All I can do is take samples and document—and with your help preserve it. Now the artifacts exposed on the surface, I'll have to collect those and send them to the state museum."

Mr. Mac removed his hat and scratched at his rim of gray hair. The corners of his mouth turned down as he half-smiled. "All I know is my grandpap died in the war, and right after that the old house burned to the ground. All the family records with it."

"Surely your father remembered something?"

"Pap wasn't much for talking. He mentioned this tenant or that, born in slavery."

"Like Aunt Charlotte," I said.

"And that's all?" Mr. Raintree asked.

Mr. Mac frowned. "I never tried to puzzle it out—about my grandpap having a slave or two." I wondered if he knew more than he was telling.

"I'd guess he owned more than a few, to provide a burying ground like this. Your grandfather was one of the wealthier plantation owners around here—would be my guess."

"Nothing—nobody—left to prove it. Not so much as a picture," Mr. Mac said.

Too poor to own slaves—that's what Mr. Mac had always said we were. Dirt farmers scraping to get ahead. Then how to explain the graveyard? I wondered, as Dr. Raintree placed first the skull, then each shell and marble and fragment of glass or porcelain atop a bed of cotton in its own cardboard box, which he handed to me to place in his truck. Someone who had a plantation—*not* a McDaniel—had used this land to bury his slaves.

For the next three days, Dr. Raintree drove out to examine the burned property. He seemed to have a knack for knowing just where to place his shovel or fall to his knees. I followed his every move.

Troy still had his eye on me. Occasionally I'd look up from the ground where we were working and there he'd be in the same spot, between Aunt Charlotte's house and the stand of bamboo. He'd be leaning to one side, presiding from a distance over our efforts. If Dr. Raintree saw him, he never said so. But I was used to being the only one who seemed to notice the old horse....A miracle-horse he was at last. There was no doubt in my mind—he had guided me to the skull. He'd done what I'd hoped for such a long time—used that blind eye, or some third eye, those trips under the earth—to locate artifacts, treasure. Now here I was, an assistant archaeologist. Miraculous.

"See," Dr. Raintree pointed, "how the graves all go west to east? They look scattered, but every single one is west to east. We're not quite sure why slaves did this—the African traditions got all mixed up with Christian ones. Some say they buried their dead facing east because that was towards Africa. Some say that the dead shouldn't have to turn around when Gabriel blows his trumpet in the eastern sunrise."

Dr. Raintree talked to me seriously, just as though I were a grown-up. He explained that the plates and cups would have been deliberately broken over each grave. "Why?" he said, before I could ask it. "Again, we don't really know. Some say breaking the objects released their spirits so they could journey to the next world to serve their owners. Others say the broken items guarded the grave, keeping the dead dead, so to speak, so they didn't return to interfere in the lives of the living. Still others say that you had to break these things, or else others in the family would die too. For whatever reason, we do know it was important to decorate the graves with items the deceased used last—like medicine bottles, spoons, dishes, even mirrors. Nobody wanted an unhappy spirit, a restless spirit, wandering in the world of the living."

Aunt Charlotte was a restless spirit, I thought. Miss Lila was a sometime-ghost, but she didn't seem restless. Miss Cass's Gabriel stayed with her somehow in the bear claw, the totem pendant that she wore. Troy was a supernatural wanderer of some sort. And Cleo? It was too soon to tell.

"What would happen," I asked, "if someone took an offering away from the grave?" I was thinking about the marble I'd found.

"Superstition has it that the spirit starts to wander, to hunt for what's missing."

"Do you believe that's what happens?"

"I think it's important to honor the dead."

"But you…"

Dr. Raintree read my mind. "I don't like taking anything—even to send to the museum, but at this point, after so many years, anything exposed will deteriorate."

He crouched and brushed off another small bottle. "See this? The family of the dead person would have placed it upside-down." He buried the mouth of the bottle in the dirt, then recorded it in his notebook. "So the medicine would go down into the grave."

"What about the shells?"

In addition to the cowrie, Dr. Raintree had found broken bits of conchs and scallop shells.

"You see lots of shells on graves nearer the coast. Again, the theories vary: the belief that shells enclose the soul…the belief that the sea brought them, the sea will take them back. The cowrie, though, that's special. It came all the way from Africa. It's a mystery how the original slaves managed to bring anything, no matter how small, and hang on to it."

He had also found two pierced coins, the engravings rubbed off.

"Cleo," I said. "Cleo who died—she wore a little coin on a wire around her ankle."

"Those were common during slavery times. It was probably passed down to her. A good-luck charm."

He'd found no other bone, not so much as a fragment. Mr. Mac was right, he said, about the acidic soil.

Early in the morning of the third day, Dr. Raintree, on his hands and knees, his face close to the dirt, called me to him. Carefully he lifted a small piece of china different from anything he'd found so far. Bits of black paint clung to a pale curved surface, and there appeared to be half an eye. "Looks like part of a china doll—maybe a hand-me-down from the planter's child. A little girl, a slave," he said, "was likely buried here. Another child or two as well," he continued, "judging from the marbles we found and the shorter length of these depressions."

I was quiet. I hadn't bargained on finding children's graves. "Do they have to have been our slaves? Couldn't another farmer have buried his slaves here?"

Dr. Raintree looked surprised. "Not a chance. During slavery, black people were buried next to the land they worked. Since this land was in your family as far back as 1800, this site is evidence that—let's count back—your great-great-great-grandparents were wealthy slave-owners. That's the amazing thing about archaeology, Etta. It brings truth to light, even when that truth has been buried for years and years."

After lunch, Dr. Raintree and I marked off the burying ground with baling twine and railroad spikes. He'd marked a total of twelve graves.

The Daily Sentinel sent out a reporter, who took pictures. Will was still too sick to join us, so it was just my father, Mr. Mac, me, and Dr. Raintree leaning on his shovel. I had smuggled in my pocket the marble I'd kept. I managed to drop it into the graveyard without anyone's noticing, and buried it with my foot. It had belonged to a child who died, who had belonged to our family.

Our phone started ringing first thing the next morning. Most of the calls were for my parents, but some were for me. Suddenly it seemed I was famous. But this was not the way I wanted to be famous. The newspaper had twisted everything. Instead of emphasizing the importance of a real slave cemetery, instead of focusing on the archaeology of the find, the reporter focused on making my family sound like the Olivers or the Vickerses or the Richardsons: plantation slave-owners.

"Family Stunned by Evidence of Antebellum Wealth." That was the front-page headline. "Local farming family committed to preserving cemetery of slaves owned by ancestors," read the caption beneath the photograph.

"According to expert Dr. Ralph Raintree, only the wealthiest families could afford to set aside land for slaves to bury their own kind....It is indeed a loss for our heritage that the McDaniel mansion burned to the ground following the War Between the States.

"According to Phil McDaniel (known locally as Mr. Mac), all records, pictorial or otherwise, vanished in the fire. But the family plans to preserve the cemetery by erecting a fence as per the historical land survey...."

Both Margot and Stephanie called me. Then came the breathy voice of a girl who didn't bother to introduce herself. She didn't need to: Joyce Ann Richardson, who had never so much as nodded my way. "To think," she said, "your family and my family were planters way back before the Civil War. Gosh, it sounds like you all owned more slaves than we did. There really are no pictures of the plantation house? That's so sad. Gone with the wind."

Joyce Ann—she'd actually called me. I could hardly believe it. Here was an invitation to join the golden circle—I would now be popular. Why, then, wasn't I elated? *Gone with the Wind*—I'd seen the movie in Marion three years ago when the theaters were making a big to-do over the one hundredth anniversary of the start of the Civil War. It did give me a thrill to picture myself, my mother and father, Will and Mr. Mac posing in front of white columns the size of tree trunks. And Cleo, too. A real plantation house—to think that it was ours!

No sooner did I think this than it occurred to me: wouldn't my mental picture make Cleo, like Mammy in *Gone with the Wind*, a slave? Mammy, whom Cleo had sometimes in manner resembled. But Cleo wasn't a slave; she was like family. Or was she? I was confused. In the movie, the *slave* Mammy was like family; she hadn't left Tara, the plantation, even when she could have gone. And Cleo—she and Starry had refused even to go on a short trip with Miss Cass to Washington, DC, to hear the Reverend King. Truth was, as I knew good and well, the McDaniels' plantation house wouldn't have been Cleo's any more than Tara was Mammy's; Cleo would have lived in a shack apart from us, my family and me, a life of her own apart from ours, a life of secrets.

I hadn't yet been to Cleo's grave, but I could picture the cemetery beside the Morning Star Holiness Church. Now, like a transparency in my Earth Science schoolbook, my family's slave burying ground laid itself down on top of the other, where Cleo lay, and the two were parts of one whole.

17: Purple Shoes

August 11, 1964

Will wasn't getting any better. His fever wouldn't go away. The surgeon in Columbia wanted to take a look at him; he might have to do some repair, but it would almost certainly be minor. Nonetheless, he said Will should come as soon as possible.

This was my chance. I could have gone along, but I begged my parents to let me stay home with Mr. Mac. Dr. Raintree was returning one more day to verify his notes. I couldn't miss it. I couldn't!

Mr. Mac's cough still sounded serious. My parents weren't sure about leaving me with him, even for a couple of nights. But they were too worn down to argue.

Since Dr. Raintree's arrival, I'd spared little time for Troy. Not wanting to lose one second of my time with the archaeologist, I would rush across the orchard to the barn as soon as the sun came up and simply hand Troy a jelly sandwich, when I used to make him work for it, and fill his bucket to the brim. He'd given me what I wanted: a find. He was on my side at last, or so I thought.

But today the slave burying ground, all that it meant, hit me. I stopped at the barn door and stared at the horse. And he stared back from inside, his head twisted to favor his seeing eye. He was just as grisly, just as eerie-looking as before. True, he had given me a find; he'd brought Dr. Raintree into my life. But the survey had taken a turn—those were no Swamp Fox relics. With the help of that blind eye that could see underground, Troy had as good as kicked at the dirt himself, crippled old devil, and dug up the graves of my family's slaves and their children. I pictured

Troy lying in the rain, spattered with mud, his scar not yet a scar but a raw-red gash that stank. There he'd sprawled, his legs stretched out, stiff as though ready for his own burial. Now he stood, as if he had himself gone into the graves and climbed back out with their contents in tow, determined for me to see what he saw. Troy shivered—horseflies were after him—then hobbled to his bucket where he waited for me.

Dr. Raintree arrived at eight o'clock. All he did was re-measure the perimeter of the graveyard and walk around, making checkmarks by his notations. He seemed to be in a hurry.

I hoped he hadn't seen the article in the local paper, which barely mentioned him and his work.

When he packed up his truck for the last time, Dr. Raintree shook hands with Mr. Mac. "Thank you for protecting the site," he said. "Not many people would go to the trouble."

He tugged on one of my braids. "Always keep your eyes open."

Then he was gone. His tires kicked up dust; Mr. Mac coughed. And I remembered that I had to stay the night in Miss Lila's room where the door and curtains were always shut, where fumes of floor polish lingered, in the bed where Miss Lila had suffered long in fever and delirium. I could imagine dead eyes staring, cold ghost-fingers brushing my face while I slept. I wished I'd gone to Columbia with Will and my parents after all.

I followed Mr. Mac back to the burying ground. "You never knew anything about these slaves? Nothing about a plantation?" My grandfather, measuring with his hands, seemed to be making mental notes about the fencing.

He looked towards Aunt Charlotte's house and shook his head. "I always thought Aunt Charlotte was a little bit odd. She claimed she was born in that house into the McDaniel family. I thought she was fooling with me."

"Doesn't it make you feel bad, though? To find out your grandfather owned slaves? He'd have owned Cleo's mama, too, maybe her papa."

"He was trying to make a living. Nothing wrong with that. And he couldn't have been too hard-hearted to give up good land like this for a cemetery."

"But Mr. Mac, *slaves*?"

"The times were what they were, Etta."

The excitement of the find had gone with Dr. Raintree, who wouldn't be returning. The burying ground—now it seemed to me a sort of wound. It would always remind me of my family's shameful history. Even so, surely Mr. Mac wanted to do more than just fence off the graveyard. Wasn't he curious, I asked, about the grandchildren of his grandfather's slaves? Maybe tenants other than Cleo's family had people buried here.

"I'm not going to pry into things people might want left alone," he said, his cigar between his teeth, the corners of his mouth turning down. "We're doing right, putting up a good iron fence. Anybody who wants to can come and pay his respects."

But how will they *know*, I wanted to ask but didn't. I sensed that I was about to get on his nerves. For Mr. Mac, feelings were not something you talked about.

When I was older and could look back with some distance, I understood that the fence probably allowed my grandfather to make amends, in his own mind, with his family's slaves and their descendants. He was able to fence off that part of the past. But not everything was so neatly set apart. Mr. Mac never would block from his memory the artillery barrage of the First World War, any more than he could shut Miss Lila in that dark front room.

❧

At Walter's Store I had just dug out two good Cokes when Mr. Mac started coughing. He coughed so hard his hat fell off and nearly his glasses. He staggered, grabbed hold of the counter. Tears ran from his eyes. His neck reddened from his collar up. Miss Cass, who right then came through the front door, rushed forward and took his arm. She sat him on the bench. Mr. Walter and the other men hadn't moved. It was as though they'd been struck with whatever paralysis had struck Cleo back when Troy kicked Trudy. Surely they didn't all have bad hearts.

Mr. Mac made a wheezing sound with every breath. I patted his back like I'd seen my father do. When he finally caught his breath, his lips looked blue.

"Mac, I'm taking you to the doctor, now don't argue," Miss Cass said.

Mr. Mac shook his head.

"I said don't argue—won't do you any good."

"Got Etta," he wheezed. "Got Etta staying with me."

"Don't worry about Etta. You're the one needs taking care of." She nodded at the farmers. "Some help, gentlemen?"

"My truck," he coughed, as the old men shuffled him out.

"It's not going anywhere," Mr. Walter said. "Be waiting right here for you."

In town, Dr. Monroe didn't hesitate. He was sending Mr. Mac straight to the hospital, where he would spend the night for observation and tests. As he walked us to the door of his office, the doctor caught sight of my face. He stooped to my level. He was a tall, stiff sort of man so that, despite my own height, this took some effort. Mr. Mac was going to be just fine, he promised. He'd be home the next day.

Miss Cass saw Mr. Mac to his hospital room. I had to stay in the waiting area. No exception this time.

I slid into the front seat of Miss Cass's red station wagon and started to cry. I cried like a big loud baby, embarrassing myself, and couldn't stop. My whole body sobbed. Miss Cass took it in stride, just as she had when Mr. Mac had his spell at the store. "You're scared. It's normal. You're thinking if Cleo can go to the hospital and die, so can Mr. Mac."

I nodded. My mother, if she were here, would make me stop crying. I imagined her hands gripping my shoulders.

Miss Cass read my mind. "He's not going to die, Etta."

"How…" I wiped my face on my shirtsleeve. "How do you know?"

"It's just one of those things I know." She reached into her big black pocketbook and gave me a handkerchief. "It's clean."

"What if he has a heart attack? Or a stroke?"

"Tell you what. This evening, you and I, we're going to pray for your granddaddy. We'll mix up some healing herbs. The Bear Clan, don't you know, are the Keepers of the Medicine. In fact, I used to be a member of the Bear Medicine Society. I promise you, Etta, he's going to be fine. Now look at me."

Miss Cass was wearing her usual man's clothes, her hair in its usual braid. The beads were just visible in the unbuttoned neck of her green checked shirt. Her face was wrinkled, but in a way that made her look smart; there were brown splotches on her cheeks and forehead, but her green eyes were young and a deeper green than ever above her shirt.

"Take a deep breath. We'll do it together. One, two, three."

I breathed deeply, filling out my chest like Miss Cass did.

"Now," she said. "We have some work to do. At least I have. You can help or not, it's up to you. Reach back there to the floorboard and grab one of those papers."

I leaned over. I hadn't even noticed, when I sat in the back seat on the way to town, the box full of paper anchored with a spearhead paperweight.

On the front was a picture of the Reverend King in a dark suit. I turned it over: "Speech Delivered at the March on Wash-

ington, August 1963: *I Have a Dream.*" It looked like a poem—
or a song. There was something about South Carolina, and
slaves and slave-owners. And children. Little children, black and
white, holding hands. I pictured the small depressions that
marked the graves of the slave children; I thought of the little
girls who were killed in that Alabama church, and Cleo's Eugene; and Juney and Will and Trudy—I could see them holding
hands. "Let freedom ring…" My eyes rested on the ending. The
words were like bells ringing: "Free at last, free at last. Thank
God Almighty, we're free at last."

"It's not the whole speech, but it's the best part. *The New
York Post* printed it, that's how I got hold of it. You should have
been there, Etta. Hard to believe it's been almost a year."

"You going to take these to the colored churches, like you
did the other one with the jail picture?"

"I am. Negroes here know Reverend King is out there
working for them. But this speech, like that letter—these are
things to keep. You must take some copies home yourself.
They're worth reading over and over."

"But…why do *you* have to do it?"

"Who else is going to? The *Sentinel* is not about to stir the
pot and print anything like this. Too many white folks around
here are happy as larks to make believe there are no bad feelings
at all between them and the Negroes. They think if they ignore
what's going on everywhere else, somehow it will never become a
problem here."

"You're not scared?"

"Scared of what?"

"People in other states are getting killed, like those boys in
Mississippi. They had a car like yours—you said so."

"That was Mississippi, not here."

"Well, the sit-in at Whaley's Drugstore was sure scary.
Some teenagers tried to hurt Evelyn and the others. Mr. Sneed

at Walter's—he said you probably gave them the idea, turned Yankee like you were, different from the rest of us."

Miss Cass laughed. "As if Evelyn and her friends don't have the sense to come up with ideas on their own? And as for Verne Sneed calling me different, well, I've been knowing him for years. I take that as a compliment."

She pulled from her handbag a two-page list of Negro churches in Marion County. "Over thirty churches have been burned so far this summer in Mississippi." She shook her head. "One thing about the Klan—those boys do love fire."

"We don't have a Klan here—do we?"

She didn't answer. Maybe she hadn't heard the question.

Why, I wondered, did my feelings sometimes swing one in one direction, then right away swing in the other? Everything *had* seemed fine before people started trying to change things, before this Reverend King started preaching and marching. Cleo had seemed happy enough. Starry, Jesse, and the other colored farm workers still seemed content. Even after the sit-in, Evelyn didn't complain. I had been safe with Cleo and in the world around me, even if I hadn't known the first thing about Cleo's past. What Miss Cass was doing didn't feel safe at all. And yet I wanted to be a part of it. Miss Cass was acting not because it was safe but because she believed it was right. She had gumption.

We visited the churches in town within the space of an hour. If the preacher happened to be there, Miss Cass gave him a handful of her fliers and explained what they were. If not, she'd leave them on a table or chair in the entrance, with a note clipped to the top.

The country churches took up the rest of the afternoon. They were spread all over the county. I had never before considered the fancy names of the colored churches: Baptized in the Spirit Holiness Church of God, AME Apostolic Church of Prayer and Deliverance, Zion Baptist Church of Faith and

Prophecy…White churches showed no imagination: First Baptist, First Presbyterian, First Methodist, Grace Episcopal.

Miss Cass had been driving slowly for some time, keeping an eye on the black sedan following us. She'd waved her arm out the window, gesturing for it to pass, but it stayed on her bumper. Craning my neck around, I could tell only that two men occupied the front seat. But with their hats pulled low over their foreheads, I couldn't see their faces. The sedan pulled off at Walter's Store. Miss Cass sighed, shaking her head.

When we turned right at Lamar Scurlock's yard, I knew where we were going. The last church on Miss Cass's list was Cleo's. The gravel changed to dirt, and the shade from the trees darkened the road. Buzzards circled over the White Horse field. Starry and Esau's house looked deserted.

I had gone with Miss Cass into all the other churches, but here at the Morning Star Holiness Church I stayed in the car. I never wanted to set foot in that church again. For me it would never again be anything but a crypt. I took a deep breath. Only the singing of birds, the chirring of insects, and distant voices of children playing broke the evening silence.

When Miss Cass returned, she brushed her hands together. "Done."

She sat and looked at me. "It's nice," she said, nodding towards the cemetery, "where Cleo's buried. Would you like to stop off for a visit?"

She made it sound like a pleasant thing to do, like going to a tea party.

"No! I mean I—I don't know."

"Of course you don't. But you loved Cleo. And she loved you. I think I'll walk over. You can stay in the car if you want."

Behind the church, the graveyard was surrounded on three sides by trees, gray-bearded with Spanish moss. Cleo's grave was in the back corner of the cemetery, in the shadow of a big oak.

The floral arrangements still remained. They were wilted, but most of the flowers still held some color. How many days had passed since the funeral? Five now? Six? So much had happened since Cleo's funeral: the fire, the discovery of the slave burying ground, Mr. Mac's really bad spell. But suddenly to me it was as though no time had passed at all. My grief was new. I felt that awful swinging bridge move beneath me with every step I took through the dry leaves and scattered yellow wildflowers.

Miss Cass reached for my hand. "Isn't it nice?" she asked.

Like many of the others, Cleo's grave was identified only by a little metal-and-glass marker with an index card inside. I frowned. She needed a real headstone.

"I believe your parents and Mr. Mac, together with Jesse and Starry, are having a stone engraved," Miss Cass said, again reading my mind.

"How did you come to know her—Cleo?" I asked.

"Long years ago when I was a girl out this way, Cleo took in washing while she looked after Aunt Charlotte. I'd ride our clothes around to her house—there was a road in those days, and I wasn't scared of a car like my mother was. This was before Cleo got married, and before I took off for New York, which I did soon as I got out of high school. We'd stand out in the yard and talk and smoke a cigarette."

At first I didn't see the pair of shoes set between a pot of drooping geraniums and a vase of black-edged roses. Cleo's purple church shoes. I pointed. "I don't understand."

Miss Cass smiled. "That was Starry's idea. She didn't like it that they left off Cleo's shoes in her casket. Her sister loved these shoes, Starry said. She would have wanted them on her feet, matching her dress. Starry decided this was the next best thing."

Miss Cass knelt and touched a bleached conch. "This was my contribution."

"Shells"—I remembered almost everything Dr. Raintree had said—"contain the soul."

Miss Cass nodded.

"That's what he said the slaves believed, the archaeologist who marked off our burying ground. The slaves put shells on graves—and other things. Sometimes they broke plates and china dolls over the graves. Dr. Raintree said it was so the dead people would stay dead, so their spirits would keep quiet."

"Those offerings back then, Etta—and these right here—they're mostly for us left behind. It's hard to let go of someone we care about. Doing this, decorating a grave, is one way people work through the letting-go. Where Cleo is now and whether or not she cares about her shoes—well, that's a mystery."

"Do you think, Miss Cass—do you think Cleo felt like she was a slave? I thought she loved us and didn't want to do anything but take care of us, Will and me. But what if she didn't? What if she felt—I don't know—trapped or plain worn down? She had this whole different life before us. A husband, a baby."

"I'm sure Cleo loved you and Will. But we live in strange times, Etta. Cleo didn't have many choices. But she chose to be near her family, a family that came to include you. What we did today, you understand, passing out that speech by Martin Luther King, that was so one day everybody—black and white, women and men—we'll all have the same choices, the same chances."

I felt around in my pocket, but all I had were fragments of Indian pottery. I took the nicest piece, one with a basket pattern, and laid it next to the shell.

I almost overlooked the little grave beside Cleo's. I knelt at the marker with its bent and rusted frame and tried to find a faded letter or two on the shred of brownish paper behind the cracked glass. "Eugene," I whispered, picturing from Cleo's collection of framed photographs the baby with the flower, and placed a shard of pottery upon his grave too.

18: Burning Cross

August 11–12, 1964

I picked sandspurs off my socks and shoelaces and tossed them out the car window. As soon as we turned out onto the main road, the black sedan that had followed us earlier began tailing us again. I thought of Troy, how he stalked me, appearing when I humiliated myself or said or even thought hurtful, shameful things, but usually for no apparent reason. I felt more than uneasy—almost scared.

I could make out only the black car's red interior, silhouettes of the same two men in front. Miss Cass looked into her rearview mirror. "Who are those lunatics? I don't recognize that car."

There was plenty of room for them to pass, but they stayed glued to the station wagon's bumper. Finally Miss Cass pulled off onto the shoulder and waved her arm for them to go on. They gunned the motor and raced past, blaring the horn.

"Fools," she said. "Some people are just fools and idiots."

"Fools," Miss Cass repeated when we reached her ranch. Across the white wooden gate, someone had used red paint to scrawl: "Nigger Lover Beware. Yankee Squaw Go Home."

I was shocked. "Aren't you going to call the police?"

"Not over this little nuisance."

Miss Cass drove to one of the outbuildings near her barn and grabbed a gallon of white paint and two brushes. She drove straight back to the gate and handed one brush to me.

"I don't know why it is, Etta, some folks got to feel like they're better than other folks. So much so they got to get right in their business. As if we don't see right through 'em. As if we can't see the truth—that they're cowards and bullies and no better than anybody."

I was putting too much paint on my brush; it dripped to the ground. Still, the letters showed through. It would take several coats to completely hide the hateful words. I longed to have gumption, like Miss Cass. I had been a coward at the sit-in. At the mule barn with Will I'd been a coward and a bully when he climbed the ladder ahead of me. Hadn't I bullied him pretty much all his life? And when not bribing Troy, I'd meant to bully him. But I'd been the worst sort of bully to Cleo—downright cruel out by the pasture fence that day in June, a day I wished had never happened. Cleo had called me mean, after I had almost used—almost *said*—the word I was trying to kill with paint, but she had been sad, not angry. My meanness grieved her. I began to tear up; I *wasn't* mean—not like *this*.

"Mr. Mac says that some people around here are scared," I said, my voice sounding high-pitched and strange. "And when people get scared they do stupid things." At that moment, I felt so scared I could hardly breathe. "But sometimes I think *he's* scared, Mr. Mac is. Scared of fighting. He won't even talk about the war."

"Can't blame him. That First World War was a wicked war. Primitive. People nowadays don't appreciate what those boys were put through." Miss Cass laid down her brush. "And now we're up to our knees in Vietnam. Wars are like quicksand, don't you know. You're over your head before you can spit twice."

Miss Cass and I ate our supper in the kitchen. The army of empty glass bottles surrounded us on the floor. Towers of magazines and newspapers leaned against the walls. Electric fans blew tufts of white dog hair here and there. To make room for our plates on the red Formica table, Miss Cass had pushed aside a dozen little dishes of dried herbs, a cluster of mason jars with baby plants rooting, and pages torn out of magazines.

Wynken, Blynken, and Nod, their little pink tongues out, sat at Miss Cass's feet, watching with their shiny black eyes every move of her hands. From time to time she'd slip a bit of food into a drooling mouth.

The dishes were familiar yet different because of the strange spices Miss Cass put into them. She served field peas that were cold and flecked with little bits of green, and she'd made a salad with fresh tomatoes and something white and soft. "Goat cheese," she explained. "I make my own." There were roasted squashes, both yellow and green, that were tiny and whole. "Babies," said Miss Cass. And cornbread fried like a pancake but so thin it was like eating crispy lace. This, I couldn't get enough of.

"I never could get used to boiling cornbread with beans in it," Miss Cass said. "That's what Gabriel liked, the kind his mother made. Tasted like mush. A ball of mush with beans."

There wasn't any meat at all, but I couldn't think how to ask about it without seeming impolite. With our dessert of leftover blueberry crisp and creamy custard poured over it, Miss Cass served her calm-down tea. I had mine with honey, but it still tasted like grass, extra-sweet grass.

Miss Cass reached both arms across the table and grasped my hands. "Now we're going to pray for your granddaddy. You first."

Except for "Now I Lay Me" at night and "God Is Great" before meals, I had never prayed out loud in front of anyone. Cleo had done it all the time. I squeezed my eyes shut and tried to hear Cleo's voice. "Precious Jesus and Father God in Heaven, please let Mr. Mac be well tomorrow. Thank you, Amen."

Miss Cass prayed in what she called the "Old Way" to the God of all living things. She called Mr. Mac her brother and prayed for his lasting health. She prayed for clear lungs and calm nerves. She asked for peace that starts in the one person and spreads out, like rings from a stone tossed into still water. I was impressed. I felt certain that even Cleo would have been impressed.

Miss Cass released my hands. She went right to work pinching herbs from one dish or another and adding them to a small measuring cup. She kept sniffing the mixture, adding this and that, until she was satisfied. She poured it into a small square of cheesecloth, rolled it, and tied both ends like a sausage. "Give this to Mr. Mac tomorrow. I'm likely to forget. Tell him to put it under his pillow."

I put the sachet to my nose. It smelled terrible, like garlic and mint and something flowery all mixed up.

"Would this work on a horse?"

She sat down and again reached for my hands. "That horse of yours—what's his name? He can't be sick, can he? Got struck by lightning and lived, must have an iron constitution. That horse'll live forever."

That's what I'm afraid of, I started to say. "He's got this ugly scar," I said. "It covers his whole side. I wish hair would grow and cover it up. And he's all lopsided, blind in one eye, and crippled." I told Miss Cass about my friends, how Stephanie had a beautiful Chestnut and I'd dreamed of a Palomino. "*My* horse never won a prize at the fair. Nobody ever rode *him* in a parade—Jim Dandy! That was the corny name he came with. I named him Troy, like he was going to become a legend or something. Now I just wish he was halfway normal."

"Normal's good?"

"Isn't it?"

Miss Cass only raised an eyebrow.

"Well, he did show me where to find that skull. I don't think Stephanie's Chestnut could do that. But it was spooky, Miss Cass—he's spooky. To know right where those slaves were buried, where that graveyard was! As if he was part ghost. That's what Cleo thought—that he was haunted. She called him a dev-il-horse."

"Is that what you think—that he's a devil?"

"Sometimes yes, sometimes no. I was glad at first, about the skull. Dr. Raintree came because of it—a real archaeologist. I helped him survey. But now I'm not sure. I hate knowing that our family had slaves."

"You know, Etta, this ranch right here was part of the original Oliver plantation."

"You mean Mr. Oliver...?"

"Bud Oliver's my big brother—you didn't know that? He got the old house and the land around it, and I got the ranch. He doesn't claim me—hasn't for years—since I married Gabriel. One day he'll come to his senses. But what I want to say is that the Olivers owned slaves, too. It's a shameful fact, but it's the truth. Now, what's important is not so much what happened back then—that can't be changed—but what we do today. Not to forget the past or dwell in it, either one, but look it in the eye, learn from it. You understand?"

I nodded. That was what archaeologists did, in a way.

"But you were telling me about your horse," she said.

"Like when that car was on our tail—that's how I some-times feel, like he's after me. Cleo said from the very start he had juju eyes. She couldn't stand the way he looked at her—maybe he made her sick. But I don't really think that. Cleo died of a heart attack." My voice cracked. "I sometimes think it was me that broke her heart." I told Miss Cass how angry I'd been after Cleo froze and Trudy might have died if I hadn't yelled at her to roll out from under the horse's hooves. "I never forgave Cleo," I said. "Then I was mean to her. I called her a...I almost called her a...bad word. I never said I was sorry. I kept on being mean, and then it was too late. I never said I was sorry, even when I wanted to."

Miss Cass moved her chair next to mine and reached her right arm around my shoulder. And there I was revealing to Miss Cass, who didn't look maternal at all, feelings I never shared with my own mother, who was, by nature it seemed, impatient with such shows of emotion and in any case too focused on Will's physical problems to spare much energy for my "moods"— there I was, almost twelve, with Miss Cass consoling me as only a mother could.

"Cleo had high blood pressure," she said. "Do you know what that is? Well, never mind; but"—she snapped her fingers— "quick as a flash, it can give you a heart attack or a stroke. It was Cleo's time; you didn't have anything to do with it—you or that horse."

"I know…Cleo had spells. I'm glad she has her shoes." I was picturing Cleo's grave. "Now she won't have to go searching."

"What do you mean?"

"She won't go wandering like Aunt Charlotte. Cleo called her a wandering spirit—that's what I think Troy is, sort of."

"Aren't we all—wandering spirits, don't you know? Look at you, here with me. And me, I grew up here, moved all the way up North, got married, and here I am down South again, with you. You don't have to be dead to be a wandering spirit." Cleo had a saying for everything; but Miss Cass, I would later think, had a wisdom that went beyond sayings.

"He's after something," I said of Troy.

"Aren't we all. Anyway, I don't think my herbs will have any power over your horse, Etta. He's the way he is for a reason— singled out by the sky. He's yours—or else you're his—for some good reason. For some *good* reason. Be patient. The answer will come."

Miss Cass looked out the window. "Oh, Etta, we have to hurry. We're going to miss it!" She rushed into the library and pulled two chairs towards the sofa beneath the windows that lined the back wall. "Prepare to be amazed." She propped her feet on the sofa cushions and gestured for me to do the same.

The sky filled with orange and pink and red. Miss Cass pulled the beads out from her shirt and fingered them. "It's a good one tonight." She nodded. Gradually the pink and orange faded, leaving streaks of red-purple. Then even they vanished, and everything was violet deepening to black. Fireflies flickered.

Miss Cass sighed and sat back, as though she'd never before seen a sunset. "Living in the city, I never got to see such a thing."

I couldn't help but smile. "Is that where you met your husband? In New York City?"

"I did. Right on the street on my way to grab a sandwich. I was an actress—not a very good one—and Gabriel was working construction."

"A chief working construction?"

"Even a chief has to make a living, don't you know?" Miss Cass giggled like a girl, a sister, I thought, an older sister. The lines around her eyes deepened. "He was an ironworker. Lots of Mohawk men were ironworkers. Still are. They're strong and graceful as dancers. And have no fear of heights. They walk those beams high on skyscrapers easy as they might walk across the floor here. Gabriel helped build the top of the Empire State Building! Oh, and he was handsome. Black hair and black eyes and such fine muscles…After we got married, we lived in the city during the week and went to his village in upstate New York most weekends. That's when I learned about healing plants and so forth. The clan took me in like a daughter, even with my yellow-red hair and green eyes." She rubbed the bear claw with her thumb, then brought it to her lips.

"When Gabriel died, I just…came unraveled. Twenty years together, that's all we had. I didn't know what to do. I tried, but I just couldn't act on the stage any longer. And I couldn't stay with his family in the village. There was another path for me. I had to clear my head in order to find it. And guess what. My path led me right back here to this ranch.

"Now, I don't know about you, but I'm worn to a frazzle. How about I get you situated in my bedroom."

"But where will you sleep?"

She patted the sofa, which was covered with dog hair. I protested, but Miss Cass reminded me that the hedgehogs would soon have free run of the house. She was used to them, but they just might startle me.

I helped move the three little dog beds into the library, then I shut the door tight. The bedroom was surprisingly spare: a single bed with a plain oak headboard and an oak chest of drawers. No mirror, no dresser. On a small table beside the bed was a photograph of Gabriel wearing normal clothes—a white shirt, a necktie. His long black hair was pulled back into a ponytail. And there, alongside it, was a grinding bowl that held dried lavender flowers. Another smaller stone sat atop the flowers. I pressed the small stone down. Suddenly pungent, the lavender perfume rose.

At first I thought I was again dreaming—this time about the fire that took our barn and trees, Troy standing in the middle of it, untouched by the flames. Then I thought it was day. Bright lights shone into my window. Car horns were blaring. Miss Cass's three dogs were yapping.

I ran to the window and looked out into the front yard. Cars lined the driveway. The headlights were flashing from high beam to low beam to high. Horns continued to blow. I squeezed my eyes shut, then opened them. I *must* be dreaming. Strange figures were emerging from the cars, tall figures made taller by pointed hoods that hid their faces. There were white robes, but also other colors—red, gold, and black—with crosses sewn over the chests. The figures seemed to be playing a practical joke—a trick, I thought, as if they were costumed up for Halloween. From somewhere they had hauled a wooden cross and stabbed it right in the middle of Miss Cass's wildflowers. Through the screen I could hear men's voices. I smelled kerosene. Two figures set fire to torches, then held them to the cross. It burst into flames. Only the Klan did this, Halloween colors or not.

I was turning away from the window to go hunt for Miss Cass when I heard her voice outside. The men had returned to their cars, but there was Miss Cass, looking like a wild woman in her loose orange-and-yellow-striped nightgown, waving to them. "Come on back," she yelled. She had a good set of lungs to make herself heard over Wynken, Blynken, and Nod, who were barking and racing back and forth from Miss Cass towards the cars. "Come on inside and have some tea. You must be thirsty after all this hard work."

I recognized the black sedan that had followed us that afternoon. Two Klansmen in gold robes had returned to its red interior. And there was Lamar Scurlock's turquoise-and-white pickup truck—it was unmistakable.

Miss Cass grabbed a water hose and aimed it at the burning cross. "Mighty bad manners from such good Christian men!"

It happened so fast, I almost missed it. From a pale car parked behind the sedan, the red-robed driver stepped out. Aiming, lifting the mask of his hood over his eyes and aiming again, he threw maybe a block of something at Miss Cass. She crumpled to the ground. The figure hesitated. For a second it seemed he might go to her. Then he hurried back into his car.

Through the house I ran, stubbing my toes on furniture and books and knocking over stacks of newspapers and magazines. Down the long hallway of the porch, I kicked fuzzy balls of what were surely hedgehogs. I ran as fast as I could, but I was moving in slow motion, or so it seemed—as though mud was sucking at my feet.

By the time I reached the door, the last of the cars was spinning up dirt, its red taillights moving away towards the road.

The cross was still flaming and giving off a lot of heat. Miss Cass had fallen almost directly beneath it. She wasn't moving.

Suddenly flames rose from the hem of her nightgown. Was she lying in spilt kerosene? I couldn't see the water hose, but I grabbed up from beside her shoulder the thing—a book—that the Klansman had thrown. Sweating, my own skin feeling scorched, I beat out the flames in the striped cloth. The burning wood creaked. I grabbed Miss Cass's arms and tried to drag her away. "Miss Cass, wake up," I begged, shaking her.

A deep groaning sound came from inside the wood. One of the cross's arms collapsed. If the other fell, it would land on Miss Cass. Again I tried to move her, to wake her. The cross began to lean. The hose had to be near. But where? I ran in circles, searching. There! Miss Cass had flung it back towards the house. I grabbed it and aimed it at the cross. From side to side I moved, soaking it and Miss Cass in the process.

I sat on the wet ground beside her. Her chest was moving. Her eyelids twitched. The dogs came whimpering and lay down at her head. She opened her eyes.

"Need to put out the fire, keep the cross standing," she said, rising up onto her elbows. "Oh." She blinked. "Did I, or did you?"

"You started, I finished."

I lifted, so that Miss Cass could see in the moonlight, the black, leather-bound Bible.

The woman put her hand to her head. "Guess you could say they threw the Book at me."

I couldn't smile. I had recognized the man who threw it. Mr. Turnage from the bank.

"Are you…all right? Your leg. It could be burned."

Miss Cass lifted the blackened hem of her nightgown and touched her leg. "Blistered a little. You got me good and wet, though. Exactly the right thing for it. Hand me that hose."

Miss Cass let the water run over her leg. "I'm all right, but those fellows aren't. Pitiful—hiding in those outfits, hiding behind the cross, turning the Good Book into a weapon, pretending their hate is—I don't know—something that's not hate."

"I thought the Klan all wore white robes."

"The leaders wear colors, I seem to recall….They looked right clownish, didn't they? I can just see them stacked in a crazy little car in some circus, juggling balls—balls of fire—can't you?" Miss Cass started giggling. I started giggling, too. We began laughing. Then, just as suddenly, we stopped. I knew that the Klan were not clowns but killers. They burned crosses and churches with people in them. I'd recognized Lamar Scurlock's truck, and I'd seen the bank president's face. I wished I hadn't.

When I woke up the next morning, Miss Cass was entertaining reporters in her front yard. Their voices had roused me. I ran to the window. What was left of the blackened cross still stood, as Miss Cass meant it to do. The yard was a mess: wildflowers trampled, the ground dug out, marked up by spinning tires. One man snapped photographs, while Miss Cass, a bandage wrapped like a turban around her head, told the other about what happened—how she was hosing down the fire when someone knocked her out cold with a Bible. "Threw the Book at me," she repeated, pointing—stamped on its cover was a white cross inside a red circle. She'd rolled one leg of her pants up to expose another bandage around her calf. She caught sight of me and waved me outside.

"If it hadn't been for Etta here," she said, "the cross would have gotten burnt to the ground. Me with it more than likely." I was rubbing my eyes. "I'm just thankful no one hurt this little girl." Miss Cass put her arm around me, and the photographer snapped our picture.

Why had she—Cassandra Bearclaw—been set on hosing down the cross? The reporter listened, scribbling onto a notepad.

"So you could put it in the paper, that's why. Everybody ought to see for themselves that the Klan is still here, in our back yards—front yard, in my case—not just in Mississippi or Alabama or Georgia. People need to see the truth."

The photographer positioned Miss Cass to one side of the cross and told her to hold the Bible straight out in front of her. I stood on the other side.

After the reporters left, the two of us sat down to breakfast. "I hope they run a great big picture in the paper. A picture is worth a thousand words," Miss Cass said, patting a *Life* magazine on the kitchen table. Soldiers in a row were wading through deep grass. "In Color," the cover said. "Ugly War in Vietnam."

She tightened her mouth. "It never ends—war. *This* war, I don't understand. All I know is it's bound to be as ugly as the headline says. People never learn." Miss Cass scratched at the edge of the binding around her forehead. "You can tell the history of the world by listing off wars—isn't that something? People, they just like to spill blood, that's all there is to it. They'll spill as much as they can—of their own and everybody else's—if they're doing it for a cause. Doesn't matter what it is, a good cause or a bad one, so long as it's a cause."

"Like the Klan?" I asked.

"Yes, like the Klan. Coming out here in the middle of the night with their crosses and their fire, not caring who all gets hurt."

Miss Cass unwound the turban from her head to expose a swollen red bruise. She'd worn the bandage just for show. "Theater!" Her mood reversed itself. She seemed exhilarated. "All the world's a stage, my dear."

I didn't feel the least bit exhilarated. The shock of last night weighed on me. I couldn't believe that Mr. Scurlock, who worked for our family, bad as he was, was *this* bad. I couldn't believe that Mr. Turnage—from the bank!—had thrown a Bible and hit Miss Cass. I would never again touch his candy cigarettes. He was as evil as the witch in "Hansel and Gretel," tricking children with sweets.

I wanted and yet didn't want to tell Miss Cass whom I'd seen. I was sure about Mr. Turnage, about Lamar Scurlock's truck. I'd never been more sure about anything in my life. Yet I wanted—I needed—to believe otherwise.

"Did you call the police?" I asked.

"I did. Right away. But they said unless I could identify someone, their hands were tied. And I couldn't see anything for the fire."

If Miss Cass with her bandage was dressing up the truth, then she was, I thought, as good as lying. Fibbing, at least. But I was lying, too, by keeping to myself what I'd seen. I had made up my mind to be brave, to have gumption like Miss Cass. But this morning, as close as I'd felt to her the night before, I felt a little let down. Would anything ever be simple again? Whatever the reason—nothing was clear to me—I couldn't bring myself to tell on the men. At least not right now, and not to Miss Cass.

It was nearly noon before we returned to the hospital to get Mr. Mac. He was pacing the floor. I ran to him and hugged his middle. "Took your sweet time," he complained. "I was about to think I'd have to walk home." He carried a sack of medicine. The x-rays looked all right, he said, and the tests came out all right too. It looked like he'd be around a few years longer.

I kept hugging him. Even as we walked to Miss Cass's car. I couldn't make myself let go.

On the way home, I leaned forward from the back seat and told Mr. Mac what had happened. "See Miss Cass's head? They threw a *Bible* and knocked her out." Telling about it, I saw Mr. Turnage clear as anything.

"Etta came to the rescue again, Mac. She hosed down that fire when the cowards knocked me unwinding."

Mr. Mac was quiet. He pulled a cigar from his shirt pocket and started chewing. He glanced at Miss Cass with icy eyes. "Seems like you could've put your—your political activities on hold for one day. I swear, Cassandra, you know you get people riled up. You could have gotten Etta hurt—and yourself hurt worse."

"It's not politics, Mac. It's doing what's right."

"There's a time and a place for everything." Mr. Mac shook his head. "You both could've been hurt bad."

When we reached Walter's Store, Miss Cass put her hand over Mr. Mac's. "You sure you feel like driving—you're up to looking after Etta? She's more than welcome to stay with me. I believe the excitement's over, for now at least."

He appreciated it, he said, but he was fine.

19: Pandora's Box

August 12, 1964

"I saw some things," I blurted, as soon as we set off to begin the chores. "I saw more than Miss Cass did. Like Mr. Scurlock's truck. And Mr. Turnage. He's the one who threw the Bible. He lifted up his hood so he could aim. He was wearing a red robe. Maybe he's special, a leader or something."

"You don't know what you saw." Mr. Mac began coughing. He drank from a brown bottle and made a face. "It was dark. You got waked up in the middle of the night."

"The moon was full. There were headlights, and the cross was burning. I know what I saw." I couldn't believe my grandfather was dismissing me. I should have told Miss Cass after all. What had made me hesitate? Miss Cass had disappointed me, exaggerating her injuries just for the newspaper. She had been play-acting. But that wasn't the only reason. Lamar Scurlock worked for our family; I'd known him and Mr. Turnage all my life. It was a sense of shame—almost as if those two men were blood kin—that had made me hold my tongue. I felt too ashamed to admit what I'd seen to anyone who wasn't a part of my family—my family who'd owned slaves. It didn't matter that Miss Cass's family, the Olivers, had owned slaves too.

"You ought to fire Mr. Scurlock. You ought to pull every bit of your money out of Mr. Turnage's bank." I was almost yelling.

My grandfather's expression was grim. "I'll look into it," he finally said.

Having lost most of the day, Mr. Mac and I fed the cows and checked the fields and barns and packhouses without taking a break. Whenever Mr. Mac started up coughing, he took a swig or two from the brown bottle and knocked his fist against his chest.

On Mr. Mac's screened porch late that afternoon, I kicked off my shoes and settled into the big oak chair he had made by hand years ago. The porch was where Will and I stayed when we visited Mr. Mac, spending much of our time bickering over who got to sit in the chair, which used to be plenty wide enough for both of us. Its cushions, made of leather that had hardened and split with age, could scratch deeply enough to draw blood. Still, to Will and me it was like a throne, worth fighting over. While Mr. Mac settled himself at his desk in the den, I grabbed up my archaeology book from the porch floor. The comic book version of *The Iliad* was still stuck inside. I couldn't remember when I'd left it here, at Mr. Mac's house. I was almost too tired to read.

In its own way, Mr. Mac's porch was as cluttered as Miss Cass's house. To the right of the door stood the wringer-washer machine that only Cleo had known how to work. Six dirt-crusted work boots of different ages and degrees of wear were lined up beside it. Near the wall beside the wooden chair rose a pyramid of paint cans as tall as I was. Against them leaned a folded card table and chairs, which Mr. Mac set up when he and Will and I played Parcheesi. There were flowerpots helter-skelter on the floor, and balls of twine, and cans of motor oil. And there was the streamer trunk. No matter how hard Will and I had begged over the years, Mr. Mac refused to open it for us. It was Miss Lila's, he explained.

This never had made sense to me. Miss Lila was long dead. Besides, who was to say she wouldn't have wanted her grand-daughter to see inside? I leaned against the open door to the den. Mr. Mac sat hunched over a ledger, chewing on his cigar. "What do you think Miss Lila put in her trunk?"

"Old papers, that sort of thing."

"Mr. Mac." I hesitated. "Are you scared?"

He looked up. "Scared of what?"

"Scared to see what's inside?"

His eyes were a soft blue; he wasn't angry. "Maybe so." He bent back to his work.

Again I flopped into the oak chair and opened my book. A breeze had picked up. Clouds, dark clouds, had begun to gather at the far edge of the sky. Troy stood just outside the mule barn swishing his tail. Tilting his head, he stared across the pasture as though he could see me even through the screen.

I looked down at the illustration of Hector's flaming funeral pyre. Again I smelled burning wood, felt the heat of the barn fire, and now, added to this, the heat of the burning cross. Again I studied Schliemann's portrait, a dark-haired man with a moustache and an intense look to his eyes, the proud face of a man who had found real treasure. Heinrich—almost the same name as Henrietta! Why had I never made that connection?

"I'm going to be like *them* when I grow up," I called out.

"Which them?"

"Dr. Raintree and Heinrich Schliemann."

"Who?"

"Schliemann. He discovered Troy and King Priam's Treasure and the Jewels of Helen and the gold Mask of Agamemnon and…" I stared at the trunk.

"You got Troy and didn't want him. And that Raintree fellow, seems to me all he finds are little bits of junk no good to anybody. You ought to go to the university and study to be a lady Perry Mason."

I put my book down and stood in the doorway. "I don't want to be a lawyer. I'm going to be an archaeologist. I've made up my mind. And I think Miss Lila would want me to see inside her trunk. I *am* almost twelve."

Mr. Mac put his cigar into his pocket, then laid down his pencil and closed the ledger. He reached into a cubbyhole at the back of his desk, pulled out a skeleton key, and rubbed it between his fingers. "Maybe she would…now you're old as you are." He held it out to me.

Together we went out onto the porch. "Look at that sky," Mr. Mac said. "Smell it? Rain's coming." Bloated gray clouds appeared to be rolling slowly towards us.

I knelt in front of the trunk and ran my fingers over the rough dusty wood. Mr. Mac unfolded a metal chair and pulled it close. I fitted the key into the rusted lock. It jammed once, then twice.

"Turn it slow. Don't force it."

Troy, who'd come all the way up to the fence, as though the trunk was his business too, whinnied. Something clicked. I pushed the lid back, and the smell of mothballs rushed out.

On the top were four yellow King Edward cigar boxes. One held brittle letters from Mr. Mac as a young man to Miss Lila; another held a small child's crude drawings and homemade valentines—my father's. The third was filled with shells. (Lila had loved the seashore, Mr. Mac explained.) The fourth box held a thick braid of dark auburn hair, silky, still beautiful. She'd cut it, Mr. Mac said, when she got too sick to take care of it. I touched one of my own frizzy braids. Not worth anyone's saving.

Beneath the boxes lay photograph albums filled with no one I recognized. Mr. Mac peered into an album whose felt cover came apart in his hand. "Looks like it's mostly her family."

"They didn't like you, did they? Papa said they didn't like you taking her from town way out here to the farm."

"They got used to it, more or less."

Nestled in a corner was something that made a jingling sound. Now *this*—the old-timey tin coin bank—was a find. I held it up so my grandfather could see. It was a small turquoise oblong box with a curved top and a "wheel of fortune" attached to its face. Alternating red and white squares made various predictions: *Good News, Present for You, Make a Friend, Going on a Journey*...A yellow disk in the open center pictured an exotic gypsy fortuneteller. Wearing a red scarf over her black wavy hair, she held out one gold-braceleted arm, her index finger pointing to the wheel. She smiled; her cheeks wore two matching spots of rouge.

I shook it—coins jangled inside. Mr. Mac handed me a penny. I stuck it into the slot, but nothing happened. I jiggled the wheel. Nothing. The wheel was stuck, having rusted or warped. Mr. Mac fiddled with it and shrugged. "*Going on a Journey.* Reckon that's your fortune."

I turned it upside down. "How do you get the money out?"

"See that little keyhole? All you have to do is find the key." He chuckled, one side of his mouth curling down. "Have to ask Lila where that is."

I tried to fit part of my pinky finger into the keyhole; I wished I had a fingernail. Again I shook the bank. I tried to force the wheel to turn, but it wouldn't budge. It didn't matter. This was a real find.

I unfolded a patchwork quilt of blue and yellow stars to reveal a porcelain doll that was falling apart. Her blonde ringlets were coming out, and her face was cracked. Her lace dress was stained and torn, and one leg had rolled off to the side.

Mr. Mac cleared his throat. "Lila's. Hers when she was a little girl."

I didn't care for dolls, had thrown away most of my own when I was nine. But this doll was like something Dr. Raintree might value. Until now Miss Lila had never been quite real to me. I'd studied the blurry photograph on Mr. Mac's dresser and seen only a pleasant, round-faced, half-smiling woman with dark hair pulled up into a loose bun—no particular beauty. Nothing in those simple eyes gave even a hint of suffering.

I carefully lifted the doll. Its eyelids fluttered, then opened to round, brown eyes. Without meaning to, I pictured Cleo—Cleo in her coffin with those wrong curls, lying like a doll in a box. My throat closed up.

I handed the doll and her leg to Mr. Mac.

"I'm thinking about Cleo," I said. "What it's going to be like without her. All my life she was here."

"You'll always have her with you."

"I don't know. She's not going anywhere now that she has her shoes."

"What are you talking about—what shoes?"

"We visited her grave, Miss Cass and I. Cleo didn't have shoes on, lying in that casket; so Starry put her church shoes—purple ones to match her dress—on the grave. We saw them. Only I wish she would come back—not to wander like Aunt Charlotte; I wish she'd be a ghost and haunt me for real. Like Miss Lila haunts you."

"She doesn't have to be a ghost to be inside there." Mr. Mac put his index finger against my chest. He pressed his own chest. "Inside here."

"All Cleo did was work for other people. Worked like a slave. She cleaned houses, did laundry. Looked after Will and me—and before us, Starry and Aunt Charlotte." My words were coming out all wrong. Thanks to Miss Cass, I saw things differently now. And because of this new way of seeing, I hated how Cleo had had to work for others. Yet I was one of those others, and I wanted Cleo back. I wanted Cleo back taking care of me, just like always.

"You think Cleo would want you talking this way? Like taking care of you is nothing? Like a giving heart is nothing?" His pale eyes focused on the wall just past me. His mouth turned down into a real frown.

"That's not what I meant. I meant…" My eyes began to fill.

Mr. Mac leaned over and lifted the heavy quilt, then let it fall to the floor. There, at the bottom of the trunk, I knew without being told, were things from the First World War: an envelope-shaped cap, a long narrow-sheathed knife, and a mask that looked like the head of a huge insect. I stuffed the dusty cap over my hair.

"I thought I tossed out all this war mess," Mr. Mac murmured. "Don't know why Lila kept it."

I lifted the bug-eyed mask from which dangled, by way of a half-rotted hose, a rectangular can scabbed with yellow paint. I held it to my face despite the coarse material that had stiffened into sharp peaks and edges. I could see nothing through the scratched and clouded green glass.

"They called that thing a gas mask," he said. "But it didn't keep the mustard out worth a durn." All my life I'd heard about the mustard gas that caused Mr. Mac's coughing spells. "First time they shelled us, I was blind for two days. I had buddies who never did see again. It got my lungs pretty good. That's why they don't let me smoke my ceegars."

I gripped the wooden handle of what I thought was a dagger. A metal arc lined with rusty pyramids shielded my knuckles. I tried to remove the sheath, but the leather was stiff and even looked rusty.

I pointed the weapon at my grandfather. "This was yours?"

He nodded, coughing.

"Can you take the leather thing off this dagger?"

He tugged the blade from its sheath. The three-sided metal was clean, without a spot of rust; it narrowed to a pin-sharp point. "This is what they called a trench knife. We used it in hand-to-hand combat."

He gave it back to me. I tapped the pyramid-shaped spikes.

"Brass knuckles," he explained.

I ran my fingers up and down the blade. "You—really fought?"

"Spent most of my time out in fields near the German border."

"Fields like ours, with tobacco or cows?"

"Look out there," he sighed, "as far as the pasture goes— farther—and imagine black smoke like from that woods fire we had, hanging low, thick as those thunderclouds between you and the sky. And see that barbed wire fence?" His hand shook when he pointed. "Imagine yards of it wound around and covering the pasture, if the mule barn and those sheds over yonder and everything else had got burnt down and nothing was left but dirt. Dirt and mud holes and black tree stumps like those over near the swamp. The rest—you don't want to know that."

I followed his gaze. Troy had moved to the middle of the pasture. He stood heading west, very still, his normal right side towards us. I could imagine soldiers with bug-eyed masks building a horse the size of a ship out of timber; and there was my old horse, like a legend, profiled against the gathering clouds that made me think of mustard gas and the smoke of cannon fire.

"No Man's Land. That's what they called it. Good name, if you ask me....We had to stay in long ditches called trenches—us and the trench rabbits and the lice."

"Rabbits?"

"Rats. Big as rabbits."

"Didn't...you get sick?"

"The only time I came close to that was when the rations were so low all they gave us to eat was tinned horsemeat—the worst looking purple mess you ever saw. The harder you chewed it, the bigger it got." He blew his cheeks out and pretended to chew. "Finally, you had to open your throat and let it roll on down. Funny thing was, no matter how hungry you got, it never got any better."

I tried to smile but I couldn't. Troy, I thought. Purple and rubbery.

"Not that the regular rations were so good. Monkey meat from the Frogs—that's what we called the French—and Willie from who knows where. Cans, cans. More cans."

"Monkeys? Willie?"

"Names we had for whatever kind of meat mess they put in those cans."

He handed me the sheath. "Careful—that blade still has a sharp edge to it."

"You didn't stab anybody for real, did you? With this knife?"

"I tried to stay in one piece. Now put the knife in the sheath."

"Did you kill anybody, Mr. Mac?" Of course he hadn't. He never hunted with the old men at the store or even with my father. He wouldn't kill a spider, a horsefly, a caterpillar. I had seen him stop in the middle of a field and turn right side up a beetle-bug that had flipped to its back, legs wiggling in the air. The turtle that had bitten Will—well, our grandfather had no choice.

Mr. Mac didn't look at me. He looked past me. "I shot at some. Don't reckon," he added, "I had much choice."

He flinched as though something was stinging him. His head and hands made jerking movements, which meant the war fits were trying to come.

"What happened to your gun?" My mouth was dry. I tried to swallow but couldn't.

"Gave it away, I reckon."

"Did you kill anybody?"

His eyes were shut; the lids were twitching. Sweat beaded his face and his lips were tight. Finally he took a deep breath and opened his eyes. But he didn't answer.

"What else was in that field?" I asked. "In No Man's Land?"

Mr. Mac staggered to his feet. Either he hadn't heard me or he was done talking about the war. He pulled his cigar from his pocket and started chewing on it. "Now we're getting ourselves in a new mess way over in the jungle somewhere. Seems like nobody learns nothing."

"Vietnam," I said.

He nodded. His hands still trembling and jerking a little, he took Lila's doll and her separate leg. "I think I can put her back together. Lila would have wanted you to have her."

I took the cap from my head and arranged it, the gas mask, and the trench knife exactly as I had found them. I added the fortuneteller bank. I folded the quilt and buried them.

I didn't want the doll. I wanted to bury it too. I never wanted to see it again, to remind me of Lila and Cleo in their deep dark graves, and of whatever soldiers my grandfather left dead in a field.

20: No Man's Land

August 12, 1964

I crammed my feet back into my Keds. From the doorway, I looked in at my grandfather, who for the first time appeared to be an old man. He sat hunched at his desk with the doll and some pliers.

"Where you off to this late?"

"Just the barn. Just for a minute."

"Don't let yourself get caught in the rain." Coughing again, he reached for his medicine.

I climbed over the gate into the pasture. What good was locking it, when Troy roamed at will wherever he wanted, materializing as if from thin air or smoke?

I wasn't about to stop at the barn. My stomach ached—how ugly I'd been to Will because of those kittens. Kittens! I should have hit my brother, beat him with the tobacco stick—that would have been kinder than my words, words that changed his face from a smirking gargoyle's into that of a sad broken doll.

One leg after another marched deeper into the pasture, towards Troy, who hadn't moved. And with every step, images of trench warfare flashed into my brain. Mr. Mac's hand shoved its brass knuckles again and again into the face of the only German man I knew of, crushing and tearing Schliemann's cheek, his mouth. The blade whipped down; Schliemann's mouth—bleeding where the teeth had been—widened into a scream. His head snapped back, his body folded into the trench. My grandfather, his blue eyes frosted over, held the knife extended as blood settled the dust of that French field.

I wished I'd never opened the trunk. Always I'd pictured Mr. Mac as a swaggering young man smoking in nightclubs— the handsome soldier from the picture in Miss Lila's bedroom who laughed and joked with his buddies, marched around in the countryside visiting famous cathedrals and tombs decorated with statues, and drank out of a canteen. He'd breathed mustard gas—which, to me, had always sounded as harmless as bitter fumes coaxed somehow from the yellow French's that came in a jar—then got sent home. It never crossed my mind that he'd really fought and even killed German soldiers, that this lay behind his war-fits. The trunk—it was like Pandora's Box in my book of myths. I had released a swarm of demons. Mosquitoes and biting flies—I slapped at them.

Too much had happened too fast: Cleo's death and funeral, the fire that exposed the skull and graveyard, the Klan—some of whom I recognized—burning a cross in Miss Cass's yard and injuring her. And now a grandfather who I felt sure had killed— killed people.

Far in the distance stood the charred posts of what had been trees: the trees of No Man's Land, the blackened remains of the cross in Miss Cass's front yard, the torched masts of Greek ships. The Trojan War—it was no longer just a fancy story but as real as any other war. The Greeks clambering down from the wooden horse; the slaughter that came after.

The gruesome images kept coming. The same soil that preserved King Priam's Treasure held the bones of the slaughtered warriors. The fields of France, reflected in my grandfather's pale eyes, revealed what he'd wanted to keep hidden from me: bodies of soldiers shot or stabbed, boys as young as he had been in his photograph. And the burying ground not far away held not only dead slaves alongside their relics but also British soldiers ambushed by the Swamp Fox, Indians killed by settlers. When I had unearthed the skull, why, I'd touched them all.

I approached the old horse. Still motionless, he appeared to be trying to prick both ears, though only the right one cooperated. Now I too heard what he surely did—the far-off thunder. Up close, his back swaying, belly drooping, rear end skin and bones, Troy looked nothing like the sturdy wooden horse in my book. I stopped close to his good side, but, as though he were focused on waiting—for what, I wasn't sure…the storm?—he paid me no attention. Why should he? I didn't have so much as a raisin in my pocket. And neither did I have anything left to say to him. Some horse of legend. Even so, as I did the day of Cleo's funeral, I longed to believe he could carry me away from wherever I was and into legend.

Once, I had known whom to trust and whom to fear. But now the entire world seemed a battlefield. And enemies disguised themselves as friends, like Mr. Turnage.

Cleo's house. That was where I was going.

I'd overheard my parents wondering if Cleo's husband would be back to collect her things. Nobody around here had set eyes on Davis R. Boston or knew how to reach him.

"We'll wait a month," my mother said. "If he doesn't show up, then Starry and Evelyn should go in and do what needs to be done."

I wanted Cleo's house to stay the same, and I wanted…I had to see it again as I remembered it. No treasure I'd ever find would set my world to rights. Only Cleo's arms could do that. I didn't want Cleo to wander like Aunt Charlotte. Neither did I want her to be a ghost. I wanted Cleo back from the dead, as Troy had come back—but not changed, not scarred. Her house was safe, a place apart from the world of storms and wounds. And if Cleo's house was the same, maybe Cleo herself was somehow there—*the same.*

Dusk was coming on fast, and rain hung in the air like the smell of green things cut up fine—a spicy, peppery smell. I began to run across the pasture. A wind was coming in fits and starts. In front of me the branches of the sweet gum railed as though they were fighting off the heavy steel-gray sky. Thunder grumbled, rolled closer. Crickets and tree frogs screamed back and forth from one cluster of trees to another.

I felt that my feet were crossing No Man's Land onto the plains of Troy and back again. Running, yes, towards Cleo's house, but also towards woods where the Swamp Fox and his men jumped from trees and ambushed the British. Where the Klan might be congregating, planning another midnight raid. Where guerilla fighters might be poised to attack, as they were this very moment in jungles halfway around the world. I'd gathered from the men at Walter's Store as well as from the *Evening News* that the new war in Vietnam was just this sort of war, one of stealth and ambush.

Where was the bridge? I had followed the path through the woods where the sweet gum marked it. But the bridge, the board that crossed the ditch right here where the footpath ended, had vanished. Underbrush too tangled for feet lay to my right and left. Someone had moved the board—my father or Mr. Mac—to keep Cleo's house safe from trespassers.

But I was not a trespasser. My chest pounded. I grabbed a nearby tree to steady myself. I belonged there, with Cleo—where the Swamp Fox never was, or even the Indians. Outside history, further back than myth. There Cleo waited, forever apart from these storms, these battles.

I would have to go the long, roundabout way—that was all there was to it. By returning to the pasture and keeping to the edge of the woods, I could reach the tobacco field. Turning towards the swamp, I should be able to follow the ditch until it reached the built-up crossway between the tobacco field and the hayfield. Then, from Aunt Charlotte's, I could find the footpath through the pines to Cleo's house. But I'd have to hurry to outrun the night. If only my shoes weren't rubbing blisters on my heels…

Mosquitoes and horseflies, even deerflies, chased me—demons from Pandora's Box. My arms ached from waving them off. Still, they found ways to bite. For once, I wished for the waxy repellent my mother loved to smear all over Will and me before our fishing trips.

Thunder growled. I was in a race with the clouds that were bringing darkness faster and faster. If only I'd thought to grab a flashlight! At last I reached the barbed wire that divided the pasture from the tobacco field. I was still small enough to climb through, but not without scratching my legs and snagging my shirt. How—and where—Troy got through, I'd given up trying to guess. I stopped to catch my breath.

"I tried to stay in one piece," Mr. Mac had said, as though that explained everything.

I saw myself cracked like the doll from the trunk. I stood panting hard, but suddenly the air seemed too heavy to breathe. It had a yellowish tint, as though from the dust of cured tobacco, or mustard gas, as I imagined it.

I turned, fully expecting—in truth, hoping—to see the old horse. But Troy, who'd stalked me for months, even Troy had abandoned me.

I sank to my knees. The demons had caught up with me; my own wickedness had ambushed me. At once I knew that Cleo wouldn't have me, wouldn't want me. Why would she? I had as good as used the forbidden word to insult her that day near the pasture gate. Unforgivable. And if that wasn't enough, what I'd said to Will in the hayloft—Cleo, with her own third eye, must somehow have known. Despite Miss Cass's assurance, despite what I *knew*, I felt for sure that my cruelty—for that's what it was—had broken Cleo's heart.

I would apologize right now. It couldn't be too late. On my knees I begged for forgiveness. I reached for the knife in my pocket, but it must have slipped out at Miss Cass's place. My hands went to the ground. An arrowhead or just a common chunk of flint would slice down my forehead and cheek, like the crack in Miss Lila's doll, or even rip through my lip and scar it like Will's. Would such a wound be atonement enough?

The wind picked up, bringing a sudden chill. Darkness was coming on fast. I could barely see, but I searched in the weeds and dirt until at last my hand curled around something rock-shaped. But the dampish clod intermixed with flecks of grass disintegrated between my fingers. I put my hand to my nose. Horse dung—Troy's. As I had done in a fit of temper and self-hatred with the clump of mud when Will won those races in the tobacco field, I mashed the manure into my face. I rubbed it on both cheeks, my forehead, my neck, my arms. I would do what-ever it took.

I pulled my blistered heels out from the backs of my shoes and stood. I shuffled forward, slapping at the horseflies that still circled my head. Thunder boomed like a cannon; the ground shook. Rain rushed down like a barrage of bullets or arrows, stinging and sharp. The heels of my shoes flopping, I ran through the weeds that bordered the ditch.

Until I found myself in the swamp, I had no idea that I'd overshot the path.

My hands shielded my eyes from the Spanish moss and bri-ers, but thorns ripped into my legs and arms. My shins kept hit-ting cypress knees. Mud oozed into my shoes. At least, thanks to the drought, the swamp was mud instead of waist-high water swimming with cottonmouths.

A commotion surrounded me. Thunder, yes, but something more. A crashing sound that seemed to come from all directions. Who? Who was it this time? Guerrilla soldiers? Convicts who really did escape and murder innocent people? The Scurlock boys with their guns? Or their father and Mr. Turnage in hoods and robes, with a cross whittled to a dagger's point? I turned around in circles, my arms out to shield me from the briers, to push away the danger. I could barely see anything. Then—the loud squawks of a great blue heron. Wing-beats. I'd stumbled too close to a nest.

Cattails stood as tall as I was. The weeds beneath were dense and waist-high. Thick ropes of briers curled around in them. Mud sucked off my right shoe. I sank to my hands and knees to try to find it, but I could see nothing and felt only muck and the slimy knees of the cypresses and roots risen to the surface. I knew they were roots, but they felt like bones—long and slick. They *were* bones. My hands—I was sick to my stomach—groped ribs, leg bones, antlers. A deer, all that was left of it.

Amid the darkness and pouring rain, I'd lost all sense of direction. To find my bearings, I had to get out of the swamp. Will's witch-trees creaked and moaned. The mossy hags had long, long fingers. Their razor-sharp nails tore my skin. They wore whip snakes for bracelets.

In front of me, illuminated by a slash of lightning, was the stretch of scorched land. Leaving the poor shelter of the trees, I threw off my other shoe and ran along what I thought was the road. Thunder shook the ground again. I ran faster until my bare foot came down on something cold and steel-sharp. I fell. Stunned, I saw myself facedown not in mud but in Troy's lightning-gashed side—my mouth, nose, and eyes filled with the thick rotten soup of the wound.

Spitting out muck, ashes and crumbs of brick, I recognized the smells of burnt wood and tobacco. The charred ruins of the barn. My forehead throbbed. My right arm had twisted under me and felt out of joint. Something—a brick?—poked into my stomach. But my foot felt strangest of all. I sat up and pulled it towards me. Another burst of lightning. Blood was swirling out as it had from Trudy's head, looking as though it would never stop, though rain kept washing it away. When lightning struck again, I made out the sharp edge of the collapsed tin roof. The rain drummed loudly.

"It's not bad," I told myself, in order to make it so. "My foot doesn't hurt—not bad, anyway."

By the sound of his hooves plodding towards me, I recognized the old horse. He thumped closer and closer until finally— the odors of blackened earth and tobacco and wet horse gathering into a swelling warmth—Troy stood over me. At first I was frightened. In the rain and lightning, his scarred side looked raw and somehow bloody. He stomped his front hooves. He could easily kick me, as Cleo had feared he might. But he only shook his mane, then lowered his head towards mine.

In that other storm, lightning-struck, he'd lain half-dead in Jesse's pen. I'd gone to him. Now he had come to me.

"Troy." My teeth were chattering. "Good boy."

How did he do it? Escape the pasture the way he did? He had powers, but not from the Devil as Cleo thought. Like Pegasus, he had wings. And he'd come, even in the storm, with his wings and his third eye, to help me. To save me. I began to feel forgiven. I pulled myself to my knees and reached up, feeling for Troy's mane. "Let me—just—hang on."

Lightning flashed, or I wouldn't have seen it happen. Quickly, more quickly than he ever did anything, Troy twisted his head, raised his lip over his teeth, and bit me. Chomped down. I gripped my right forearm. He stumbled off and vanished behind the curtain of rain and dark.

I pulled myself to standing. "Don't think. Just walk," I said out loud. The rain tasted odd, salty.

With every step, I could sense the wound in my foot tearing, deepening. I began to feel lightheaded. Was this what fainting was like? "I *am* a hard rock," I repeated. I couldn't allow myself to faint.

My foot throbbed. It had a rhythm of its own. My arm throbbed and burned where the horse had bitten me. It had a separate rhythm. I tried to pretend that I was not myself but a companion to this drenched, limping girl trailing blood. As calmly as I had told Trudy to roll out from under Troy's hooves, I told the girl to keep walking. All you need to do, I said, is keep to a furrow. Row after row, when lightning struck, the bare stalks of tobacco shook like skeletons.

I heard a wheezing sound. It was coming from me. Inside my chest, a runaway horse. Then, the reins in my hands. I curled my fingers around them and pulled back, slow and steady. I reoriented myself.

My thigh hit the edge of the porch. Not comprehending at first, I groped at the wooden planks. Then I hoisted myself up and crawled forward on hands and knees. And almost made it through the door.

When I came to, I was lying on my side in a shallow pool. Half of me was inside Aunt Charlotte's house, my legs still out on the porch. My fingers were a sticky mass of something that felt like spider webs, and the taste of salt and vomit were in my mouth. How long had I lain like this? Rain poured through the roof, swelling the pool.

My foot pounded. Wiping off my trembling fingers as best I could, I brought my foot into my lap. Too dark to see. Just as well—I could feel the heat of my blood spilling through my fingers and onto my thigh. Pressure. I needed a bandage. All I had was what I wore—t-shirt, shorts, underpants. I pulled off my shirt, and pain shot through my shoulder and arm. I wound the shirt around my foot. How deep was Troy's bite I couldn't tell. It wasn't gushing blood.

I *needed* to get to Cleo's house. Surely I'd suffered enough for her to take pity on me. It was an easy path, even in the dark, even in the rain. I stood. Then sat. How was I going to walk with a shirt around my foot? Besides, bees had gotten into my head. The buzzing wouldn't stop.

I crawled inside through the doorway, around the water funneling down from a hole in the roof, and found a dry corner. "I'm sorry, Cleo." I shivered. "I tried to reach you."

Though the whinny startled me, I wasn't surprised. There in the strobe-like bursts of lightning, thrust in through a window opening—Troy's head. The old horse stared at me. His entire muzzle had turned white; around his eyes was white. And his blind eye, the pupil completely gone, a milky globe. Again he whinnied. He kicked at the house. He rolled his head from side to side, shaking his mane, showing his teeth. Now he neighed and kicked as though to break through the wall. I crouched in my corner. "Get on!" I whispered.

Gone. Then back, this time in the doorway. The crippled horse had climbed onto the porch. He stomped at the floorboards, which cracked beneath his hooves.

The lightning was so violent, the peal of thunder so deafening, Aunt Charlotte's house shuddered around me. I thought it was struck. Why, I could smell it—the sickening mix of smells from Jesse's pen the day lightning had felled Troy. Fire. How in all this rain could the house catch fire? I had to get out.

Troy had vanished. I crawled onto the porch, then dropped into the mud; I kept crawling towards the path to Cleo's house.

The rain slowed to a drizzle. Tree frogs began complaining, bullfrogs bellowing along with them. I stopped and looked back, but I saw no flames. The full moon came out from a hole in the clouds. A dense fog—a moving blanket—hovered over the tall grass. Was I dreaming? It seemed to hold a thousand spirits swaying and singing. I tried to sing with them, but my voice came out a whisper. "The storm is passing over…" I could just make them out in the fog, the figures—African slaves in long ragged dresses and bare feet, the Swamp Fox wearing a tri-cornered hat with a fox tail attached, black-haired Indians with ropes of beads.…There were more: the war dead risen with shields and spears from the plains of Troy and from the trenches in France with rifles and bayonets, and those three murdered men in Mississippi—two white, one black—the little girls in Alabama wearing their Sunday best, Aunt Charlotte and Cleo in turbans and aprons. Then, as though a spell was lifted, thousands of frogs, hardly bigger than raindrops, leapt where the spirits had been.

Cleo shook out a quilt and laid it over me. She put her hand on my forehead. I took a deep breath. "I couldn't get to you, but you came to me. Aunt Charlotte…She must have told you I was here."

With Cleo I was sheltered now, far beyond the commotion, the riot of spirits surrounding us. "Head hurts. Do I have a fever?" I murmured.

Cleo lifted me and held me in her lap and rocked me. "The storm is passing over," she sang, then hummed. She smelled just like herself, of wood smoke and peaches.

But it was Mr. Mac's arms that held me, Cleo's smells mingling with that of cigar and sweat and, faintly, Old Spice aftershave. My grandfather laid me on the seat of his truck. He fumbled with my foot. Then he wrapped something around my arm and put…perhaps it was his handkerchief on my forehead.

"I got hurt." I squinted against the light of his cab. "Don't get stuck, Mr. Mac," I mumbled and tried to smile.

❦

I lay flat on a table under the too-bright lights of the emergency room. A doctor was giving me shots, which I could hardly feel. I had to keep still while he stitched up first my foot and then my forehead. I'd gashed it deeply at the hairline; it was my own blood that had turned the rain salty. My shoulder, he said, was sprained. As for Troy's bite, it was shallow. Still, I'd have to watch that it didn't become inflamed.

Mr. Mac tugged on one of my braids. "I saw that old horse where he wasn't supposed to be," he said and smiled, the corners of his mouth turning down. "I figured I'd find you there too."

21: Golden Leaf

Not even a week later, in the gray light of the mid-August dawn, Will and I were riding with Mr. Mac in the big farm truck. Bundles of tobacco wrapped in burlap filled the back of it, and Jesse was following us in a tractor, hauling a trailer that was just as full. On the opening day of the tobacco market—late because of the summer's drought—all the world seemed to be pouring into Mullins. Only five miles from Marion (our high schools were football rivals), the town was famous for its warehouses and for the good prices promised at market. The highway looked like a parade of farmers.

The preceding Saturday, there had been a real parade down Main Street to celebrate the Tobacco Festival. My whole family had gone, except Mr. Mac. The mayor of Mullins led off in his shiny red tractor, hauling one huge burlap-wrapped pile of cured tobacco. The mayor of Marion eased past in a big black convertible. There were marching bands from Mullins High School, then Marion High School; cheerleaders turned cartwheels alongside them. Next came the colored marching bands who stepped high and kept together and stayed on key. Their cheerleaders danced, moving their hips. Miss Golden Leaf and her court rode on a float fancy with pink and yellow tissue paper flowers and real cured tobacco leaves. Mr. Tomlinson from the Purina Feed and Seed Store drove his Model-T. Mr. Ajax marched beside him and blew his whistle. Miss Mullins, Miss Marion, Miss Farm Bureau, and even Miss South Carolina rode on floats. United States Senator Thurmond and State Senator Gasque waved from their own long convertibles. There were other fancy cars—among them a black sedan like the car that had followed Miss Cass and me, the one that had come to Miss Cass's house that night. I recognized the red interior. But it couldn't be the same one. Two school principals, grammar and high school, waved from the windows.

As early as it was this opening morning, already stray leaves of tobacco littered the roads. Other farmers had hauled their crops during the night. I leaned out the window and waved back to Jesse. On the market floor, for the buyers' inspection, he could arrange the leaves on top of the piles like an artist, fanning them out in perfect spirals.

Once we turned onto the road leading to the warehouses, trucks and tractors followed each other at a crawl. Mr. Mac eased past Brick Warehouse, then Liberty. Around the corner were Twin States and—finally—the Golden Leaf Warehouse. Mr. Mac preferred Golden Leaf because he was friends from way back with Mr. Teasley, the auctioneer who worked there. He knew by name all the women who worked in the brightly lit office. He joked with them as he did sometimes with the farm workers.

It was my birthday. Yesterday I'd had a party with just my family and Stephanie and Margot. Stephanie gave me *A Hard Day's Night*, the new Beatles album, and Margot brought a bottle of bubble bath. My parents had gotten a display case that fit perfectly in one corner of my room. "For your treasures," Mama had said.

Mr. Mac brought me Lila's doll. He had managed to stick her leg back on, but she was still a mess with her cracked face, her tattered dress, her head bald in patches.

"She's a real antique!" Stephanie said.

"She can go in your cabinet," Margot added.

"We might be able to find a new dress for her," my mother offered. "Perhaps even some shoes."

Now, as soon as the truck pulled up to the warehouse, Will and I jumped out. We knew we had to stay together—and stay out of the way. I grabbed Will's hand and led him to a spot right in front of the office. There we sat and ate boiled peanuts out of little soggy brown bags. Workers rushed all over the place, wheeling into the huge warehouse bundles of tobacco on flat carts and placing them in rows. Once Mr. Mac and Jesse got the tobacco in, our grandfather would come find us. Then we would walk around and visit with the other farmers until the auction started.

The smell of cured leaf grew stronger by the minute. It would permeate the whole town before the day was out. People joked that it smelled like money.

"Remember the story of King Midas, Will? Everything he touched turned to gold. On the farm, we cured the tobacco; we turned these leaves gold. Now they're turning everything gold. Don't you see?"

Will nodded. He was busy with his peanuts. The doctor in Columbia had brought his fever down. He seemed to feel just fine, though his upper lip was red and tender.

I wished the market would go on forever. Then I took it back. I knew that when the Midas touch turned everything gold, everything died. Sort of like the kudzu I saw every day of my life. Miles of trees, the two blacksmith's shops, the one-room schoolhouse where Miss Lila had taught, an old country store—kudzu vines smothered them, turning them all into leafy burial mounds. People could be like that, holding on to things, trying to keep change from happening. The old men at Walter's Store—in fact, most of the white people I knew—were like that with colored people. I had been like that in my own way, with Will and Cleo. What was more, I had been selfish, not wanting to let go of Cleo—not wanting to let her go and be with the spirits.

The warehouse was getting noisier by the minute. Electric fans roared. More and more people were pouring in, some of the farmers in coats and ties, bending over their crops, making sure everything looked right.

Mr. Mac stood in front of us, grinning. "Better come with me, else you might get auctioned off." He wore a short-sleeved white dress shirt and suspenders, but that was as far as he'd gone towards dressing up.

Near the middle of the warehouse, Jesse was busy arranging the leaves of our tobacco from the center out, like spokes of a wheel. I leaned against a pile still covered in burlap and took the weight off my right foot. Still bandaged because of the stitches and sore, it had begun to throb.

My parents had not seemed surprised or even upset when they got home to find me fresh out of the emergency room and with a stitched forehead, arm and foot wound thick with bandages. They were too worn out to dwell on my injuries, my "war wounds," as I came to think of them. They knew only what Mr. Mac told them—that I had stayed out too late on the farm, got caught in the rain, lost my shoes, and had a little accident. As for the horse bite, I confessed that I'd aggravated Troy. Nor was Will impressed by the five stitches in my forehead or the eight in my foot. "You have scars where nobody will notice," he'd said. "You have the good kind of scars."

But the next morning, my parents had been shocked to see me once again on the front page of the paper—Miss Cass and me flanking the charred one-armed cross. I had to explain about Mr. Mac and the hospital and Miss Cass and the Klan. Mama, tearing up, blamed herself for letting me stay home. When I told Papa about Lamar Scurlock and Mr. Turnage, he hit the wall with his fist.

Once again the phone rang all morning. My parents' friends were glad I was safe, but what on earth was I doing spending the night with Cassandra Bearclaw? (Of course, the older ones said "Cassandra Oliver.") No one seemed particularly surprised that the Klan had paid her a visit. After all, she was an eccentric bound and determined to stir up trouble. People seemed almost to blame her for the incident.

Stephanie phoned to say that she'd just seen Joyce Ann Richardson at the stables. Several of the popular girls had begun taking riding lessons. I was showing off, Joyce Ann had said. Worse, she'd called Cassandra Bearclaw—"*Bearclaw,* can you believe that name?" Stephanie quoted her—an Indian queen taking up for the colored. And I was her papoose, both of us out to make trouble.

I wasn't hurt by Joyce Ann's comments. They were predictable. But I was upset that Stephanie was now riding with the popular group. Once school started, she would throw me over, I suspected.

I did end up with one scar that was both visible and permanent. Troy's bite was shallow, the doctor had said. He didn't think it would become inflamed. In fact, the wound got infected right away. The red, puss-filled crescent on the back of my arm did eventually heal and lighten in color, but a raised scar would be with me, just above my wrist, for the rest of my life.

At the warehouse, Will and I followed Mr. Mac around while he chatted with the other farmers about the disappointing North Carolina crop, the price of the Georgia leaf, the drought, the recent rain.

I grabbed Will's elbow. There she was—right by the front entrance—Miss South Carolina. She wore a crown and a sash with her title written in glitter. Her short dress was a delicate-looking pale yellow chiffon, and she had high heels to match. Reporters taking flash pictures crowded around her while she posed near various piles. She'd pick up a few leaves here and there, raise them to her little turned-up nose, smile and nod.

"She ought to come smell our tobacco," I told Will. "Ours is the best and the prettiest."

"Well, go get her," he said.

But I couldn't move. With her jeweled crown and floating dress, Miss South Carolina was far too beautiful for me to even think of approaching her.

Suddenly, it was starting. Lines formed on either side of the row of tobacco piles nearest the right wall. Mr. Teasley, in his straw hat and red bow tie, took the lead. His rapid chanting was a mix of song and speech that the buyers and no one else could understand. Next came those men in dark suits, the buyers from Philip Morris, American, R. J. Reynolds—the "fat cats," as Mr. Mac called them. They winked and nodded and made little signs with their hands. The farmer whose crop was being auctioned followed. Then came the other farmers, murmuring among themselves. Most were smoking nervously or chewing tobacco. A solid year of hard work—here's where it finally paid off, where the Bright Leaf more or less literally turned to gold. Or didn't.

It would take at least an hour before the procession, snaking along row after row, reached our tobacco, so Will and I kept towards the end of the line with Mr. Mac. Our father, in the tan suit he wore to his office, joined us. He and Mr. Mac seemed to be relaxing a little. That meant the leaf was selling well.

I began to limp, and Will was tired. So Papa walked us back around to the McDaniel crop. He picked us up and sat us each on top of a pile. It was the best leaf there; I had heard other farmers, playing the leaves in their hands, compliment the color, the weight. I lay back on the soft dusty tobacco, proud that it had come from my family. Will copied me. What a shame, I thought, that this beautiful hard-won crop would be hauled off to factories and ground by machines into brown stuffing for cigarettes.

"Well, looky who's here. I had a feeling I'd see you."

Miss Cass was dressed as usual, like a man but with that gigantic black pocketbook. A purplish-green bruise showed beneath the brim of her straw hat. She grabbed my wrist and lifted an edge of my bandage to peek at the bite mark. "I heard about your run-in. The old horse got you good, didn't he? Battle scars are marks of courage, don't you know? What do you think, Will? They show you've fought your way out; you're strong—the hero."

Miss Cass ruffled Will's hair. "You'll have to come see me soon, Will. You like animals? Of course you do. It's like a zoo at my ranch, isn't it, Etta? A regular menagerie."

"I didn't know you grew tobacco, too." My eyes went straight to Miss Cass's neck. The beads were nearly hidden beneath her shirt collar.

"Don't. But this is the biggest party in the state. I wouldn't miss it for the world, would you?"

"It's even my birthday, and I wouldn't miss it."

"Well, my land, happy birthday! And what fine timing. I have a little present for you." She reached her arm far down into the mouth of her pocketbook. "I've been wanting to give you something ever since you saved Nod's life—even before you rescued me from the Klan."

She held out the sachet of smelly herbs. "But, we forgot to give this to Mr. Mac. Hand it to him after the auction, please, ma'am."

She then produced my pocketknife. "Found this in my bed."

Miss Cass turned towards Will. "Did you know your sister saved my little precious puppy from a certain miserable death? Well, she did. And I'm sure you know all about the 'late unpleasantness.'" She patted the lump on her head.

Miss Cass reached back into her bag. She withdrew, threaded through her callused fingers, a strand of beads from which hung a smooth pendant resembling in its crooked tornado-like shape the jawbone of a miniature horse. I had seen in Cherokee a rattle made from a horse's jawbone. I held my breath.

"That skinny spirally part—that's the heart of the shell. Columella they call it. The beads are made from shells, too, don't you know—the purple ones from clams, the whitish ones from whelks. Bear left me a shoebox half-full of old wampum beads. Shame to keep them stored away. Now *these*"—she fingered the pair of brownish-gray cylinders half the length of cigarettes that flanked the pendant—"these I found myself, back beside my barn of all places. Color of dirt. Hard as heck to find. Mr. Walter's the only other person I know of around here that has any Pee Dee beads."

I had never imagined that the drab tubes on the plaque in Walter's Store were beads. No wonder I'd never found any myself. I hadn't known what to look for.

"I found that worn-down shell for the pendant down at Pawley's Island….Fine tobacco here." She patted the fanned-out stack next to me. "Mac and your papa grow the best."

I lowered the beads over my head. I couldn't stop grinning. I remembered what the small beads meant—white for knowledge and purity, purple for what made us human and imperfect. The longer brownish beads would connect me to the land and its history. But the heart of the shell, what would it signify? My soul?—as Dr. Raintree might have suggested? I rubbed its polished surface.

"That's where the song begins," Miss Cass said, as if reading my mind. "Put it up to your ear." I pressed the cupped top of the pendant to my ear. But I heard nothing beyond the auctioneer's nasal singing and the jumbled chattering that echoed throughout the warehouse. "The heart and the spirit—the breath of the song, don't you know—joining together," whispered Miss Cass. "Now when you get home, you grab some hair from your horse's mane and tie it around the top of the shell. That'll give you good luck."

Troy. He had been missing since the storm, for six days now. Mr. Mac said his headlights had caught the horse standing right beside me in the mud, but I had no recollection of that. I'd last seen him acting like a wild thing in the doorway of Aunt Charlotte's house. I figured he was wandering. He would wander back to the mule barn when he was good and ready. I touched the swollen bite that burned and throbbed. As far as I was concerned, he could take his time.

Miss Cass turned to Will. "Your sister looks like an Indian princess, doesn't she? Prettier than that beauty queen in her yellow dress." Will rolled his eyes.

I didn't know what to say. No one besides my parents and Cleo had ever called me pretty, and they didn't count. With Miss Cass it was different. "Indian princess," she had said. "A hero," she had also said, with "marks of courage."

Miss Cass looked over to the procession of buyers and farmers. "Time to join the crowd. You two come see me, now."

The auctioneer's song grew louder. It was like a sort of spiritual, the music winding up and down. The buyers responded—two fingers up, three fingers down, a wink, a nod. I touched the beads that lay on my breastbone. The Jewels of Helen.

I felt surrounded by treasure. All this Bright Leaf—and now Indian beads of my very own.

"Can I see?" Will was jealous.

I handed him the strand. "Wow," he said. "Real wampum."

Will's swelling was down. But our mother had been right. He still didn't look like everybody else. I wanted to think that school would be better for him this year. That maybe there would be some new friends who saw past his face to his sweet temper'ment, as Cleo would have said—though I suspected that his temperament was not a whole lot different from anyone else's. But the odds of Will's making friends were slim. Slim to none.

At least for now his spirits were as high as anybody's. All eyes were on the Bright Leaf. Nothing else mattered.

22: Treasure

June 25, 2005

I had no way of knowing on my twelfth birthday that the days of the tobacco auctions were numbered, that the long green rows and dense fields of Bright Leaf, which gave the region its special look, would disappear. Never did it occur to me that my father would one day sell off our own fields until all that remained was the land just behind my parents' and Mr. Mac's houses—land that included little more than the burying ground, the Aunt Charlotte field, and what remained of Cleo's house.

By the 1970s it was all but impossible for family-owned tobacco farms like ours to survive. Of course by then the harmful effects of smoking were widely known, and even the manufacturers of cigarettes had to admit the connection between tobacco use and cancer. So, here in Marion County, one family farm after another disappeared.

Papa's talk of moving to a city never amounted to anything more than talk. Once I grew up, however, I lived in many cities. But every summer I returned to the farm to visit my parents and Will, who was raising his own family in the house that had been Mr. Mac's. I came from Virginia, Massachusetts, even Greece and Italy, where I lived and worked—not as an archaeologist who discovered treasures but rather a curator who preserved them in museums, who held to the light whatever truth they revealed—the ugly as well as the beautiful—and placed them within the jigsaw puzzle of history.

Alone in my childhood room, I often took stock of the hodge-podge of mementos that filled the shelves behind the glass doors of my display case. *For your treasures*, my mother had said. Indeed. I had, like Miss Lila with her trunk, assembled a treasure box of memories.

This particular visit in the summer of 2005 was no different from any other, except for the recent event that plunged me back into that summer when I turned twelve and my journey into the world began in earnest. Edgar Ray "Preacher" Killen, the ringleader of the Mississippi Klansmen who murdered the three civil rights workers, had finally been sent to jail. He was convicted on June 21, forty-one years to the day after he and more than a dozen others killed Michael Schwerner, James Chaney, and Andrew Goodman. It had taken that long. He was eighty, the age my grandfather was when he died.

No one had believed Mr. Mac, short of breath as he was, could beat the odds and live so long. I pulled from my cabinet the photograph I'd eventually taken from Miss Lila's room: Mr. Mac, young and dashing in his dress uniform from the First World War. His eyes stared out like new silver coins. Soon enough, gas would cripple his lungs, the bursting of shells would fray his nerves, his young wife would die. I lifted carefully Miss Lila's doll, with her battle scars, as Miss Cass would have called them.

Once I started, I couldn't stop pulling things from my cabinet. A sheaf, a "hand," of cured Bright Leaf, now brown and crumbling but still smelling faintly of the barns of my childhood—this was a souvenir from 1978, the last year our family farmed tobacco. I'd spent that summer at home helping my mother look after Papa. He'd lost half a lung to cancer. A survivor, he too had beaten the odds.

A jar of preserves—Cleo's—had gradually turned black. The envelope beside it was stained and brittle. I emptied its contents onto my bed. I hoped, inhaling, to find once again the complex odors from Cleo's house, the last time I ever set foot in it. But I smelled only the musty scent of old photographs.

❧

It was in October 1964, two months after Cleo's death, when my parents finally tracked down Davis R. Boston at a county fair in Conway. I didn't get to meet him, so he never seemed a real person to me. In a hurry, according to my mother, and making a mess in the process, he packed up the pictures and most of Cleo's jars of preserves and pickles. Also some odds and ends from the armoire. He wasn't interested, he said, in the furniture. He was a traveling man.

Starry and Evelyn borrowed the farm truck to haul off the rest. My mother and Jesse helped them. Cleo's clothes, her record player, most of the furniture, her pots and pans…Evelyn was getting married soon, but not to Roscoe who, I supposed, was in Germany by now, or else in Vietnam. Evelyn took what she could to help set up housekeeping.

At last, after everyone else in the world had been there, my mother agreed to take me to Cleo's house. Will didn't have any interest, especially since Mr. Mac had promised to show him the World War I artifacts in the trunk. Will was having bad stomachaches; they had started right after school began. Sometimes he threw up. Dr. Monroe suspected ulcers, but I knew better: kids were picking on him.

The weather had cooled. That Saturday's sky was as bright and blue as it had been the morning of Cleo's funeral. My mother, turning her station wagon off the highway into an almost invisible opening in the pines, crept along over ruts and bumps. Even when Cleo was alive, the road was rarely used. The rusting shell of a car was off to one side, almost hidden in the brush. I kept fingering the beads Miss Cass had given me. Afraid that I might break or lose them, I wore them only on special occasions.

Cleo's house looked shabbier than I remembered. Already the yard was wild with weeds. Had the front porch always sagged? Several windowpanes were cracked. "Moving accidents," Mama explained. Still, the chinaberry trees that flanked it looked like gold clouds, brilliant against the blue of the sky.

My mother opened the front door. "Watch for snakes now. And spiders."

I had to stop just inside the doorway. Cleo *was* here. The smell was faint but familiar—a smoke-tinged mixture of peaches and cloves. I shut my eyes and took a deep breath.

Everything left behind was in a mess. Cleo's mattress was pushed up in front of the fireplace. Starry and Evelyn had taken the white-painted metal frame and headboard. The table that had held the photographs was on its side, one leg broken off and lying beside it. A half-dozen record sleeves littered the floor where the record player had sat. But the wardrobe remained intact, doors ajar.

"It was just too big," my mother said. "Too big and heavy to move. Even Jesse couldn't budge it. I wonder where on earth it came from." She shook her head. "I don't like seeing Cleo's house like this. I know it doesn't matter, but I'm going to sweep a little. And tidy the kitchen. You go ahead and look around. Just keep an eye out for snakes and—"

"I know. I *know*."

I ran my hands along the wall near the wardrobe. "Can I— would it be all right if I take something? Just to remember her by?"

"I think Cleo would be pleased."

As carefully as I could, without tearing through it, I removed the picture of Martin Luther King in his jail cell. I knelt to gather the records, but they were only cardboard jackets, empty inside.

My mother was in the kitchen now, shutting drawers, opening and closing cabinets.

I peered into the wardrobe. It appeared empty, but since the sun was coming in at a low and blinding angle, I couldn't tell for sure. I would know only by reaching in with my hands. And—Mama was right—there could well be spiders or even snakes.

Still, this was my one chance. Since the night I ended up at Aunt Charlotte's house, soaking wet and bleeding, my fingers sticky with webs or blood or both, I was somehow less afraid of spiders—though I was far from fond of them. I slipped my beads inside the neck of my t-shirt. They were cold against my skin, the pendant bulky. The strands of Troy's mane I'd added, as Miss Cass suggested, felt scratchy.

Slowly, on tiptoes, I stretched my arm across the top shelf and patted the entire surface. Nothing. Only dust. And a loose button. Plastic, not valuable. I held my breath and swallowed hard. I felt along the second shelf. Again, nothing. The third and fourth were empty as well. I had to sit on the floor to explore the fifth and bottom shelf. It was especially dusty and gritty. Three more ordinary buttons turned up, but not one coin, not even one piece of the jewelry from Davis R. Boston's picture-taking business.

I rocked back and hugged my knees. The wardrobe sat on four squatty legs. I sprawled flat on my stomach and reached as far as I could underneath it. The beads and shell pendant pressed almost painfully into my chest. My hand and arm raked over grit and what felt like cobwebs. I clenched my teeth. I touched something flat, something that rustled. An envelope. When I could catch my breath, I brushed off the dirt and shook out the contents. Photographs. Perhaps in his haste, Davis R. Boston had let the envelope slip, then accidentally kicked it. Or had Cleo slid it underneath the wardrobe herself, for me to find?

My mother sat beside me and set a jar between us. "Fig preserves. Way back in a cabinet. Mr. Boston must have overlooked it. The only thing left that Cleo made."

Together we went through the pictures. Wearing necklaces and a head cloth, similar to the one I had seen earlier, there was Cleo in the dotted swiss dress.

"Do you think this is her wedding outfit?" I whispered.

"Maybe. But I've never seen a veil like that," Mama said.

Another print, badly faded, showed Cleo and a man, holding hands. "Mr. Boston?"

It looked like him, she said, but of course he was years older now and had white hair.

There were several snapshots, from the chest up, of the man wearing a dark jacket and a hat—some serious, some smiling. He was handsome; his smile put me in mind of Evelyn's old boyfriend, Roscoe. My mother nodded. "That's definitely Mr. Boston."

In one print a pair of young girls were holding hands in front of a tobacco barn, one tall and thin, the other short and chubby. Starry and Cleo. Had to be. The girls grinned straight into the camera. In another, a very black and lean old woman in a long dress and huge white apron sat on a porch. I knew that porch.

"Aunt Charlotte?"

"I bet so. We'll ask Mr. Mac," my mother said.

Finally I held a print that was fading at the edges. It was of Cleo's baby sleeping, a flower in his hands, a duplicate of the one she had kept on her table. I angled it in order to catch the light.

"Oh, Etta," Mama said. "It's a funeral portrait. People used to do that. Take pictures of their loved ones, especially children, before they buried them."

I felt a little sick. I'd never heard of such a thing. And yet I was fascinated. I searched every inch of the small photograph for something—anything—to signify death. I stared at Eugene's closed eyelids and long lashes, his full lower lip meeting the top one in a slight pout. His small fingers were positioned around a lily. The lace that rose to his dimpled chin was a little blurry, as though there had been a breath just when the camera's shutter clicked. The only clue was that the bed beneath the infant resembled the satin mattress of a casket. But that was all. Everything on the surface signified sleep. I tried to stop looking, but I only looked harder. In pale script, scrawled across the lower left corner, was the photographer's name—D. R. Boston. My mother took the picture from me and slipped it back into the envelope.

We sat for a few more minutes. Inside the heavy beam of sunlight falling onto the floor danced millions of dust motes. The birds had not yet left for winter and still chattered in the trees. I listened for a sound beyond. But Cleo's spirit was silent. Perhaps she was with Eugene and her mama and daddy after all.

As soon as I got back to my room, I placed inside my curio cabinet the few things I'd salvaged from Cleo's house. The envelope held a Cleo I had never known, a past that I had not been a part of. And that was all right now.

"Look!" Without knocking, Will rushed into my room. He wore Mr. Mac's cap and held the gas mask up to his face. He looked more like a gargoyle than ever. "Mr. Mac's gonna give me the knife when I'm sixteen. You know it's sharp as a razor."

I fought back a sudden wave of jealousy. I hadn't thought I'd want the army things—I'd had no desire to see them again. But for Will to own them instead of me...when *I* was the one who'd suffered the trenches of France, the plains of Troy.

Girl. That awful time in the mule barn when Will had found the kittens, he'd turned the word—most likely imitating members of his little league team—into an insult. And I, blindsided, had felt it.

All right, then. I was a girl, but not the sort of girl Will had implied. I was getting over my fear of spiders; I'd proved it at Cleo's house. I'd never be prissy like Stephanie and snooty Joyce

Ann and the popular girls. Neither could I imagine being like my mother or Cleo: nursing a sick child all summer long and picking up after others. Look at Miss Cass. Mr. Mac called her an odd duck; people talked about her behind her back. But she lived the way she wanted. She *lived*.

Even Mr. Mac could see me as a lawyer—at least a "lady" lawyer. But Dr. Raintree—now, he had taken me seriously. I was already an archaeologist-in-training. I was strong, a "hard rock" for real. Think of the rescuing I'd done in just one year. From Trudy to Miss Cass's dog to Miss Cass herself. Think of how I'd survived that thunderstorm. Like a hero, Miss Cass had said.

So what if Will got the gas mask. I had Miss Lila's doll, not a thing to play with but an object from history, an artifact. Of course the mask was an artifact as well. I'd have kept it safe in my cabinet; Will would treat it as a toy and tear it up.

I pictured Cleo, hands on her hips, giving me a stern look for my selfishness. I rolled my eyes at my brother. "You look like a big mosquito in that mask. Now shoo."

"Wait, I forgot something." He ran out and ran in again. "I almost forgot. Mr. Mac didn't want you to feel left out." He held out to me the thing I'd really wanted from Miss Lila's trunk, the tin fortune-telling bank. "Mr. Mac couldn't find the key to unlock it."

The cheerful gypsy still pointed to "Going on a Journey." I slipped a penny into the slot and shook the bank, hoping to jar loose the mechanism that turned the wheel. "Present for You," I whispered. "Come on."

Nothing moved. Again I shook it, jangling the coins inside, coins that Miss Lila must have saved, but still the wheel didn't budge. "Lucky Find," "Pleasure Ahead," "Surprise Coming"— these were just a few of the other possibilities. But the smiling fortune-teller with her rouged cheeks insisted on the journey. She pointed, her bejeweled arm sure of itself.

Will giggled. "You'll never get the money out, not without the key."

⚜

The bank was full. It had been for years and years. But I—even grown up—always tried to add one more penny. The wheel never budged. The fortune-teller with her red scarf and gaudy jewelry had sealed my fate. And the coins inside, some Miss Lila's, most of them mine, would stay, a hidden treasure.

If the wheel *had* to stay frozen, I'd always wished as a girl that the gypsy would point at "Present for You." Then I'd always be getting a present. A perpetual present—this, of course, was what the journey was, which had begun with Troy.

Here in my cabinet was the dull pocketknife, and here my cross with the tooth marks—the only thing made of real gold. Here were the newspaper clippings that had made me famous, though never popular, and here a piece of the burnt cross from Miss Cass's yard. (I was never able to see relics of the True Cross in Rome and Venice without recalling my own charred fragment.) And there in a tacky frame, topped with a yellow plastic horse's head and tiny plastic horseshoes glued to the sides, was a picture of me at eleven, forcing a smile, sitting on Troy's back. In it Troy had not yet kicked anyone or been struck by lightning. He was just an ordinary ill-tempered old horse, his head lowered in resentment or, at best, boredom.

The gift that wouldn't be ungiven. Out of habit, I rubbed the raised scar on my forearm. Troy had seemed to exist half in the world of the living and half in the world of the dead underground—he'd wandered with the spirits. So often he'd taken me by surprise, appearing as if from nowhere.

The low-slung belly of my Trojan horse had been both treasure chest and Pandora's Box. It was impossible for me to recall that year of Trudy's accident and Miss Cass's burning cross, the discovery of the burying ground and Cleo's "spells," which hinted at her coming death, without connecting it to the turmoil to come: other assassinations, the demonstrations and riots of the 1960s, the punishing war in Vietnam—events that swept through my adolescence.

Who said what to whom I didn't know, but after the summer when I turned twelve, Lamar Scurlock never sharecropped with Mr. Mac again. He stayed with Aubrey in his trailer and farmed his one field. His older sons joined the army. And as for Mr. Turnage, my parents and grandfather kept their money in his bank only until a second one moved into town. And never again did I go with Mr. Mac into that dark office with its polished desk and candy cigarettes.

I wondered from time to time if the dramatic incident with Miss Cass had ended the local Klan. At any rate, the Klansmen never appeared in public again. The few other sit-ins, the one march down Main Street, remained peaceful. (Finding out about them only after the fact, I never had another chance to join in.) Perhaps the *Evening News*, importing violence into everyone's home at dinnertime, was enough. From marchers beaten and bloodied in Alabama to burning buildings in California to military planes dropping bombs over Vietnam—all of this was more than enough.

I remembered going with Mr. Mac to Walter's Store one Saturday late that fall of 1964. It was the first cool snap of the season, and the potbelly stove was burning orange. The men— once I was grown, they formed in my memory a sort of Greek chorus—were still going on about the cross-burning in Miss Cass's yard. They seemed to have forgotten I had been there.

"Cassandra planning to stay on, you reckon?" Mr. Sneed rubbed his hands on his knees. He was wearing a stretched-out brown sweater and a red knit scarf, but he still seemed to be cold.

"Take more than a bonfire and a whack on the head to scare her off," Mr. Mac said.

Mr. Sneed turned to Mr. Oliver, blinking behind his thick glasses. "She's your sister, ain't she? You can't talk sense into her?"

"She's a strange bird, no question," Mr. Hamm piped up. He held a cigarette with the thumb and forefinger of his talon-like hand and leaned towards the stove. "But she does have a way with tomatoes." He tilted his head towards Mr. Mac. "Dangdest thing the way she keeps 'em growing all fall. Reckon it's that compost heap she keeps out by her barn?"

"She ain't got the sense of a mule, you ask me," Mr. Sneed said. "But she's stubborn as one, that's for sure."

"Verne, you need to shut your mouth." Finally Mr. Sneed had gotten Mr. Mac worked up enough to say something. "Her head wasn't any harder than yours to begin with. It was the Klan made it harder. Cass don't look at things the way other people do. She never will. But what difference does that make? Everything just—got out of hand."

"Cass lives here, belongs here, right where she started from," Mr. Oliver said, finally coming to her defense. His ears reddened and began to wag. "Same as you and me. The ranch is hers, left by her daddy and mine. Leave her be."

So Miss Cass was one of *them*; she belonged. It was her place to be among them as the eccentric, the subject of gossip, and that—I suspected—suited her just fine.

Mad Cassandra. Now, a lifetime later, I smiled at the thought. In mythology, the daughter of Troy's King Priam had both the gift of foresight and the curse that her predictions were never believed.

But I had taken to heart Miss Cass's prophecy—what she had said about totems.

Fate, it seemed, had never meant for me to unreceive the present of that old horse. At eleven, as secure in my child's world as within the walled city of Troy, I'd welcomed him. There was no returning him. I had begun my travels on his back, collecting along the way these souvenirs, a treasure to no one but myself—photographs and artifacts that pieced my life together with other lives.

I had devoted to one entire shelf of the curio cabinet my best specimens of pottery and all of my unbroken arrowheads and spear points, a collection that couldn't compare with Mr. Walter's. Here were trinkets from our family trip to Cherokee: a painted gourd that rattled, and the belt decorated with brightly colored plastic beads I'd used to mark the skull. Here was the sachet of Miss Cass's healing herbs that Mr. Mac refused to accept, even from me. And here also, draped over the death mask of King Tut on the faded cover of *Ancient Wonders of the World*, was my one authentic treasure, the one collector's item that I owned: the string of genuine beads, Mohawk and Pee Dee together. White for knowledge and purity, purple for human failings. In the center, the worn shell and the knotted strands from Troy's mane.

On the afternoon of my twelfth birthday, the day of the tobacco market when Miss Cass had given me the beads, I went with Mr. Mac in his truck to look for Troy. My grandfather assumed that the storm had blown a tree down onto the fence, giving Troy an opening to escape the pasture. It made sense to begin our search at Aunt Charlotte's house, where Mr. Mac claimed to have seen him last. "He stood there leaning like he always does. Right over you almost. Don't know how he got away so fast, once I stepped out my truck to fetch you."

But when we reached the shack, we forgot for a time about Troy. Aunt Charlotte's house had collapsed into a pile of splintered boards. The roof had caved in, taking all four walls with it. Anyone inside would have been crushed. *I* would have been crushed. Mr. Mac and I got out of the truck and stared.

"Must have happened right after I found you," Mr. Mac said. "Reckon the storm was too much for it. You were out, thank the good Lord."

I recalled the nearly constant lightning, the horse's frenzy, the deafening crack of thunder, the way the walls had shaken, the smells that brought to mind the old horse struck by lightning in Jesse's pen. The house was on fire; I'd been convinced of it.

There was a rustling in the bamboo. Already calling Troy's name, I turned.

Some were circling low over the bamboo; some, with their greasy black feathers and hunched shoulders and naked heads, were half-hidden inside the thick stand, tending a large dark-reddish mound. Mr. Mac grabbed my shirt to stop me from running straight into the bamboo.

Late that afternoon, Jesse came with a tractor and chains. Mr. Mac, leaning on a cypress walking stick, supervised the locking of the hooves, the dragging of the body out from the bamboo to a spot in the already burnt clearing where fire wouldn't spread. Bandanas covered our mouths and noses.

Had Troy been lightning-struck a second time? No way to tell for sure—the buzzards had worked him over.

I helped Jesse dig a channel for hay and wood, then stood back and watched as he pulled Troy over it. With Jesse and Mr. Mac, I covered the horse with more wood and hay. A proper pyre. Just before Jesse drenched everything with gasoline, I borrowed Mr. Mac's sharp pocketknife and cut off a piece of Troy's mane.

My first thought was that Troy had drawn the lightning meant for me, and while I'd never believe it wasn't his ghost that showed Mr. Mac where I was lying, now it came to me that from the very start the horse had been the target. And Troy—not any mere horse but one chosen...could it be by Zeus, who hurled the lightning?—had chosen me. My scar was proof.

"If you're lucky, one will find you," Miss Cass had said of totems. That old horse was my totem, and his true name was Journey.

As the flames rose, I recalled my vision of Troy standing untouched in the fire that had revealed the burial ground. But this fire *was* Troy—the heat, the orange-gold flames, the smells of burning wood and flesh, the smoke that rippled skyward, like a dark stream carrying millions of sparks into the deep-red clouds of sunset, into the purple dusk, finally into the black night. I could have sworn I saw them—the sparks becoming stars, storying the sky with constellations.

∽

As I'd taken to doing whenever I slept in my childhood room, I opened my curtains to the night sky. A moonless night of glittering constellations. Pegasus. As if I were speaking of Troy whose presence outside my window I could almost feel, I recited aloud a description of that constellation by the Roman poet Ovid, which I had known by heart for many years. An ancient passage, it was like an artifact that told of a mythical past: *And now when the stars shall spangle the blue sky, look up: you will see the neck of the steed. Now he enjoys the sky, to which he soared on wings, and he sparkles bright with fifteen stars.*

I placed the beads over my head and felt their weight on my chest. Even now I saw in my mind the image of Schliemann's wife decked out in the Jewels of Helen. Wrapping the loose strands from Troy's mane around my fingers and pressing the heart of the conch to my ear, I cupped my hand around it to form a sort of mouth, the missing lips of the shell.

The heart of the song, that's what Miss Cass had called it. As with other conchs—shells that were whole—I heard the distant tide, the wind, the surge of waves. Or was it the rising and falling tides of my own fortune, the echo of my ever-wandering steps? Around that bonelike shape, the air surrounding me gathered within the mouth of my hand—a tightly whirling storm. And I heard the sounds that had emerged from the fog that faraway night at Aunt Charlotte's: the many spirits of the field singing, Cleo humming her forgiveness, the ineffable horse who had marked me for life, huffing and stomping.

THE END

Acknowledgments

In writing this book I wished to recreate as honestly as I could a particular time and place. Though the characters of *Lightningstruck* and what happens to them are fictional, the novel is rooted in history. Much of its background stems from my personal knowledge of the landscape and people of Marion County, South Carolina, during the Civil Rights Era in the 1960s. For factual and anecdotal material, I found especially useful (and entertaining) the following sources: Robert D. Bass's *Swamp Fox: The Life and Campaigns of General Francis Marion* (1959), Debi Hacker and Michael Trinkley's *Indians, Slaves, and Freedmen in the Pee Dee Region of South Carolina* (1993), Dubose Heyward's *The Half-Pint Flask* (1929), the Historic Marion Revitalization Association's *Images of America: Marion* (1999), Joseph Mitchell's "The Mohawks in High Steel" (1949), Ovid's *Fasti* (Book 3), Eldred E. Prince's *Long Green: The Rise and Fall of Tobacco in South Carolina* (2000), *Life* magazines (January–December 1964), the SC ETV film *The Last Auction* (2004), *The Carter-Klan Documentary Project* (2006–2007), and the South Carolina Tobacco Museum in Mullins, South Carolina.

I would like to express my gratitude to Marsha Taylor and Carla Clark, early readers and wise critics of this manuscript, and to Susan Jaques, who donated the perfect hideaway for me to rough out the first draft. For technical information and personal reminiscences, I wish to thank my brother Steve Mace and my friend Maeolda Calhoun, both of whom spent far more time "working tobacco" than I did. Many, many thanks to my father, Bob Mace, for his patience with my questions and for his rich accounts of the tobacco industry in the early 1960s. And to the end of my days I will be grateful to my husband, the poet David Havird, who devoted countless hours to reading and rereading drafts—tirelessly advising, editing, and encouraging me. *The gift is the journey.*

About the Author

Ashley Mace Havird grew up on a tobacco farm in South Carolina. She has published three collections of poems, including *The Garden of the Fugitives* (Texas Review Press, 2014), which won the 2013 X. J. Kennedy Prize. Her poems and short stories have appeared in many journals including *Shenandoah*, *The Southern Review*, and *The Virginia Quarterly Review*, and in anthologies such as *The Southern Poetry Anthology IV: Louisiana* and *Hard Lines: Rough South Poetry*. A recipient of a Louisiana Division of the Arts Fellowship, she lives with her husband, the poet David Havird, in Shreveport, Louisiana. *Lightningstruck* is her first novel.